Four Lindos

John Wilton

ISBN: 978-1-916596-75-7

Copyright © 2023

All rights reserved, including the right to reproduce this book, or portions thereof in any form. No part of this text may be reproduced, transmitted, downloaded, decompiled, reverse engineered, or stored, in any form or introduced into any information storage and retrieval system, in any form or by any means, whether electronic or mechanical without the express written permission of the author.

This is a work of fiction. All names and characters are the product of the author's imagination and any resemblance to actual persons, living or dead, is entirely coincidental.

PublishNation

www.publishnation.co.uk

Acknowledgements:

I would like to say another huge thank you to all my friends in beautiful Lindos. My warm thanks go to my good friends Jack Koliais and Janis Woodward Bowles, both of whom encouraged me greatly to get on and write my first Lindos novel, published in 2015.

My thanks also go to everyone in Lindos and beyond, including the many regular Lindos visitors, who have said and written such nice things about all my previous novels.

Much appreciation also goes to all those readers of my previous novels who have encouraged and inspired me to once more write a story based not only on Lindos.

Endless gratitude goes to my proof-reader Fiona Ensor for her tireless efforts on all my novels in identifying my errors. Any that remain are entirely my responsibility.

Needless to say, this story is total fiction. However, without the magical village of Lindos, and the people in it, this novel could never have been written. For that reason, as with all my previous Lindos novels, I will always be eternally grateful to the people there, my friends in that magical paradise.

Author's website: www.johnwilton.yolasite.com

Previous novels by John (all available on Amazon and Kindle):

The Hope (2014)   *Lindos Retribution* (2015)

Lindos Aletheia (2016)   *Lindian Summers* (2018)

Lindos Affairs (2019)   *Lindian Odyssey* (2020)

Lindos Eros and Hades (2021)

Karagoulis. Lindos life and times (2022)

MAP OF LINDOS

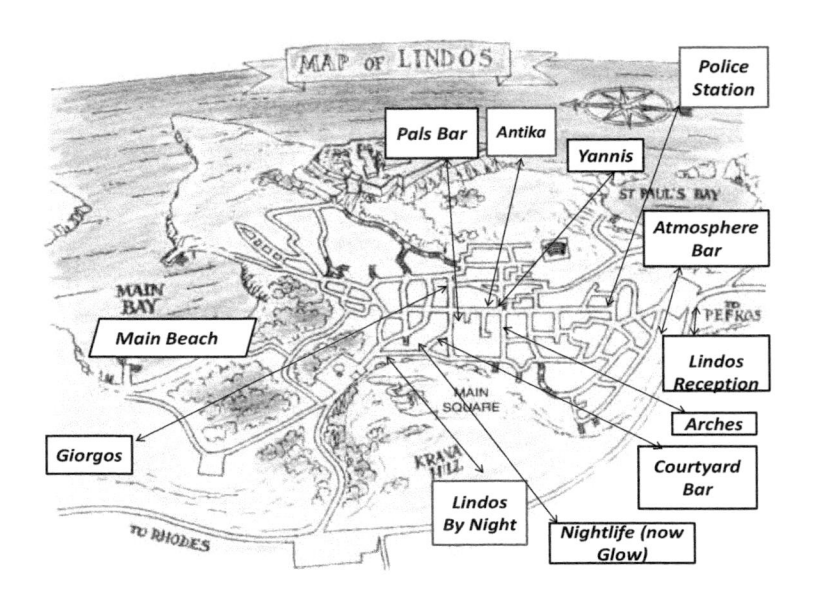

- Police Station
- Pals Bar
- Antika
- Yannis
- Atmosphere Bar
- Main Beach
- Lindos Reception
- Arches
- Giorgos
- Courtyard Bar
- Lindos By Night
- Nightlife (now Glow)

PART ONE:

THE INVESTIGATION

1

Ημέρα Ενα (Day 1)
Saturday July 2nd 2022: the mobile phone

Bzzz … bzzz … bzzz.

There was a persistent annoying low buzzing sound penetrating the alcohol induced haze in his head. It felt like it went on for hours. In reality it was only a few minutes that time. As he very slowly forced his eyes open slightly into a squint he was greeted by the bright sunlight of the Lindos mid-afternoon hot July sun streaming through the small gaps between the slats of the shutters into the bedroom of his flat.

"Agh … ouch."

Trying to raise his head from the pillow brought only a deep dull ache in his temple, causing him to wince and blink, trying to adjust to the sunlight. Why had he drunk so much last night, or more accurately, into the early hours of Saturday morning? At that point, as he questioned that lack of judgement, his complete lack of any sensible action and decisions, vague, blurry, disconnected snapshots of what occurred during that previous evening and early morning intermittently flooded into his brain. He had no idea at all quite what the actual order of those occurrences had been, and certainly not how accurate they were. He was sure there were three women. Certain of that at least. Tourists, English and in their forties, maybe mid-forties. Through the blurry alcoholic hangover haze he vaguely remembered estimating that was their ages when he was introduced to them. He knew there had been Pal's Bar, where he and his friend Ken had met them. Well initially Ken, who engaged them in conversation. Then there had been the club,

Arches Plus, the open air club down towards the Main Beach. He remembered that much and was sure of that. In between all those brief remembered snapshots though there was nothing, except that he knew it was daylight when he and Ken left the club, although not with the women, he recalled. They must have left earlier. Through the aching fog in his brain though, he'd no clear memory of that or what time. When it came to recalling getting back to his flat in the centre of the village and desperately getting into his inviting bed, as he obviously must have done? Nothing at all. There was nothing in his brain about that.

Bzzz ... bzzz ... bzzz. The annoying noise continued. It needed to be stopped. It was aggravating the pain in his head. As he sat up in the bed and slowly turned his head towards the direction of the annoying sound his blinking blurred vision eventually focused on a mobile phone on the bedside table. It wasn't his. He had no idea whose it was. Even in his drunken state though he had obviously managed to connect it to a charging cable and plug that into the wall socket. Now he realised the annoying sound was someone calling it. Through his narrowed blinking eyes he roughly made out there was no name of the caller on the screen, but there were other earlier missed call notifications on it, as well as what looked like a voicemail sign. He tried to answer it by touching the screen, but the phone was locked. So, he was unable to even turn it off. He tried unsuccessfully a few times. So, the annoying buzz continued until the caller gave up and rang off. According to what was showing on the phone's screen the annoying buzz must have occurred a few times earlier, although being in the depth of his drunken sleepy state he never heard those. They never disturbed him. There had been a number of earlier calls, including a couple from someone named Michael, plus some from what was showing as 'unknown number'. They were clearly from someone, or some people, not in the phone's directory of contacts of whoever it belonged to.

2

Saturday July 2nd 2022: the body

"Good morning Christof."

"Morning Yiannis. Good of you and your Sergeant to eventually show up all the way down here. Couldn't your killer at least have had the decency to dump the body in the north of the island, a bit nearer to Rhodes Town, rather making me traipse all the way down here to the arse end of nowhere? And on a bloody Saturday morning."

Not exactly the friendliest of greetings, but Inspector Papadoulis knew from experience not to expect much else from the police pathologist that early, even though it was actually now just before ten. Papadoulis had got the early call from the Rhodes Town station just after eight that morning informing him that a body had been discovered in Gennadi, near one of the roads from the village down to the long pebble beach. The Inspector was from Rhodes and married to a local girl he'd met when they were both training at the Hellenic Police Officers School. They had two teenage children. He'd spent his entire police career on the island, being promoted from Sergeant to Inspector following the killing of his superior officer, Inspector Dimitris Karagoulis, during a murder case investigation in 2010. Consequently, he'd become quite familiar over the years with the pathologist's often gruff and grumpy manner.

Yiannis Papadoulis was a quite tall, upright man, relatively slim, and with thick swept back, typically Greek, dark hair. Although having just turned fifty that was displaying traces of beginning to slightly grey at the edges. He was a regulation policeman. Very organised, he played everything methodically by the book in his profession, in contrast to his more unorthodox murdered previous boss, Inspector Dimitris

Karagoulis. Karagoulis was from Athens and had been transferred to Rhodes against his will in the year 2000 after he made a fatal mistake on an Athens murder case. He was given an ultimatum after being suspended for that, transfer to Rhodes or retire. Financially Karagoulis had no choice but to accept the transfer. During his ten years in the force on the island he became well known for his quirky methods of investigation, often based on his obsession with Greek Mythology, much of which he sometimes employed in trying to solve cases. Initially that irritated him, but gradually Papadoulis grew to like it, so much so that he even occasionally dipped into some of it for his off duty leisure time reading. At times the Greek Mythology applied approach of Karagoulis even made him smile, and an excellent relaxed working relationship developed between the two men. However, Yiannis Papadoulis generally usually wasn't one to delve into philosophy or Greek Mythology when it came to trying to solve cases following his promotion to Inspector from Sergeant after Karagoulis was killed. He preferred to simply deal more methodically with the facts, what he saw, and what he and his officers discovered in their investigations.

Papadoulis picked up his Sergeant, Antonis Georgiou, at the Rhodes Town police station just after nine. Gennadi was on the south east coast of Rhodes, over sixty kilometres from the islands capital, Rhodes Town, about an hour's drive. It was a working village, as well as a tourist destination, and it had an air about it that was a bit different to the usual tourist resorts on the island. There was more of a feel for the Greek way of life, whilst still having facilities like bars and restaurants, as well as supermarkets and a bakery. The hotels ranged from the small locally owned guest houses and apartments found in the main village itself to huge hotel complexes with multiple pools and all-inclusive options, mainly on the outskirts of the village or along the coastal area. One of the most attractive things about Gennadi was its huge long pebble beach, around five hundred metres or so from the centre of the village. The beach stretched uninterrupted for over ten kilometres so it was always easy to find an unpopulated spot. The village was fairly quiet in the daytime during the week, but was famed for its summer Sunday beach parties pre-Covid, when DJs played chilled music at hip seafront bars. In the summer evenings the few open-air tavernas and bars buzzed with what tourists there were staying in Gennadi itself.

By the time the two police officers arrived at the spot where the body had been discovered the pathologist had already started his examination of the crime scene and initial examination of the body. He'd obviously received the call even earlier than Papadoulis and so Christof Costas was clearly not in the best of moods through his weekend being interrupted. He was a stout man of medium height in his early fifties. Even though he'd been born and bred in Rhodes Town and had qualified in Athens he was clearly not immune to the midsummer early July heat. This was already a particularly hot July morning, unusually hot even for that time of year, with not a hint of a cloud in the clear blue sky. The small wet patches on his pale blue short sleeved shirt betrayed his unfit physical condition, as well as the slightly larger ones under his armpits. In the Rhodes police force he was known as someone who enjoyed more than his share of Mythos and Alfa Greek cold beer, something that obviously contributed to his poor physical condition. Nevertheless, most of the officers recognised that he was good at his job, including Papadoulis.

The two police officers left their car on the road and made their way through the few trees to the place where the body was discovered. It wasn't more than thirty metres from the road. Over the years the Inspector had learned that Christof Costas, as the chief police pathologist on Rhodes, was someone whose investigation and examination should be listened to and studied carefully, even though he'd also learned from experience that the pathologist was not always the most pleasant of men or the easiest to get along with. Costas could be a blunt man who didn't suffer fools gladly, particularly ones who were police officers. He did appear to focus more of his impatience and rudeness though on more junior officers, rather than the senior ones. However, his initial comments to Papadoulis on this particular Saturday morning over his obvious displeasure at having his midsummer weekend interrupted had seemingly suggested that he was temporarily abandoning his discrimination between ranks. The Inspector ignored them and simply asked, "Dumped?"

"What?" the pathologist replied as he looked up at the policeman from his position crouching down examining the crime scene.

"Dumped, you said dumped, Christof."

"Yes, dumped, not killed here. There's a wound from a blow to the back of the head, but no blood around, not even dried blood on the ground. There's some matted in her hair around the wound of course, and some small spots around the back of the neck of her light blue t-shirt, no doubt splatters from the blow. I won't be sure until I get the body back to the lab, but it's likely that the blow to the head wasn't the fatal one. There are marks and bruises on the neck, so it looks like strangulation. Nevertheless, I'd be pretty sure the victim was killed somewhere else, then the body moved here and dumped in these bushes."

"Moved to Gennadi? Why here? It's pretty desolate."

"Yes, perhaps, although the murder could have taken place back in the village and the body just dumped here. I've no idea why here, Yiannis. That's your job, to find out, remember."

There was a mixture of sarcasm and an echo his bad mood in the pathologist's voice.

"As you will have seen the road is concreted, and goes all the way to the beach down there."

He pointed towards the beach and the sea before continuing, "So, we aren't going to get anything that could be identified as tyre tracks. And I expect this road from the village is used by quite a few vehicles, people going to the beach, as well as vehicles making deliveries to the few bars and cafes down there. There is a small holiday apartment complex just a bit further down towards the beach, so someone may have heard a vehicle in the early hours this morning. There are some faint and quite rough footprints from the road to here where the body was found. We may be able to get something from them, although as I said they are quite faint and it doesn't mean they are necessarily the killer's of course. Could be anybody's really, even tourists making some kind of short-cut back to the village from the beach."

"Ok, I'll get the local officer to knock on doors in the apartment complex. Who found the body?"

"A local guy walking his dog early this morning, apparently the dog discovered it in the bushes. Says he owns one of the small cafes in the village. The officer from the Gennadi police station recognised him and confirmed that. He's over there taking some more details from him."

The pathologist pointed to the guy with the dog and the local officer about thirty metres away on the road and Papadoulis told his Sergeant to go over and join them to see what else he could find out from the guy.

As Georgiou turned to go over the pathologist added, "The Crime Scene Team are on their way down here from Rhodes Town so be careful where you are walking Sergeant. We don't want you and your Inspector here tramping all over the crime scene do we?"

Papadoulis looked at his Sergeant and simply shook his head slightly. Clearly Costas' mood was not improving in the increasingly hot sun. Even though the two Rhodes policemen obviously knew better than to disturb the crime scene, even accidentally, Papadoulis thought it best to just not bother to respond. Instead he simply asked, "What can you tell me so far about the victim, Christof. Other than, as you said before, they weren't killed here?"

The pathologist stood up from examining the body and told him, "Female, I'd guess around mid-forties, and from her appearance obviously not Greek. Possibly English tourist I'd say and not staying in Gennadi, but in Lindos, or at least near there-"

"Where did you get that from? There's no handbag with the body?" Papadoulis interrupted.

"No, but there was a hotel room key card in the pocket of her jeans, Lindos Memories, but nothing else except a few Euro notes. No phone."

"Lindos Memories? Why the hell would the killer pick here to dump the body if she was killed somewhere else? Maybe she had some connection with the village?"

As Papadoulis shook his head slightly and rubbed the back of his head with the palm of his right hand the pathologist told him, "Perhaps, Yiannis, but the guy over there who found the body said he didn't recognise her, never seen her before. Gennadi is only a small place and as he said he owns a café I'm guessing he would see a fair few people in the village, even if they were only tourists. And anyway, as I said, the hotel key card indicates that she hasn't been staying anywhere in the village, but near Lindos. I think it's more likely it was the killer who had some sort of connection to this part of the island, and knew this as a likely spot to dump a body, obviously mistakenly thinking it wouldn't be easily or quickly discovered in the bushes."

"Hang on, I ..."

Now it was the Inspector who leaned down, almost on his knees, to peer intently at the victim's face.

"What?" Costas asked. "What is it?"

"I ... I think I know her. She looks slightly different if it is her. Her hair was a different colour I think, dark and longer, not short and blonde, but I'm pretty sure it's her."

"Who, her who, Yiannis?"

The Inspector's indecision was doing nothing to improve the pathologist's mood.

"Regan, her name is Regan, and she's not English. She's Irish, or I should say, was. She had an Irish first name, Aileen, if I remember rightly. I thought she was saying Eileen, but she corrected me with the Irish version."

"Well, if you're right, and it is her, she certainly can't do that now, Yiannis."

Papadoulis stopped speaking and peered down into her face for a long few seconds.

"And?" the impatient Costas asked agitatedly. "When, when did you meet her?"

"Oh yes, sorry Costas. I interviewed her about six years ago over a murder case in Lindos. At least we thought it was a murder case initially, but eventually it was put down as an accident. The body of a man was found in an alley by some steps leading down from the top alley in Lindos. It did look at first as though he'd had too much to drink and fell on the rough steps in the dark – it's not very well lit up there – and cracked his head against a wall. But the autopsy found there wasn't excessive alcohol in his bloodstream and for a while though we thought it might be murder."

"I remember that case, Yiannis, but I never worked on it. I was seconded to work on a big crime case in Thessaloniki at the time."

"When I interviewed her she told me she lived in Boston. She said she had a business there, but was in Lindos trying to trace her birth father. Apparently he was Greek. Her mother had recently died. She was Irish too, her mother. She'd worked in Lindos for two summers in the mid-seventies and got pregnant. She told me her birth certificate said 'Father unknown'. Her mother wouldn't tell her anything about him before she died, but this woman, Regan, told me she had some idea from what little her mother did tell her that her father was Greek, from Lindos."

"And the murder or accident? Was she involved?"

"No, no we didn't think so. The guy who was killed, or died in an accident, was English. One of the bar staff in one of the bars told us that he was asking about an Irish woman in the village on one night before the body was found."

"Her?"

The pathologist pointed to the body.

"I don't know. She was renting a flat in the centre of the village. It could have been her, but she said she'd never seen the guy, and pointed out that there were quite a few Irish tourists staying in Lindos at that time of year, which was true. She said she had no idea why anyone would be looking for her in particular, and she seemed sure that it couldn't have been her he was looking for. We did some searches, social media and the rest on her, but couldn't find anything. She said she had an American passport, but the U.S. Consulate in Athens couldn't trace one for her. That was odd. And then shortly after that I got a call from the Chief of the Hellenic Police in Athens ordering me to release the guy's body, which was in the Rhodes Town mortuary, to the British Consul, and informing me that there was no need for any further investigation of what was obviously a nasty accident."

"Very odd," the pathologist scratched the back of his head.

Papadoulis nodded slightly and added, "Yes, I thought so, Christof, but that was the end of the case. Consequently, officially it was recorded as an accident, not a murder, and we never got to the bottom of whether this woman was involved or not. I heard she left the island a short time after. How she's ended up dead in Gennadi though is a further mystery, and this definitely looks like a murder and not an accident. From my interview with her I don't recall her having any connection with Gennadi, never mentioned this place I'm sure."

The Inspector shook his head slightly in bemusement and then added, "Any idea on time of death?"

"First impression from the condition of the body would be sometime in the early hours of the morning, maybe between four and five. The guy found the body just before eight. Assuming she was killed somewhere else, possibly in or near Lindos, in a car it would be around thirty minutes to get here from there at that time of the morning. Quite quick, the roads would be empty. My initial quick examination of the body when I got here, just after nine, sometime before you two of course, Yiannis" – he wasn't letting his annoyance at the policemen's later arrival subside – "was that death had occurred four or five hours before that. So, between four and five this morning, but I'll have a clearer idea once I get the body back to the lab and do a full examination."

"Looks like we have a murder in or around Lindos in the early hours of this morning then?"

"Yes, you do, Yiannis. That should keep you busy for a while and stop you disturbing any more of my weekend. I'll email you my fuller report later this afternoon. Here's the Crime Scene Team arriving now, so if you'll kindly leave me to it I'll finish up what I need to do here, leave them to do the rest, and get this poor woman back to the comfort of my lab in Rhodes Town for a full autopsy. If by any chance we find anything around here that looks like it was used to cause the blow to the head I'll let you know straightaway, but, as I said, there's no sign of any dried blood around here so I'm pretty sure she was killed elsewhere and whatever was used to administer the blow to the head will have been disposed of there or somewhere else, not around here."

At that point Papadoulis walked over to join his Sergeant just as he'd finished interviewing the guy who found the body, now leaving with his dog.

"Anything further from him?"

"No, not really, sir, only that he hadn't seen the woman around the village at all. He owns a café there and-"

"That's what Christof said he'd told him. It's only a small place so I'm sure if she'd been in the village at all, even as a tourist, he may have seen her. Christof said he found a hotel key card in her pocket for Lindos Memories. She was obviously staying there, but there were only a few euros in her pocket with that and no phone or handbag. However, I think I know her name, Aileen Regan. I interviewed her on that case in Lindos six years ago."

"I remember that case, sir. We thought it was murder. I remember you interviewed her, but I wasn't with you when you did. I never met her, so couldn't be sure our victim her, Regan. Although if you say so-"

The Inspector cut him short.

"That's what we thought at the time. That it was murder, but it's on record as an accident following the Hellenic Chief of Police ordering us to shut it down as that if you recall. I'll remind you of more about it on our way to the hotel she was staying at now."

"Lindos Memories will be our place to start then?"

"It will, Sergeant, it will. I hope you didn't have a nice weekend planned."

3

The identity?

Lindos Memories Hotel was a short way outside Lindos, slightly under a mile, and to the left just off the road to Pefkos. It was approaching twelve noon, and the baking hot midday Rhodes sun was bearing down, reaching its peak as Papadoulis and his Sergeant parked at the front of the hotel.

The hotel was a smart looking, low rise, light sandstone block complex of only two stories, with an impressive vista out over the swimming pool to Navarone Bay. It had become known as that due to sequences of the 1961 Second World War movie 'The Guns of Navarone' having been shot there. The whole setting was very picturesque and gave off a very relaxing atmosphere as the two policemen, far from relaxed, made their way directly to the reception block.

As they approached the reception desk the Inspector took out his identification badge and introduced the two officers to the young receptionist. The name badge on her uniform informed them she was Maria Castellanos. Returning his identification to the inside pocket of his jacket Papadoulis replaced it from there with a transparent evidence bag containing the hotel electronic door key card found in the victim's pocket and asked the receptionist to check the room number and its registered current occupier. It wasn't easy through the evidence bag. It needed to be swiped on the reception computer pad, but when Maria asked for it to be removed from the bag Papadoulis explained that wasn't possible as it was evidence. Eventually, after three attempts, she succeeded in swiping the card and informed the two policemen it was for room 209, occupied by a Kathleen O'Mara.

"Only her, no one with her," the Inspector asked.

"No, no one sharing the room. Just her, although the room was booked by another woman staying here. There are three of them, three English women, her and ..."

The receptionist hesitated for a moment while she checked the computer screen. Meanwhile Papadoulis briefly glanced sideways at the Sergeant, both exhibiting surprise and confusion across their faces that the room wasn't occupied by Aileen Regan.

"Odd, sir," Georgiou commented and appeared to about to go on, but the Inspector just raised his index finger to his lips and shook his head slightly.

"Err ... yes, here it is. Suzanne Carmichael made the booking, for her, Miss O'Mara and Alison Lees."

"Not an Aileen Regan?" Papadoulis asked.

Now the receptionist looked confused.

"No, Inspector, just those three."

"Perhaps you were mistaken, sir, and it wasn't her after all," the Sergeant suggested.

Papadoulis rubbed the back of his neck for a moment and then shook his head slightly before replying, "No, I'm sure it's her."

He asked the receptionist, "How long is the booking for and would you know if the three women are present in the hotel at the moment?"

The receptionist glanced back at the screen before telling him, "Four nights. They arrived and checked in at three yesterday afternoon. I have no idea if they are in the hotel at the moment though, Inspector. If they are I would guess they are around the pool. It's through those glass doors there," she pointed to the left of the reception area, "and just straight down the broad plaza between the hotel room blocks."

"Is there anyone who could identify them for us? Could you?"

"I wasn't on duty yesterday when they checked in, but the luggage porter, Giannis, perhaps could. He was working yesterday afternoon. Just a moment."

She turned and disappeared through a door to her right into the back office. A few seconds later she reappeared with a man dressed in black trousers, an open neck white shirt and a black waistcoat with a small Lindos Memories motif on its left side.

Before Papadoulis could ask if he could point the women out the porter told him, "They are by the pool. Well, two of them are. I haven't seen the third one this morning."

"Good, could you show us please?" Papadoulis asked.

"Of course."

With that the two policemen followed him through the glass doors into the bright hot sunlight again and down towards the beautiful setting of the pool, with its small hotel taverna to the right hand side and the lovely panoramic view out over the blue sea in Navarone Bay. The porter stopped briefly to scan the pool area as they reached the top of the small flight of steps finally leading down to it and then after a few seconds pointed to the left, telling the policemen, "There they are. Over there. Well, two of them anyway."

"Thanks. We'll take it from here," Papadoulis told him.

With that they walked away from him in the direction of the two sunbeds on which the women were lazing in the hot sun. Papadoulis' initial impression as they got closer was that they were both in their mid-forties. One was blonde haired, which was tied back. What was instantly clearly evident was that it was dyed. Some of the darker roots were creeping through. The other woman was a brunette, with shorter curly hair. Both were not unattractive. The one with the dyed blonde hair still retained her good figure, displayed nicely by her bright yellow bikini. Even though reclining on the sunbed she appeared somewhat taller than the brunette, who had a few extra pounds protruding over her green bikini bottom. There was no mistaking that they both exhibited the instant impression they were the sort of British females of a certain age who undoubtedly enjoyed lazing in the hot Mediterranean sun, in this case the hot Rhodes sun.

When they got close to the sunbeds Papadoulis again produced his police identification and asked, "Alison Lees and Suzanne Carmichael, I'm Inspector Papadoulis, Rhodes Police."

The taller of the two sat up and propped her sunglasses on to the top of her head before answering in what is usually described as an 'estuary accent' associated with south-east England, particularly along the River Thames in London.

"Yes, I'm Alison Lees." She pointed to her brunette friend adding, "she's Suzanne Carmichael. Is there something wrong Inspector?"

Papadoulis ignored her question and instead swopped it for another of his own.

"The receptionist told us there were three of you, three women in your party?"

The woman blinked in the sunlight and raised her left hand to her forehead to shield the bright sun as she looked up at him.

"Yes, there is, but what's this about?"

"Is the third woman in your party here in the hotel at the moment?"

"We haven't seen Kathleen this morning. She's probably sleeping off a hangover. That's what we assume. We had rather a frantic crazy first night, and way too much alcohol," the brunette volunteered. "No doubt she'll surface eventually, when she needs food. What's she done?"

"Nothing," the Inspector answered. "Do you have a photo of her by any chance?"

"Yes, but, what-"

Papadoulis didn't let her finish.

"Can you show me one please?"

The two women looked confused. Why were the Rhodes police asking about their friend and wanting to see a photo of her?

Alison Lees took a deep breath and then reached into the small beach bag beside her sunbed to produce her phone. She swiped the screen a couple of times and then held it up towards Papadoulis and Georgiou.

"That's her, sir," the Sergeant said straightaway, which drew a look of displeasure towards him from Papadoulis before the Inspector asked the woman, "So, that's Kathleen O'Mara?"

"Yes, that's Kathleen. What's this about?"

Once again the policeman avoided answering and simply asked, "Have you ever heard of or met an Irish woman called Aileen Regan?"

The two women briefly exchanged glances before both replying almost simultaneously, "No."

"Who is she, and what's she got to do with Kathleen or us?" the dyed blonde asked.

"Probably nothing," Papadoulis replied, but before he could go on Georgiou commented, "You must have been mistaken then, sir."

That drew another sideways look of displeasure in the direction of his Sergeant, and a further confusing look on the faces of the two women.

"So, when was the last time you saw Kathleen O'Mara?" he asked them.

"Err ... last night, or to be more precise the early hours of this morning I guess," the brunette replied. "Around four maybe. We'd had quite a few drinks and I didn't really check the time. We lost track."

"Yes that's probably about right. I do remember glancing at my watch as we left the club and that was just before four," the woman with the dyed blonde hair added.

"Club, which club?" Papadoulis asked.

"Erm ... Arches something or other."

"Arches Plus?"

"Yes, that was it, Inspector. Down by the beach apparently, although it was too dark to actually know if it was the beach nearby."

"And did the three of you leave the club together, and with anyone else?"

"No, I mean yes we all left together, and got a taxi in the square to the hotel, but no there was no one else with us. When we got back here we went straight to our rooms and our beds. We needed them."

"So, the last time you saw Miss O'Mara was around four this morning, going into her room?"

"Yes, our three rooms are altogether and mine is next to Kathleen's," the brunette confirmed. "But please tell us what this is about? You should go and ask Kathleen. She'll be in her room sleeping off her hangover, I guess. She was drinking even more heavily than us two. It's room 209."

"Yes, the receptionist told us her room number." Papadoulis paused for a moment. "But I'm afraid she won't be there. I'm sorry to have to tell you that her body was found this morning just off a road at a place called Gennadi in the south of the island."

A look of shock raced across the faces of the two women. One of them lifted her hands up to her face while the other simply said in a voice broken with shock, "What? No, it can't be. It can't be. She came back here to the hotel with us. You must be mistaken, Inspector. She'll be in her room."

"I'm sorry, but it is. The body is that of the woman you just showed me in that photo, I'm afraid."

A small tear trickled down Alison Lees' face as her friend asked, "But what, what happened, and when? We were only with her last night enjoying our holiday and then she went off to her bed here. It was to celebrate her birthday, the holiday. How far away is this place where her body was found?"

Papadoulis again said, "I'm sorry," and added in reply, "Gennadi is about forty minutes from here. The body was discovered just before eight this morning. I'm sorry to have to tell you that it looks like your friend was murdered."

The look of horror quickly spread over the faces of the women once again. For a long moment they were speechless. Then the brunette said very quietly, "Murdered, but …"

"I'm afraid so. We are pretty certain. Obviously our forensic team and pathologist will have to do a full examination of the body and the crime scene, but initially it looks pretty much that way."

"How?" Alison Lees asked. "Murdered how?"

"That's all I can tell you at the moment you understand, and we will need to look at Miss O'Mara's room now. It is probably best if one of you or both of you if you wish, accompanies us while we do that, but please don't touch anything in there."

They both nodded in agreement, got up from their sunbeds to put on their robes and flip flops as Alison Lees told him, "We will both come."

Papadoulis sent his Sergeant off to reception to get the hotel Manager for him to let them into the victim's room, while he made his way with the two women to room 209. Five minutes later the Manager was standing with them just inside the doorway to the room while the two policemen put on their latex gloves and made a preliminary investigation of its contents. During a brief ten minutes they discovered nothing out of the ordinary and Papadoulis instructed his Sergeant to call the pathologist to get a forensic team to come and inspect the room more thoroughly. Then he asked the Manager to get whatever was required to over-ride the code which Kathleen O'Mara had obviously keyed in to use and lock the safe so they could examine whatever was inside, including hopefully her passport. He was still clinging to the hope that any passport that they discovered would actually be for an Aileen Regan and not Kathleen O'Mara. The Manager returned with an electronic device which he said should be pressed onto a small magnetic looking disc on the front of the safe so as to open it. After Papadoulis told him to touch nothing in doing just that the Manager opened the safe and the Inspector removed its contents with his forensic gloved hand. There was an Irish passport, along with some euros in a small plastic wallet, but when the Inspector opened it to check it was, indeed, in the name of Kathleen O'Mara. He shook his head slowly slightly and shrugged his shoulders as he told Georgiou again quietly that he'd been certain the woman's body was Aileen Regan. He shrugged once more and then turned to tell the Manager that the room would have to be locked and sealed as a possible crime scene until the forensic team arrived.

"My Sergeant will need to take a formal statement from each of you," the Inspector told the two women as they all left the room. "He can do it here in the hotel in the Manager's office rather than at the police station in Lindos, if you prefer."

"Here will be fine, if that's ok," Suzanne Carmichael replied, and her friend nodded in agreement, adding, "I think we will feel more at ease if we go to our rooms first, get out of our bikinis Inspector and put on some proper clothes. Somehow it seems more appropriate."

"Sure, no problem. The Sergeant will take your formal statements separately in your rooms instead then in fifteen minutes, starting with you Miss Carmichael."

The two women nodded,

After they left Papadoulis commented, "There was no sign of any struggle in the O'Mara woman's room."

"Nor, any sign of anything that looked like blood, sir."

Papadoulis rubbed his chin with his left hand before saying, "No, and I didn't get the feeling that these two women were in any way involved in the murder. I may be wrong, but they did seem genuinely shocked. Ask them again about the name Aileen Regan though. Push them on it. I'm certain it's the same woman. Find out how they know the victim, and particularly for how long. I'll head back to the station in Lindos. Call me when you're done taking their statements and I'll get the local police to send a car to pick you up."

"Ok, sir."

"So, just what happened here, or even elsewhere if the victim went out after the other two women had gone to bed and thought she had also. What happened in those three hours or so between when they last saw her between four and five and when the body was found in Gennadi at eight, and how the bloody hell did it get there?"

The Inspector was just voicing his thoughts aloud. Something Georgiou had come to understand he was prone to do. The Sergeant simply shook his head slightly in bemused agreement.

4

The known and the unknown: the 'Socratic method' and Sherlock Holmes

By the time Georgiou had finished taking the statements and arrived at Lindos police station Papadoulis had written on a white Incident Board pretty much what he'd voiced previously to his Sergeant, what they knew, but mostly queries about what they didn't know. Kathleen O'Mara was written in block capital letters on the top of the board with Aileen Regan in brackets next to it and a question mark.

The police station was a low single story white building just off one of the main alleyways through the village, towards the top at one end of it, where the Atmosphere Bar and the Lindos Reception was located. Lindos Reception was a café where the tourist coaches dropped off and picked up their arriving and departing holidaymakers as no vehicles were allowed in the narrow alleyways throughout the village.

The white Incident Board was in a small office at the rear of the station which the two officers had been allocated whilst carrying out their investigation. It had been updated a few years earlier, which basically meant a new, much more up-to-date computer and a coat of magnolia paint on the mostly bare, decidedly unfriendly looking walls. The two metal desks, which had seen better times, had clearly retained their status during the updating having not been replaced, despite each acquiring a considerably more comfortable looking new chair. The only things that broke up the monotony of the bare walls were the fair sized Incident Board and a new air-conditioning unit high up on one wall that faced onto the outside alley. There was not even a small window through which the bright Lindos sunlight could intrude upon the monopoly of the artificial strip lighting, but at least the air-conditioning unit kept the office at a bearable temperature, even in high summer.

As Georgiou went straight across the office to fill the kettle and make a coffee he spotted the name and commented, "You haven't given up on that then, sir? Aileen Regan."

"No, not yet, I'm not convinced yet we should."

With that Papadoulis got up from his chair behind the small metal desk and walked across the office to write the names Alison Lees and Suzanne Carmichael on the board beneath the victim's. Then he turned back to ask, "What did they tell you? Anything useful or interesting?"

"Mostly background. Nothing really revealing that might help us in the case."

The Inspector shook his head once as he propped himself on the corner of the desk.

"They said the three of them worked together for a marketing company in London. They have each been there for eight years and ten years, but the victim only started there a year ago. The three of them became friends not long after she joined the company. She was Irish, which we know now from her passport anyway, but Lees and Carmichael are English, with British passports."

"So, did you press them about-"

"About your woman, Aileen Regan?"

Georgiou interrupted, anticipating precisely what his Inspector was going to ask.

"I did, sir, but their answer was the same as before. They both said they'd never heard of her. Alison Lees did seem more intrigued as to why we were so interested in her. She asked who she was, and what she had to do with the victim, even asking if that was who we suspected was the murderer."

"What did you say?"

"Just that it was a name that had popped up in our enquiries. Then I changed the subject by asking both of them what had made them choose Lindos for their holiday and had any of them been here before, plus whose choice Lindos was?"

"Good. We'll keep quiet about anything more on Aileen Regan for now. What did they say?"

Carmichael said she got a deal for the trip for the three of them. Something to do with one of their clients at the marketing company where they work and some link they had to the Mitsis hotel chain that Lindos Memories is part of. So, she got the client to get a discount for them. She didn't really choose the hotel or Lindos. It was just the one their company's client could get a good discount on for them. She said the trip was a surprise for O'Mara's birthday, for them to celebrate it with a five day break at Memories."

"Sounds like the three of them were good friends then, considering the victim had only been at the company a year."

The Inspector was rubbing his chin with his right hand as he said that while wandering over towards the Incident Board.

"That's what I thought, sir. So I asked Carmichael about it, being good friends. She said they just all got on really well almost as soon as O'Mara started working at the company. Her and Lees are both divorced and she said O'Mara told them she'd never been married. So, they all lived alone in London and over the year since O'Mara started working with them they'd spent quite a lot of nights out together in London, especially at weekends, even went away for a couple of spa weekends in England. She said they just all hit it off straightaway, all three of them, and enjoyed each other's company. Lees told me much the same thing when I asked her about the relationships and friendships between them."

"Doesn't sound like either of those two, or even both of them, are our killer then?"

"No, sir, not really, unless one of them had a blazing row with O'Mara when they got back to the hotel?"

"Well, at the moment, as far as we know, they were the last persons to see her alive as they all went to their rooms at the hotel, so perhaps-"

"They were, sir, but their three rooms are all next to one another. So, if Lees or Carmichael had a blazing argument with the victim surely the other one would have heard something, and they both told me separately that they never heard anything unusual."

Papadoulis was pacing slowly across the small office as he said, "So, unless the two of them were in it together, killing her, but why would you organise a trip for a friend's birthday to Lindos to then kill her? Why not just do it in London?"

"Maybe it wasn't pre-meditated, sir, although we checked out Carmichael's and Lees' rooms and there was no sign of any struggle having taken place in either of them, nor anything that indicated that the murder took place there, in either of them. And, as we saw, there was no sign of any struggle in O'Mara's room. Also, I spoke to the chamber maid who cleaned Lees' and Carmichael's rooms this morning and she said that apart from some of the women's clothes lying around the rooms everything was normal, just what she usually expected to find in a guest's room."

"Hmm ... so, no sign of any struggle or blood in any of the women's rooms."

The Inspector slowly paced back and forth across the room as he repeated what his Sergeant had just told him.

"Nor in the rest of the hotel, sir. I've had four officers checking all of the hotel grounds and public areas, including down on the beach, but there's nothing."

Papadoulis stopped and turned to glare at the Incident Board.

"So, our victim doesn't appear to have been forcibly removed from her room and the hotel and-"

"Unless of course it was by gunpoint, sir."

"What?"

He turned to look into Georgiou face.

"Yes, that's a possibility, I suppose. But aside from that she either left of her own accord, alone, and went to meet her killer or ..."

His voice tailed off in mid-sentence as he hesitated for a moment and walked over to stare once again at the Incident Board for a long minute in silence.

"Or, sir?" the Sergeant eventually asked.

Papadoulis took a deep breath and puffed out his cheeks as he exhaled in exasperation.

"Or she knew her killer when he or she turned up at her room after she'd said goodnight to the other two women, and then she left with him of her own free will."

"Or her, sir."

"What? Oh yes, ok, or her, Sergeant."

"And with the open layout of the hotel the two of them leaving wouldn't necessarily be seen by the night receptionist, even if they were actually awake and not just sleeping during the hotel quiet night hours."

"Well, it would be easy to come out of one of the rooms, go around the side of the reception block and not be seen as you left the hotel, sir. It's possible."

"CCTV by any chance?"

"Yes, sir, but not for all areas. There are some blind spots, so it's possible to leave without being picked up on the cameras."

Papadoulis turned back to face his Sergeant as he asked, "The room electronic key card."

"What about it, sir?"

"The hotel must have a record of when it was last used. It won't tell us when she left the room, with or without her killer, but it will give us an accurate time that she left the other two women and went to her room."

"Ok, I'll check. One other thing though, sir, that might be of interest. Carmichael said that O'Mara took quite a bit of persuading to come on the trip, even though it was arranged for her birthday. Seems odd. Her birthday celebration with supposedly good friends and she was reluctant. Carmichael even thought she detected something in the impression O'Mara gave that she wasn't keen on coming to Lindos at all."

"Really?" The Inspector raised his eyebrows. "Did she have any idea why that was? Did she think it was because Regan ..."

He stopped himself.

"I mean O'Mara, had been here before? Did she say she get any inkling of that?"

Now it was the Sergeant who was shaking his head slightly.

"No, sir, she said that when she pressed her on it O'Mara told her she thought it would just be too hot. However, she got the impression it was more than that. Carmichael said none of the three of them had been to Lindos before when I asked her previously. Maybe they just fell out on their first night here? After all they did say they'd had quite a bit to drink. Maybe it was over a guy. Both Lees and Carmichael told me they met

25

two men in Pal's Bar in the village, and they took them to that club they told us they went to, Arches Plus. An open air club down towards the main beach."

Papadoulis spun around with a look of annoyance on his face as he told his Sergeant, "Why didn't you say that earlier that they met two men?"

"I ... err ... you asked-"

The Inspector wasn't about to let him finish. He stared straight into Georgiou's face as he added, "So, there were two other people who saw our victim and associated with her last night. Had they, the three women, been anywhere else in the village last night? You did ask Carmichael and Lees that I hope, Sergeant?"

There was now a hint of frustration and rising anger in the Inspector's voice.

"They said they were in the Courtyard Bar before, just up the alleyway from Pal's Bar. It was recommended to them by the receptionist at the hotel. But it was just the two bars and dinner at the Village House restaurant."

Papadoulis let out a sigh of exasperation over his Sergeant only just informing him of that and shook his head vigorously.

"Right, well we need to go and talk to the staff and the owners of those bars Sergeant, as well as of the restaurant, and see what they can tell us about the three women. Were they alone in all of them? Did they eat alone? Did they have any conversations with the staff or the owners? Did you ask them that?"

"No, not really, sir."

The Inspector's patience was disappearing fast.

"What about the two men they went to the club with? Surely you got their names?"

Georgiou flipped over the pages of his small black notebook nervously as he replied, "Yes, sir, I did, but only their first names. That's all they told the women when the men introduced themselves."

He looked back down at his notebook and then added, "Err ... yes, here it is, Ken and Daniel."

"And did the women have any idea if they were tourists and where they were staying?"

"No, sir, they thought it was somewhere in the village, but neither of them could be sure, although both Carmichael and Lees thought they were regular tourist visitors to Lindos as the two men seemed quite familiar with the owner of the club and the staff in Pal's Bar."

Papadoulis slammed his fist down on the metal desk in anger. His patience had run out.

"Jesus, Sergeant. Don't you think this was the first thing you should have told me? These two men were obviously among the last people to see O'Mara alive, and if one, or both of them, turns out to be our killers they could be long gone, off the island by now. Were they British, English?"

"The women said so, sir, yes, English."

"Ok, we need to find them. Get some officers knocking on the rented apartment doors throughout the village. Hopefully, the staff and owners in Pal's and the Courtyard Bar, as well as the club, will be able to identify them and where they are staying. We need to go and interview all of them."

"Now, sir?"

"No, unless things have changed from our enquiry here six years ago when I interviewed the Regan woman the bars won't open till around seven. The restaurant will be a little earlier. We'll go there at six. Get the door to door throughout the village organised with the local officers now. While you do that I'll go to the small café, Café Melia, in the old Amphitheatre Square just off the main alley through the village. If I remember correctly they do very good feta and spinach pies. I'll get us a couple of them for lunch. We've got nearly three hours before the Village House restaurant might be open and we can interview the owner and the staff, and it'll be a long night once we go to the other two bars after. Better grab some food now while we've got a bit of a gap."

Georgiou was somewhat bemused by his Inspector's apparent change of tone. His anger had quickly disappeared it seemed, replaced by a moment of generosity in offering to get him some food, but the Sergeant wasn't about to turn that down.

"Ok sir, thanks."

Georgiou had seen those sorts of mood swings before and had almost grown used to them. He'd learned to accommodate them. To some extent he'd put it down to the fact that Papadoulis was a very methodical, play it by the book, sort of policeman, even though his own previous Inspector, Dimitris Karagoulis, had been far from that. Consequently, Papadoulis consistently came down quite heavy on any errors or omissions by his officers. Georgiou understood well though that what brought the Inspector and him together, put them on the same wave length, was a driving desire to solve crimes. There was more to the Inspector's generous offer over the pies than met the eye, however.

Café Melia was in a pleasant spot on one corner of the old Amphitheatre Square, opposite the slightly sloping narrow road that led down out of the village towards the postcard picturesque St. Paul's Bay. From its position there it benefitted from passing tourist trade on their way to, or returning from, the popular small beaches in the bay. It was a prime spot to buy freshly made filled baguettes, as well as various Greek pies and cold drinks to take for lunch for a day on the beach. Alternatively it was perfect for a cold drink for tourists on their way back from the beaches into the village and their accommodation. In addition to the half-a-dozen tables inside the café there was a range of small tables and larger comfortable looking cushioned couches in a small area outside offering a pleasant outlook over the square. It was a great place to sit over coffee and watch people passing by, largely tourists. The enjoyment of that pastime was only slightly diminished by the occasional vehicles arriving up the road to park in the square so that their driver could off-load its large stocks of food or drink onto various trolleys in order to then manoeuvre the trolley with its load down one of the village alleyways to deliver to one of the shops or restaurants.

Throughout the summer Café Melia was a very popular spot in the village, for both tourists and some of the locals, as well as many of the Brit ex-pats. Today was no exception. Most of the seats inside and out were taken. Papadoulis joined the queue of two people ahead of him waiting to order food and drinks to takeaway. Serving them were two women. One was dark haired, Greek looking, and probably in her late teens. She was clearly younger than the other, who looked to be in her mid-thirties.

She had what is usually described as dirty blonde hair, cut in a bob down to her neck, and was wearing a quite tight fitting revealing bright royal blue sleeveless vest type top that showed off her slim figure perfectly, as well as a dark blue short skirt. She was busy looking down at the till while taking out the change of the customer she'd just served immediately ahead of Papadoulis reaching the front of the queue. As she handed the customer her change and noticed the Inspector her eyes widened and a wide smile spread across her glossed lips.

"Long time, no see, Yiannis. To what do we owe this pleasure?"

Her accent betrayed straightaway she was English. An expat who had lived and worked in Lindos and nearby for years.

"Work, a case unfortunately, Sally, oh, and your excellent feta pies of course." As he finished he returned her smile.

"Of course, although if they are that good I'm surprised you've managed to resist coming by for them for so long. What's it been? Five years at least?"

Her smile turned to a frown and he started to awkwardly shift his weight from foot to foot as he replied, "Err ... erm ... must be, I guess, five or six. I ... err ... I was wondering if you'd still be here."

While she reached into the glass fronted cabinet under the counter with some tongs for the pies she told him, "You know me, Yiannis. Love it here. Why would I leave? Even the winters are better here than Manchester. Not so much rain for a start. Don't think I'm ever going back. No reason to. I heard you were in the village today, knew you'd be in, couldn't resist."

She smiled and tilted her head slightly as she told him that, then asked, "How many of these pies do you want? We're closed from November to March, but I can usually find some work in Lardos or even Rhodes Town. I know plenty of people in both of those. I guess this is my home now."

"Right, that's good. Yes, two please. I've got a Sergeant from Rhodes Town here with me back at the station. News travels fast in Lindos then, you knowing I was in the village. Who told you?"

"Oh, you know, Yiannis, as you said, it's a village. It was probably someone who came in earlier. You're still in Rhodes Town then?"

"Yes, yes, still there."

She handed him the bag with the two pies and took his five euro note. As she looked at him out the top of her eyes from her slightly bowed head she asked, "And your wife?"

"Dimitra ... oh, yes, yes err ... yes, she's still in Rhodes Town, We, I mean ... err ... we both are, of course."

"What about you? You with anyone now? Living in Lindos now?"

Her bright smile was back. She knew very well why he was asking and shook her head slightly as she told him, "No, and no, Yiannis, no one, no one will have me. Damaged goods, remember."

He did and he knew precisely what she meant. It was about her and him.

"I'm in Lardos not here in the village," she added

His awkwardness returned.

"Well, I err ... I'd better get these back to my Sergeant."

There was no one in any queue behind him. No other customers who needed serving, but nevertheless he attempted to cover his awkwardness with, "And better let you get on and serve some more people."

This time she let out a small chuckle and then told him, "Yes, because as you can see, Yiannis, there's quite a queue."

Her chuckle developed into another broad smile as she added, "I suppose that's why you're such a good detective. You notice things don't you. I could always see that, remember that."

He didn't know how to reply, other than, "Ok, good to see you, Sally."

He understood perfectly well what their whole conversation had really been about. She did too, of course, because that was what she set out to do, was determined to do as soon as she saw him. She was a tease and good at it, and she knew exactly how to use that to unsettle men, to the point sometimes of making them very uncomfortable. Yiannis Papadoulis may have been a correct, methodical, do things by the book, Police Inspector, but to her he was no different to other men who'd been in her personal life in that respect. He'd always been someone easy to tease and easy to unsettle, unbalance. She'd realised that, done that, right from the first time they met in 2016 and she definitely hadn't changed, nor had he.

He puffed out his cheeks as he headed to leave, but before he got through the open doorway he heard her call across the cafe, "Yiannis."

He turned his head back into the café towards her as in an invitingly, questioning, almost seductive tone of voice he knew only too well she rattled off, "Later? A catch up? It's been a while. A drink? Lardos maybe? On your way back to Rhodes Town later?"

What he felt now was way past awkward. He knew she could always disorientate him, usually with her sudden unexpected suggestions. He'd experienced right from the beginning of their past affair how she could unbalance him. She had that effect on him all along and she knew it. Clearly she still had.

"Err ... well ... well ..."

He turned around towards her across the café as he finally managed, "Well ... the thing is Sally-"

She didn't let him finish. Much better to keep the policeman off balance and disorientated she was thinking.

"Call me later. The number's the same. When you're finished here tonight, call me. Doesn't matter how late. They'll be somewhere in Lardos we can get a drink, I'm sure."

While she told him that she was determinedly giving off a sort of matter of fact air by simultaneously wiping down part of the counter with a cloth nonchalantly while occasionally very briefly glancing up out of the top of her eyes checking his reaction. Her body language was one of 'take it or leave it', her invitation. She knew he wouldn't 'leave it'. She could see that she easily got the reaction she was seeking. She was so sure he'd still have her number. She was a confident woman who knew he would. She was right.

He never actually answered, just nodded slightly and left with the pies to head back to the station and his Sergeant. Did he only suggest getting the pies because he knew she'd still be working there or at least hoped she would be? That was what was running through his detective brain as he made his way up the slightly sloping alley and to Lindos police station just off it. She looked good though – bright, bubbly and tanned. He couldn't get her out of his mind as he walked back to the station. He needed to get his head back on the case though.

Over their late snack lunch, with more coffee the Inspector told Georgiou in a seemingly more conciliatory tone, "I forgot to ask about one thing from your interview with the two women. What about O'Mara's phone. Did you ask if either of them had any idea why she didn't have it with her, or even where it might be? It wasn't in her room safe. Presumably she had one?"

The Sergeant had the last part of his pie in his mouth. Papadoulis waited for him to swallow it and reply.

"Sorry ... no, I mean yes she had one, sir. I told them it wasn't with the body and we couldn't find it in her room, but no they had no idea why she wouldn't have had it with her or where it might be now. One of them said she was sure she had it with her in the village last night while they were out, even took some photos. I did get the number from them though. I tried it a couple of times, but there was no answer. It was switched on though. It just went to voicemail. I thought it best not to leave any message in case the killer has it and it might alert them."

"Good thinking."

The Inspector's mood had changed a little. Maybe it was the effect of the feta and spinach pie, or maybe something else that afternoon, or more accurately, someone else?

"So, someone must have it, and I'm guessing they won't be able to turn it off if it's locked."

"Or maybe the battery will run out, sir, unless for some reason they put it on charge."

Papadoulis looked sideways from his chair across at his Sergeant as he asked. "Why would the killer do that, put it on charge?"

"No idea, sir. It was just a thought."

The Inspector raised his eyebrows and shook his head slightly once more, indicating that he couldn't fathom the logic of his Sergeant's comment. After a short silence he told him,

"Get on to the tech bods in Rhodes Town station and give them her number. Tell them to put a track on the phone straightaway. If the killer does have it we want to know where it is and where they are as soon as we can."

Georgiou wiped his chin with the napkin that had been wrapped around his pie and then walked over to the phone on one of the desks to make the call. While he did so the Inspector went over to write everything they'd discovered so far about the case on the Incident Board, including the word 'PHONE' in capital letters under Kathleen O'Mara's name, followed by a question mark.

After his call to Rhodes Town Police Station Georgiou called Lindos Memories Hotel to ask them to check the time Kathleen O'Mara's room key card was registered as being last used. When he finished the call he told Papadoulis, who wrote on the board under her name '04.12 last time O'Mara used hotel room key card – time Carmichael and Lees last saw her?' He stepped back a pace and after a few seconds glaring in silence at the now quite full white board he momentarily scratched the back of his head and told Georgiou, "Ok, let's go over what we do know, what we don't know, and what we need to find out."

The Sergeant had experienced this method with him before on other cases in Rhodes Town. It was the Inspector's way of methodically reviewing the case with him, discussing it with him, going over it verbally to get a bigger picture and trying to ascertain the way forward; the direction in which their enquiries should focus.

Papadoulis was a great believer in this what was known as the 'Socratic method'; an approach based on a search for general commonly held truths that shape beliefs and then scrutinizes them in order to determine their consistency with other beliefs. The basic form is a series of questions formulated as tests of logic and fact intended to help a person or group discover their beliefs about some topic, explore definitions, and identify general characteristics shared by various particular instances and situations. In an investigation it was about what actually happened in the case, what they knew about that and what they didn't know. It was a method of hypothesis elimination, in that better hypotheses are found by steadily identifying and eliminating those that lead to contradictions. As the name suggests, it was originally developed by the Classical Greek philosopher Socrates.

Georgiou had got used to it, and, although not as much a methodological policeman himself he had grown to like it, not least because his Inspector had been quite successful in eventually solving cases in this way. He joined Papadoulis standing in front of the board as he reeled off what was written on it, expanding on parts of it.

Alongside the Inspector's belief in, and use of, a sometimes quite rigid methodological approach to investigation, as well as appeals to Classical Greek beliefs his former boss Inspector Karagoulis would have approved of, he wasn't above occasionally throwing in comments from less academic sources. As the two policemen stood in front of the Incident Board he rubbed the back of his neck and said, "Eliminate the impossible and whatever remains, however improbable, must be the truth. Sir Arthur Conan Doyle, Sergeant."

"Sherlock Holmes, sir?"

"Yes, Georgiou, quite a detective."

The Sergeant raised his eyebrows slightly as his Inspector continued.

"So, we have a victim, Kathleen O'Mara, possibly also known as Aileen Regan," the Inspector began and glanced sideways at his Sergeant expecting an interruption from him challenging the fact that Papadoulis was obviously still clinging on to his belief that he recognised the victim from a case six years previously.

But it never came. Georgiou stayed silent, thinking better of it.

"The body was discovered by a local man walking his dog in Gennadi on some rough ground under some trees approximately thirty metres from the road at around eight o'clock this morning. Preliminary pathologist estimate is that the murder took place between four and five, but not where the body was found-"

"Not in Gennadi, sir," Georgiou interrupted.

"What?" Papadoulis was irritated by his Sergeant's interruption, disturbing the flow of his thought process, and he showed it in his sharp response, as well as his body language in the way he quickly spun round away from the board to glare at the Sergeant.

"How do you know that?" he snapped back at him.

"Well, the hotel key card, so-"

"So, what, Sergeant? The murder could still have taken place in Gennadi couldn't it, just not where the body was found there? The victim could actually have gone to Gennadi willingly with her killer."

"I suppose ... yes ..." Georgiou decided it was best not to continue any response, but simply wait for his Inspector to continue.

"The victim is in her mid-forties, according to the initial pathologist estimate," the Inspector turned back to face the board and continued. "Her passport, her Irish passport, which we discovered in her hotel room safe shows she was forty-four. All that was found on her body was a small amount of euros and a Lindos Memories Hotel room electronic key card, which we now know was last used to enter the room, presumably by her, at twelve minutes past four this morning. She was staying at the hotel with two female friends from work, Alison Lees and Suzanne Carmichael."

He pointed to the names of the two women on the board.

"It was their first night in the hotel, their first night in Lindos, and according to Suzanne Carmichael none of them had been to Lindos before. The women said they returned to the hotel together at around four after a night out in Lindos and all went to their rooms and bed. So, presumably when Kathleen O'Mara's key card was used at twelve minutes past four to enter the room she was alone."

"Yes, presumably, sir," Georgiou agreed.

"Consequently, she must have left the room soon after, if the time of death is accurate, either alone or with someone, her killer, and-"

"Who may, of course, have been waiting in the room for her, sir, having broken in perhaps?"

The Inspector scratched the back of his head again and this time was more receptive to his Sergeant's interruption and suggestion.

"Yes ... yes, they could have been, I suppose. Either way we know she wasn't killed in the room or anywhere else in the hotel it seems."

He stepped back a bit and stared at the board once more in silence. Eventually he sighed slightly and told the Sergeant, "It's just a pity we don't have full CCTV coverage of the entire hotel."

"It is, sir, but as there was no sign of any struggle in the room doesn't that suggest she knew her killer?"

"Yes it does, unless the killer took her from the hotel at gunpoint, as you suggested earlier remember Sergeant."

Georgiou sheepishly agreed. "Yes, I did, didn't I?"

"Hang on," Papadoulis started to say as he walked over closer to the board again. "What about the car park?"

"The car park, sir? It's at the front of the hotel, quite a large area."

The Inspector turned to stare at his Sergeant once again.

"I know that, Sergeant, but there must be CCTV coverage there surely, and anyone leaving with the victim would have to have had a vehicle, whether she went at gunpoint or of her own free will."

"I ... I suppose so, sir." Georgiou knew what the next question would be and it wasn't going to be good.

"You did ask and check?"

The Sergeant hesitated long enough for Papadoulis to draw his own conclusion.

"You bloody didn't, did you?" His anger had returned.

"Erm ... err ... no, sir, unfortunately I didn't."

The Inspector took a deep breath trying to contain his anger. He was barely successful."

"Do it now, as soon as we've finished this," Papadoulis barked at him.

"Yes, sir, I will, of course."

The Inspector took another deep breath and turning back towards the board shook his head once more, indicating his annoyance at what he perceived was his Sergeant's incompetence. He walked over to the part of the board that had the word 'PHONE?' written on it.

"The victim had no mobile phone with her, nothing on the body, although we know from her friends that she had it with her that night in Lindos and we know from the times that you rang the number that it was still active at that time, although the battery may have run out by now of course. So, where is it? Who has it, if anyone, or did she simply drop it somewhere and lose it. It wasn't in her hotel room. Presumably therefore she took it with her or still had it on her from the women's night out when she left the hotel with the killer. Hopefully, the tech guys in Rhodes will be able to get a trace on it and track it down if it's still active and the battery hasn't died by now. While we're waiting for that we need to also track down her phone service provider, presumably in Ireland or the U.K., as we know from the other two women she was living and working in London, and get her call records for the past month. I'll do that while you're checking the hotel for their car park CCTV. We need to check it from all last night and through to six this morning, just in case the killer did break into her room while the women were in Lindos."

"Ok, sir."

Ten minutes later the Sergeant reported that the Hotel Security Officer was going to send him the CCTV coverage of the car park that they wanted by email attachment in the next half-an-hour.

"Good, so that means at least the hotel has some coverage of the car park," Papadoulis commented, adding, "and I've just told the Rhodes Station tech officers to get on identifying O'Mara's phone service provider and get her phone records for the past month while they are trying to trace her phone."

The Inspector perched himself on the corner of the desk and rubbed the back of his neck with his right hand as he finished telling Georgiou that and was now once more peering intently across the small office at all that he had written on the Incident Board. Georgiou knew better than to interrupt his thought process, if there was one. Consequently, he simply stood in silence also peering at the board and the now much greater amount of information written upon it.

Finally Papadoulis eased himself off the corner of the desk, saying in a much more active and urgent voice as he once more pointed to part of the board, "Right, Sergeant, we need to go back to basics. Let's start by retracing the victim's movements last night."

He pointed to part of the board and continued, "We know she and her two friends, Lees and Carmichael, were in these two bars, Pal's Bar and the Courtyard Bar, as well as the Village House Restaurant for dinner first. We'll interview the owners and staff in them as soon as they open tonight and see what they remember about the women, if anything. One of the women said when we first saw them at the hotel pool, Carmichael I think, that they'd all had quite a bit to drink last night and she thought O'Mara was in her room sleeping off a hangover. We know she wasn't then, but if they had so much to drink surely someone in one of the two bars, one of the staff perhaps, will remember them."

Georgiou nodded and added, "And the two men, sir, the two men who took them to the club, Ken and Daniel. We need to find out more about them. Whether they are locals or tourists? The owners or staff in the bars may be able to help us with that, especially as one of the women told me that they thought the two guys were regular Lindos visitors. The bar staff tend to get to know their regular customers."

Georgiou's computer pinged as the Inspector replied, "Yes, we need to find and talk to them, and hopefully the staff will be able to help,"

The Sergeant glanced at the screen and confirmed it was the hotel CCTV car park coverage.

"Good, start trawling through that straightaway, but start first with around four, when the women got back to the hotel, and then after look at the earlier times last night to see if there's anything suspicious. While you're doing that I'll get on to Kyriakopoulis back at Rhodes Town station to do some background checks on the victim under both names, as well as on the other two women, their stuff on social media and the rest, plus the Irish police and passport office about the victim, as well as any financial records he can dig up."

Georgiou looked up from the computer screen while the CCTV files were downloading to ask something he guessed he knew the answer to.

"Under both names, don't you mean all three?"

Papadoulis responded sharply. "No, I mean all four. Suzanne Carmichael and Alison Lees, plus both the names Kathleen O'Mara and Aileen Regan."

He glared across the small office at Georgiou as his voice rose to emphasise the name Aileen Regan. He still wasn't giving up on his suspicion.

The Sergeant thought it best at that point to keep his head down and get on with checking the CCTV while his Inspector called Sergeant Kyriakopoulis about the background checks. Although he'd grown used to Papadoulis operating in this way during the time they'd worked together he was still unable to determine and decide if it was stubbornness on the Inspector's part or just a case of investigating and covering every angle and possibility. However, he wasn't about to dwell on that question now. Instead, he decided to simply peer intently at the CCTV images on the computer while the Inspector made his call to Kyriakopoulis back at Rhodes Town station.

Just over twenty minutes later though he broke the silence with, "Look at this, sir." Papadoulis went across to look over his shoulder as the Sergeant rolled back the CCTV film.

"There, there, stop it there," Papadoulis instructed him

"Yes, that's what I meant," Georgiou told him as he briefly glanced away from the screen and up at him over his shoulder.

"It's not very clear. It's the far side of the car park, furthest away from the camera, but it's definitely two people and one of them looks like a woman, and the time is about right, sir, four-twenty. Can't really make out the other one, but I guess it's a man. There surely can't be many people leaving the hotel at that time of night, so I reckon the woman must be O'Mara."

"Is that the only camera?"

"Yes unfortunately, just the one at the front of the hotel. I checked."

Papadoulis leaned closer to the screen as he asked, "Can you zoom in?"

"I can, but it just gets even less clear. See ..." Georgiou zoomed the frame in to confirm that, but then added, "But if I roll it on they get into what looks like some type of SUV model, dark coloured maybe black, although again the camera is too far away to get any image of the registration or even a clear make of the car."

He did just that and the Inspector agreed, shaking his head slightly as he added, "Damn."

"We can try and get the tech guys at Rhodes on it though, sir, and see if they can enhance the images in any way to make them clearer."

"Ok, get on to them about that."

As Papadoulis wandered slowly back over to his desk rubbing his chin with the palm of his left hand the Sergeant tried to offer some consolation for the lack of clear images.

"At least from this we have some better idea of the time O'Mara left the hotel, around four-twenty, and with what looks like a man, someone who must have been waiting for her somewhere in the hotel, or in his car in the car park, obviously waiting for her to return from the women's night out in Lindos."

"That's true. Have a look at the CCTV for the hours before that. See if it picks up a man on his own arriving at the hotel, or at least what looks like the same car arriving in the car park."

Georgiou went back to once more peering at the computer screen to do just that, but before that he took another look at the CCTV still image of the two people heading towards the car.

"It's not easy to see and be sure, sir. It's not very clear and quite dark in that part of the car park, but there doesn't seem to be any sign of anything in what I assume is the man's hand, like a gun for instance. It does look like the woman is wearing a light coloured t-shirt and dark trousers which could be jeans, just like the clothes on the body, and her hair looks light coloured, which could be blonde like O'Mara's. I'd be pretty certain it's her."

"What about the other person. What does it look like they are wearing? Can you make it out?" Papadoulis asked.

"Just dark clothes. Looks like a dark t-shirt maybe, and dark trousers, plus some sort of dark cap pulled down almost over their eyes I'd say. They are slightly taller than O'Mara, if it is her, and look quite slim, but really it's all a bit of a guess because of the bleary nature of the image, sir."

Papadoulis shook his head slightly once again, telling the Sergeant, "Ok, start looking at the earlier footage to see if you can spot anything, probably going back to midnight."

Slightly over an hour later the Sergeant reported, "Nothing, sir. No sign of anyone arriving alone or anything that looks like that black saloon in the later footage arriving in the car park. I've gone back to midnight, shall I keep looking?"

As the Inspector told him, with some hesitation, "Err ... yes, ok, look at another couple of hours, back to ten," his computer pinged. Glancing at his screen he added, "Christof's preliminary autopsy report."

It was just after four, prompting Papadoulis to think that the pathologist had obviously wasted no time, wanting to preserve what was left of his weekend. His thought was confirmed when he opened the email and Christof had written, "Here is my preliminary report in the attachment. Hope you won't need to bother me again this weekend, Yiannis."

He opened the attachment and started to scan the report, commenting and reading aloud parts of it.

"Female, around mid-forties, body looks in good condition, so obviously kept herself reasonably fit. Perhaps worked out regularly. Hair dyed blonde... time of death between four and five a.m. ... Some fibres were found on the victim's clothing, not from her clothes. They appear to be carpet fibres or from car seat covers, suggesting the body was moved in a vehicle after death or the victim was in a vehicle shortly before her death. It's as he said at the scene, the wound to the back of the head wasn't the cause of death. But hang on. In the report he states that strangulation wasn't either, despite the marks and bruises on her neck, and what he thought at the place the body was found."

As the Inspector stopped speaking to carry on scanning the report on the screen Georgiou asked, "What was then?"

Papadoulis sat back in his chair and stopped scanning the report as he frowned and told his Sergeant, "KCN, she was poisoned."

"KCN, sir?"

"Potassium cyanide. Christof says that preliminary blood tests show that is what killed her."

The Inspector looked back at the screen and started to read aloud from the report again. Potassium cyanide releases hydrogen cyanide gas, a highly toxic chemical asphyxiant that interferes with the body's ability to use oxygen. Exposure to potassium cyanide can be rapidly fatal. In addition there was quite an amount of alcohol in the victim's blood ... which fits with what the other two women told us from their night out in Lindos."

As he finished speaking he sat back once more in his chair and started to slowly scratch the back of his head looking confused.

"They said she was drunk and that they thought she was sleeping off a hangover when we saw them this morning, so that would account for the alcohol in the bloodstream, but cyanide, sir?"

Georgiou was equally confused.

The Inspector agreed on the alcohol. "Hmm ... yes ... although the female in the CCTV footage seemed to be walking ok. If it was O'Mara, maybe she wasn't that drunk, or had some type of high tolerance level?"

"Used to it, perhaps, sir, that kind of lifestyle?"

"Nothing discovered at the scene which could have been used to cause the blow to the head ... a full toxicology report requested and victim's clothes being checked for DNA." Papadoulis continued to read from the screen, and then scanned down through the further parts of the report in silence until adding a minute or so later, "This is also interesting, although I'm not sure what it tells us."

"What, sir?"

"A small tattoo on the inside of her upper right thigh, a flag, an Irish tricolour."

"Well we know she was Irish. She had an Irish passport. Perhaps obviously just a patriot."

"Perhaps, Georgiou, but seems a bit extreme don't you think, and to hide it away there is a bit odd too?"

"Maybe, sir, but-"

Papadoulis didn't let him finish. "And this ..."

He stopped for a moment as he read the next part of the report on the screen, eventually relaying again what he read.

"Christof says it's likely that the blow to the head came before the strangulation attempt, followed then by the poison being administered while she was in a state of less consciousness."

The Sergeant sat in silence while his Inspector once more slumped back in his chair before adding, "So, our killer had access to cyanide, or at least a cyanide tablet. In the report it says that Potassium cyanide is a compound with the formula KCN, a colourless crystalline salt, similar in appearance to sugar. It is highly soluble in water."

"So, it would have been relatively easy to administer it to the semi-unconscious victim in something like a bottle of water."

"Looks like it, Sergeant, and if our killer is carrying around a cyanide tablet in the appearance of a sugar cube I think we can assume this was a pre-planned murder and not some random attack in the early hours of this morning, particularly if the two people on the CCTV seen leaving the hotel were O'Mara and her killer."

He, if it is a he, and we can assume possibly it was from the CCTV, sir, obviously had the whole thing well planned and knew exactly where O'Mara was staying and would be."

"Did Carmichael and Lees say for certain that the three of them were all together the whole evening?" Papadoulis asked.

"Err ... I assumed that was the case, sir, although I never actually asked either of them that directly."

The Inspector glanced sideways at him and as he shook his head slightly told his Sergeant, " Right, you need to check with the other two women if she was with them the whole evening before they returned to the hotel, or did she go off to meet someone and perhaps arranged for them to come to her hotel later? Presumably, if she did it was likely to be someone she knew. They said that they all returned to the hotel together. Give one of them a call now."

While Georgiou reached for the phone to call Alison Lees the Inspector wandered back over to the Incident Board to write a note under Kathleen O'Mara's name on it about the cyanide as cause of death, as well as the flag tattoo, and then stood gazing at it in silence for a full five minutes more, scanning it from side to side. Then he wrote 'CAR PARK IMAGES 4.20' on it to one side. Eventually, Georgiou interrupted the silence filling the office.

"Lees said the three of them were altogether all evening. When I asked if she was certain of that, pointing out that after all they said they all had quite a bit to drink and maybe wouldn't have noticed if O'Mara had disappeared for a short time, especially in the club which would have been crowded at that time on a Friday night, she seemed a bit agitated and said I could check with Carmichael if I didn't believe her, but she was sure she would confirm it. So, should I, sir?"

"What, should you what?"

Papadoulis was distracted, deep in thought and still scanning the Incident Board.

"Check with Carmichael that they were altogether all evening."

"Maybe later, but if Lees is so adamant Carmichael will likely just confirm that what she told you was true."

With that the Inspector turned back to the board, thoughtfully scanned all the information on it for a good few minutes more, and then briefly scratched the back of his head with his left hand before saying in a much lower tone of voice than usual, "So, what's the key to all this?"

"Key, sir?" Georgiou asked as he looked across at him from his desk.

"Yes, Sergeant, what links all this, all these things together? We have a dead woman, who I am still certain is not who she claims to be, or perhaps was not who she claimed to be in Lindos six years ago. We have her two friends, her women holiday companions. Her dead body found in Gennadi, but not necessarily killed there. Why did the killer dump the body there. Was it because they knew the area or just a random choice, and why all the way down there in the south of the island when the victim was staying near Lindos. Then we have what appear to be the victim and another person on the hotel car park CCTV leaving at four-twenty, which could account for the fibres found on the victim's clothes as per the Pathologist report. So, what's her connection to that person, especially as she appears to be leaving with them willingly? How did he or she know O'Mara was there, staying at that hotel? Was that someone she met in

Lindos earlier, a local or a tourist? And why does O'Mara leave with them at that time, barely the early hours of the morning, especially when the other two women were so positive that the victim had had a lot to drink; so positive that they clearly thought when we first approached them at the hotel pool this morning that O'Mara was still sleeping off a hangover. It definitely didn't look on the CCTV that the woman leaving the hotel was walking across the car park in any unsteady way. And-"

Georgiou attempted to interrupt with, "But we've been through all this, sir, and ..."

His voice tailed off as the Inspector turned his head away from the board and fixed a glare across the office at him for a few seconds. The Sergeant knew better than to repeat what he said. He'd seen Papadoulis do this before on other cases. It was obviously something he felt he had to do, some sort of methodical routine that he believed helped his thinking and analysis of cases. Georgiou was right.

"I was about to say, Sergeant."

There was a trace of annoyance in his voice as he added, "And then there's her phone. We know she had it with her in Lindos last night, at least according to her two friends. It wasn't on the dead body so where is it now?"

He stood there in front of the Incident Board in silence for a few seconds more before turning to go back and sit at his desk. Now he was rubbing his forehead with the fingers of his right hand in puzzlement. Georgiou thought it best to maintain the silence.

After another full couple of minutes Papadoulis bit his bottom lip faintly and told his Sergeant, "Perhaps we are looking at all this the wrong way."

"Georgiou looked bemused but remained silent. He wanted to ask just what his Inspector meant, but determined it was best to keep silent and let his vocal thought pattern run on.

"Perhaps we need to look at it all in a different way."

"How, sir?" Georgiou decided he could at least ask.

"If you only look at a problem, a case, one way, then you will get stuck, or at least, could get stuck if there is no obvious pattern to all the circumstances, for instance the victim leaving the hotel with someone when she was supposedly drunk, and in the early hours of the morning. Where were they going?"

Papadoulis got up from his desk and walked over to the Incident Board once more before continuing, "Instead of looking at a problem or a case one way therefore you should sometimes turn it around, sometimes by a hundred and eighty degrees. Then you can perhaps see things from another angle in order to solve it, or at least get a clearer picture of it, look at it differently."

Georgiou simply nodded to indicate some form of slight agreement. What he was actually thinking though was just how did his current boss the methodical Inspector Papadoulis ever work so well as a Sergeant with his murdered, much more chaotic, Greek Mythology obsessed Inspector Dimitris Karagoulis?

"So if, as you said earlier, because of the cyanide the murder was obviously not a spur of the moment thing, sir, but was pre-planned, then by looking at the sequence of events differently we can conclude that our killer isn't someone O'Mara met last night in Lindos for the first time, but someone who had tracked her movements, knew exactly where she was going to be staying, at the Memories hotel and arranged to meet her there?"

"Yes, Sergeant, but someone who knew her, or at least knew of her, and that's why the killer took her phone. If the killer is someone she knew or knew of her then presumably there could be messages or calls on her phone linking them to their meeting with her. So, instead of it being a crime in a moment of anger and rage, perhaps brought about over her refusal to have sex with the killer, sex with someone she'd only just met in Lindos last night, it was a case of the killer hitting her with an object and trying to strangle her to silence her, and then eventually poisoning her while she was semi-conscious. That means it was a pre-planned murder by someone who knew exactly where she would be, where she was staying, where to find her."

Now the Sergeant was nodding in agreement with much more agitation.

Papadoulis turned away from the board as he said, "That's why we need to find her phone. That's what we need to focus on. We can check whether any of the staff in the two bars and the restaurant saw her with it last night, and staff in the club, when we interview them tonight. And we need to go back and ask Carmichael and Lees who they think O'Mara might have told where they were staying, both last night in Lindos and before they left London."

He checked his watch and then added, "We'll start in the restaurant, Village House, in an hour. In the meantime though, get an officer here to dig out that 2016 Lindos case file. Officially it was recorded as an accident, but let's have a look at that so that I can remind myself about the case, all of what we found, particularly about Aileen Regan and what she told me when I interviewed her, before we got orders from higher up to abruptly close it and record it officially as an accident.

The Sergeant simply nodded reluctantly once more, hiding any disapproval that the Inspector still hadn't completely given up on his theory that Kathleen O'Mara and Aileen Regan was one and the same person, or at least, had been.

5

Daniel Bird

Just at the point where Papadoulis was clearly getting more and more agitated, waiting for any information on the victim's phone from Rhodes Town – walking backwards and forwards across the small office and muttering, "What's taking them so long?" – the phone rang on the desk Georgiou was using.

After he identified himself to the caller he placed his left hand over the receiver and told the Inspector, "It's Rhodes, sir," then after listening for a few more seconds said to the caller, "Ok, yes, got it, so-"

"Have they located it?" Papadoulis interrupted.

Once more the Sergeant placed his hand over the receiver saying, "Hang on, sir."

"Right, good, so that's as close as you can get?" Georgiou asked the caller.

Meanwhile his Inspector was getting even more agitated, anxious to know what they'd found, while his Sergeant listened to the caller for a further half-a-minute or so.

"Ok, I see, so definitely in that part of the village and up to about five metres if we're lucky. Thanks."

As he rang off the Inspector's patience had all but run out. Georgiou did not even get to replace the receiver before he asked firmly, "Well?"

"The phone's signal pinged in Lindos village ten minutes ago, down towards the centre of the village, near to the square by the old Amphitheatre."

"And? Is that the best they-"

The Inspector's agitation wasn't subsiding, but Georgiou didn't let him finish.

"They explained that GPS location data can be very accurate and precise under certain conditions sir, mostly in outdoor locations. In the best instances they said the signal can be reliable down to within a five metre radius under open sky. However, GPS and internet connections are not exactly great in some parts of the village. So, one of the alleys off that square is the best they can do at the moment. The tech guy pointed out that the one good thing is that the phone is still turned on and that obviously the battery has not died. If it's our killer that has it they haven't bothered to turn it off. For some reason they've left it on."

"Right, there are a few tourist apartments around that square, and nearby going down towards St. Paul's Bay," Papadoulis started to tell his Sergeant. "And there's Café Melia, so I suppose it's a long shot and unlikely, but our killer could be having something in there. Get some officers checking those apartments and the café, and give them the number of the phone. Tell them to call it sporadically, just in case they are near enough to hear it ringing by any chance. There are two alleys that run off the square. Get them to also check the apartments in the one closest to the Amphitheatre which goes all the way down to Giorgos Bar. You and I will check the one alongside Café Melia and the Italian restaurant that bends round and up to the main alleyway through the top of the village past the Olympia Restaurant. There's an alley just off that one, just after you get around the bend. It goes up to the centre of the village and comes out near Bar404 and Yannis Bar. If I remember rightly there are a few more apartments in that alley, so we should also check them out."

"You seem to have got to know the layout of the village very well, sir."

"Well, we did spend quite a few days here six years ago investigating that so-called accident remember, Sergeant. Now come on, get those officers sorted doing door to door, and don't forget to give them O'Mara's phone number. We can get started checking that other alley. No time to waste in case our killer disappears with the phone."

Fifteen minutes later, while three officers checked the apartments around the square and leading down to St. Paul's Bay, Papadoulis and Georgiou were climbing the three small steps leading up to the alley just around the bend from the square. The square was busy with some of the children of the

Greek residents playing, as it was on most late afternoons and early evenings in the summer, while staff of the Italian restaurant on one side of the square, Gatto Bianco, was busy setting up tables for the evening on the restaurant's small front terrace. The heat of the July day was gradually giving way to an only slightly cooler early evening as the hot sun faded slowly behind the Acropolis looming over the village. For many of the tourists this was the nicest part of the day. Some were sat outside Café Melia having an alcoholic drink or an iced coffee on their way back from a day on Lindos Main Beach or the smaller Pallas Beach, before showering and changing in their apartments and heading out later for dinner in one of the many rooftop restaurants. It appeared to Papadoulis that the grim discovery early that morning in Gennadi had not yet reached Lindos, not to the tourists at least, not enough to affect the tourist trade.

After climbing the three steps Papadoulis and his Sergeant came to a halt. There were three pairs of large wooden doors on the left hand side of the alley. The first pair had a small wooden plaque on the wall next to them with the name Erato Apartments, obviously tourist apartments. The other two pairs of doors further down the alley on that side had nothing similar, not even a number on them. To the right, about ten metres from the steps, was a short alley of about twenty metres with a dead end and a couple of single doors, but with no names or numbers. Further along that side of the alley was another pair of large wooden double doors and then in the corner at the far end three more small steps leading up to a pair of arch shaped wooden doors. The Perspex plaque on the wall next to them showed that they too were tourist apartments.

After the two policemen walked the thirty metres or so to the far end of the alley the Inspector turned back to look along it and then briefly scratch the back of his head.

"Should we just knock on all of them, sir? Shall I take one side and you the other?" Georgiou asked.

Papadoulis glanced sideways at him and then let out a small sigh.

"Let's think about this for a moment, Sergeant. If our killer is in one of these apartments or behind one of these doors with

O'Mara's phone they are hardly going to just admit they have it, give it up to us, and also admit to the murder just because we happen to be two Greek policemen knocking on their door are they?"

"So, sir, what do we do? The tech guys at Rhodes station said that the track is only reliable down to within a five metre radius."

After a few seconds silence the Inspector nodded to himself a little and then told Georgiou, "Look, we know according to those guys the phone is somewhere around here, in one of the apartments in this alley or in one of them around the square down there."

He pointed towards the end of the alley and continued.

"And we know that the phone is still switched on, or at least has recently been switched on."

The Sergeant looked confused until Papadoulis added "So, Sergeant, we go and stand halfway down the alley and then you call it. Call O'Mara's number and if we get lucky we may be able to hear it ringing as it's obviously switched on. We just have to hope the volume control is turned up enough."

With that the two men moved to halfway down the alley and Georgiou made the call. After ten seconds or so he said, "It's ringing, sir, so the phone is on, but it's not being answered."

"Leave it to ring for a while," Papadoulis told him and then began to slowly walk along the alley back towards the far end, back towards the apartments on the corner with the three small steps and the Perspex plaque. Ten metres from them he stopped, saying, "Listen, can you hear that? It's a phone ringing."

They were now standing beneath a shuttered pair of windows close to the pair of double doors on the left hand side of the alley between those of the Erato Apartments and the pair of doors nearest the end of the alley.

"It is, sir, but it could be any phone. We don't know if-"

Georgiou was interrupted by his Inspector telling him, "Ring off now. Stop the call."

The ringing they could hear stopped.

Papadoulis pointed. "It's here, behind those doors, which must lead to whatever is behind those shutters. That's where

O'Mara's phone is and perhaps our killer. Call the other officers and tell them to stop their search and come here now."

Georgiou nodded. As he was starting to make the call he pointed out that, "Even if the phone is here, sir, we don't know that the killer is in there of course, but shouldn't we wait for back-up from the three officers in the square anyway, just in case?"

However, the Inspector wasn't waiting. On one of the doors was a large old fashioned iron door knocker. He went straight over to it and banged it aggressively three times. Initially no one answered, so Papadoulis banged the knocker again three more times. Georgiou suggested that they were probably tourist apartments behind the door and whoever was staying there was likely to have been off on one of the Lindos beaches for the day and still making their way back to the apartments.

The Inspector glanced back, telling him, "Whoever it is they left O'Mara's phone in there. That why we heard it ringing."

Just as the three back-up officers came running up the alley one of the doors swung open. Papadoulis and Georgiou were faced with a bleary eyed, dishevelled looking, quite tall, long thin faced, dark haired guy in his mid-forties wearing a dark blue t-shirt, beige shorts and flip flops.

The two policemen produced their police identification credentials and introduced themselves, followed by Papadoulis asking, "Can we come in, sir."

"What ... why ... what's this about?" the man asked.

"Can we just come inside please, sir and I'll explain."

The guy held the door open for them and the two police officers went into what was a small enclosed courtyard with a high white wall to the right hand side. Straight ahead of them was a closed door to what was obviously an apartment and to the left was another apartment door, this time open, obviously left like that by the guy while answering the Inspector's knocks on the courtyard door. Also to the left was a flight of wrought iron stairs up to a small terrace and another apartment door which was also closed. Papadoulis quickly estimated that the shuttered double window under which they were standing when they heard the phone ringing - O'Mara's phone – was part of the ground floor apartment to the left, the one the guy had emerged from to let them in. He nodded slightly in the direction of the open door to that apartment and then told Georgiou firmly, "Make the call again, Sergeant."

Within seconds the sound of a phone ringing – O'Mara's phone - came from the guy's flat.

"Is that your phone ringing, sir?" Papadoulis asked, knowing full well it wasn't his.

"What? ... err ... what ... erm, no, no it's not."

He looked the worse for wear, clearly very hungover and confused, and was now rubbing the back of his neck with his left hand while the Inspector watched his actions and reactions carefully.

"It's ringing in your apartment, sir. So, is that your phone?"

The guy sat down on one of the white plastic chairs by the small table in one corner of the courtyard as the Inspector began to ask again. "Sir, is that-"

"No, I mean yes it is a phone ringing in my apartment. It's been ringing all bloody night, well since the early hours of this morning when I got back here. But, no, no, it's not mine. But what's this-"

Papadoulis didn't let him finish.

"Who's is it then, sir?"

"Erm ..."

He was rubbing the back of his neck again as the Inspector pulled out one of the other chairs from under the table and sat down opposite, prompting him once more with, "Sir?"

"Erm .... I'm not really sure. I think it belongs to one of the women I met in the village last night."

"Which woman? Did you get her name, and why do you have her phone?"

The Inspector leaned forward onto the table, staring straight across into the man's face as he asked that.

The guy shook his bleary head slightly as he replied, "No I didn't get their names. There were three of them. Not their full names at least."

He shook his head slightly again and bit his bottom lip trying to remember before he added, "Err ... Ali ... and err ... Suzy and ... err ..."

He hesitated, trying to remember the third name through the haze of his hangover.

The Inspector glanced up at the still standing Georgiou and then asked, "And, sir, the third one?"

Now the guy rubbed his forehead with his right hand while he simultaneously leaned forward to rest his other elbow on the table and support his chin.

"I'm a bit hungover, so it's all a bit blurred. That sort of long Lindos night hangover, if you know what I mean."

"Not really, sir, but I can imagine. The name? It is quite important."

"Yes, yes, but what's all this about? And what's the phone got to do with it and me, what's-?"

"The name, sir, the name of the third woman?"

His interruption and slightly raised voice indicated that Papadoulis' patience was rapidly running out.

"Yes, err ... erm ... Katherine, I think ... erm ... no, no, Kathleen maybe."

The Inspector glanced up at his Sergeant once more, raising his eyebrows before asking, "So, how do you come to have this woman Kathleen's phone?"

Even though it was well past five in the afternoon the guy still appeared to be suffering from his hangover. Instead of answering the Inspector's question immediately he first asked, "Look, do you mind if I get some water?"

Papadoulis sat back in his chair and nodded. Before the guy emerged back into the courtyard with a large bottle of water Georgiou commented, "Seems odd, sir. If he's our killer he's very hungover. On the CCTV footage from the hotel car park O'Mara didn't appear to be walking unsteadily, didn't appear drunk, but nor did the guy she left with."

The man took a long drink from the bottle after he sat back down at the table, then shook his head vigorously for a few seconds as if he was trying to regain some of his hungover dulled senses.

Papadoulis waited, assuming he would now get an answer to his last question as to why the guy had O'Mara's phone.

Instead though all he got was another, "Just what is all this about, Inspector?"

54

He ignored it and again asked, "Why do you have the woman's phone, sir?"

Again the guy ignored the question and instead reached out his left hand on to the table towards the bottle to take another swig of the water. The Inspector's patience had expired. Before the guy's hand could reach the bottle he grabbed his wrist and in a raised voice asked, "Who the bloody hell are you? What are you doing here in Lindos?"

The guy freed his wrist and sprang back in the chair. Badly hungover he might have been, but his senses were still functioning well enough to comprehend the policeman's growing impatience and anger. He obviously was certainly not making any allowance for the guy's hungover state.

The guy blurted out rapidly, "Daniel Bird, my name's Daniel Bird. I'm a regular visitor to Lindos. I'm just here on holiday for two weeks. I don't understand what this is about, that's all."

Papadoulis leaned forward onto the table once more, stared directly into the guy's face, and again asked in a very firm menacing tone, "So, why have you got the woman Kathleen's bloody phone then, Daniel Bird?"

Throughout all of this the Sergeant remained standing and mostly silent, taking full note of, and admiring, his Inspector's interrogation technique; how he was purposely not informing the guy what this was all about, not telling him about Kathleen O'Mara's body being discovered and her murder. He clearly wanted to get as much information out of him before Daniel Bird was aware of how serious the situation was, in the hope that he might actually divulge something that he wished later he hadn't when he'd perhaps had time to get his story straight. It was an interesting and useful technique. Georgiou was learning from his superior all the time.

"Ok, ok," from Papadoulis' growing agitation he was at last starting to realise the seriousness of the situation. He took another swig of water before saying, "As I said before, the phone belongs to one of the three women I, we, met in the village last night, Suzy, Ali and Kathleen, I think the third one's name was. But I didn't know which one until you just told me. I just knew it, remembered it belonged to one of them, but I had no idea which."

He was looking straight across at the Inspector and was about to continue when Papadoulis asked, "We?"

"We what?"

"You said we. So, it wasn't just you who met them?"

"Oh, no."

He took another swig from the bottle.

"So, who else?" the Inspector asked.

"Ken."

"Ken who? A friend of yours? What's his last name?"

"I ... err ..."

He hesitated for a few seconds and rubbed the back of his neck once again.

"Well, he's not really a friend, just someone I've seen in the village and spoken to on a few nights. A regular Lindos holiday visitor, he said, but I don't know his surname, just know him as Ken."

"Where's he staying?"

He shook his head slightly once more in a very gentle manner, as if he was trying to remember, but that was actually making his head ache even more.

"Not sure. I think he said it was out of the village, up the top in Krana, one of the hotel and studio complexes up there I think. He told me he stays in a few places up there, and sometimes in the village."

"Which one, Mr. Bird? There are quite a few," Papadoulis pressed him once more.

"As I said, I can't be sure, Horizon maybe, Lindos Horizon rings a bell, but-"

The Inspector got up out of the chair, turned away from him and slowly walked to the opposite side of the courtyard, then turned and leaned against the high white wall.

"Let me get this straight, Mr. Bird," he began. "You have the phone of a woman you say you only met last night, and who you only know as Kathleen. In fact, you didn't even know it was hers before I informed you of that. Prior to that you thought it could belong to any one of the three women you met last night, one whom you think was called Kathleen but wasn't exactly clear on, or one of her two friends, Ali and Suzy."

Bird stared across at him, unsure quite where he was going with this.

"And then you say it wasn't just you who met the three women, one of whose phone you now have, but also a man called Ken, who you only know as Ken and don't know his full name, but you think he is a regular tourist visitor to Lindos, but you aren't really sure where he is staying, although you think it is up at Krana and could be Lindos Horizon."

"But I'd bet he'll certainly be in Pal's Bar later tonight though. He always is I believe. That's what he told me before anyway," Daniel Bird interjected.

Papadoulis walked back over to again sit at the table opposite him as he quite softly told him, "All a bit vague though isn't it, Mr. Bird?"

"Yes, but I had quite a lot to drink, and anyway you still haven't told me what this is all-"

The Inspector didn't let him finish. He leaned across the table once again and told him in a quite low, but firm voice, "She's dead, Mr. Bird. The woman Kathleen, who's phone you happen to have, was found murdered early this morning just off a road to the beach at Gennadi. And by the way her name, her full name, in case you are remotely interested, is Kathleen O'Mara. And you have her phone, Mr. Bird. Now why would that be?"

A look of shock spread over Daniel Bird's face. If it was possible, given his hungover state, even more blood appeared to be rapidly draining from it. After a few seconds all he could mutter was yet another, "What?"

His head slumped into his hands as he rested his elbows on the table. Meanwhile, Papadoulis glanced up at his Sergeant as they both closely observed Bird's reaction. Georgiou frowned, but the Inspector wasn't about to give the hungover man any respite. He remained leaning across the table as he raised his voice again and demanded, "Now, Mr. Bird, tell us how you come to have Kathleen O'Mara's bloody phone. Stop pissing us around."

Bird lifted his head up from out of his hands, shook it vigorously a couple of times and then muttered, "Ok, ok,

Inspector, I'll try. From what I can remember this is what happened."

For a moment the two policemen fleetingly thought he was about to admit to the murder. They quickly exchanged glances suggesting that is what they both anticipated. They were wrong.

"We, me and Ken, and I really don't know his last name, met the three women in Pal's Bar late on. Well, actually Ken met them first, was talking to them first. I must have nodded hello to him when I came into the bar, but never spoke to him, if I remember rightly. I was at the bar and he was a few feet behind me talking to the three of them, the women. I think I heard him say, 'I'm sure Daniel will take you there', or something like that. So, hearing my name I went over to them and Ken."

"What time was that?" Georgiou interrupted, which drew a disapproving glance from the Inspector who obviously preferred that they simply let Bird relay what he knew.

"Err .." He rubbed the back of his neck yet again. "Couldn't say exactly. Must have been past one as the music had gone off so-"

"Music had gone off? What's that got to do with the time?" the Sergeant interrupted again.

"It's a local by-law. The music in the bars has to be turned off at one o'clock, Sergeant," Papadoulis told him, accompanied with another glare of annoyance, followed by, "So, where, where was this guy Ken telling the women you'd take them?"

Bird looked across at them both and then went on, "Yes, so anyway probably around half-past one, I guess it was. There were still quite a few people in the bar having late drinks. That's what usually happens, but apparently the women wanted to go to a club. It was their first time in Lindos, first night, so they were asking Ken if there was one and where. He told them Arches Plus, the open air club down towards the Main Beach. It's only open on a Friday and Saturday night."

"Why you? Why did Ken say you'd take them?" Papadoulis asked.

"He knew that I knew the owner, Valasi, because I've been coming here for quite a lot of summers."

"This guy Ken didn't want to go? So, you took the women there?"

"No, he wanted to go alright. He was just using it, me taking them, as a way to get to talk to them. We all went when they'd finished their drinks, including Ken. As I said, I think he wanted to go all along. He was just ... oh, I'm not sure what he was doing ... maybe just playing a game to get them there, making out he wasn't going to go. He was quite drunk. He'd been doing shots with them in Pal's I think. Anyway, he came. I actually hadn't been down there to Arches Plus for years, four or five maybe. It would have been before Covid, before the pandemic."

He was rambling a bit, the lingering effect of the hangover. As he reached for and took another drink from the bottle of water Papadoulis' patience was running out once again.

"What happened at the club, Mr. Bird? The phone, how did you come to have it?"

"It was packed. Soon as we got in there Ken got us all drinks, not that we really needed any more, but he insisted. We just talked between us. I spent most of the time talking to one of the women alone, Ali. It must have been a couple of hours, perhaps approaching four, when the women said they were going to leave. Ken tried to persuade them to stay for one more drink, but one of them, it was that woman Kathleen I think, said something like it had been a long day, what with the travelling, and she was clearly determined to leave."

"Did the other two agree?"

"They seemed a bit reluctant at first, but soon agreed. I suppose because they would have to share a taxi back to their hotel."

"You knew they weren't staying in the village then?"

"Yes, yes, Memories, they were staying at Lindos Memories. I think I asked them, one of them anyway, probably Ali, before we left Pal's."

The Inspector shot a quick glance at Georgiou before he asked, "Why?"

"Why what, Inspector?" Bird looked puzzled.

"Why were you so interested in where they were staying?"

Georgiou clearly realised that Papadoulis was checking in case perhaps Bird was the man who later was on the hotel car park CCTV leaving with the victim.

Bird still looked bemused.

"Just something you ask here generally, Inspector. You talk to someone in a bar here, or anywhere on holiday I suppose, and you ask how long are you here for, where are you staying? Just small talk."

"Is that all, the only reason?"

"Well, I suppose I was checking that if they came to the club, and it would obviously be quite late when they left, that they could then get back to where they were staying easily enough, that's all."

"You weren't hoping to go back there, to their hotel, with one of them then?"

A very slight glimpse of a smile crept across Bird's lips.

"No, Inspector. I was quite drunk by the time we got to the club, and they were all quite drunk it seemed. Not really my style to try anything on in those type of situations."

"What is your style here in Lindos then?" Papadoulis asked.

Now it was Daniel Bird who was frowning.

"Style, what's my style? I don't have one, Inspector. It was a figure of speech."

"OK, so they left, the women. But you still haven't explained how you come to have Kathleen O'Mara's phone?"

"Valasi, the owner, when he saw me coming in, all five of us, he kindly showed us to what they call the VIP area in the club. It's an area slightly higher up that looks down over the rest of the club and one of the staff comes to take your order for drinks so you don't have to queue at the bar, which is always crowded. There are some table and chairs there and we, me, Ken and the three women, were stood by one of the low tables. After the women left Ken suggested we had one more drink, so we ordered one. After that we both had had enough so agreed we'd leave. We both said we needed some food, and there's a place just along the road from the club where you can always get some late-"

"What time was that?"

"Phew! Four-thirty or nearer five perhaps. I vaguely remember thinking as we left 'Christ it'll be light soon'. So maybe even after five. I really couldn't be sure, Inspector. Possibly someone at the club might remember, Michalis maybe, the Manager. He knows me and was the one serving us drinks."

"And where do we find him?"

"Arches, the club in the centre of the village. He works there during the week, and then Arches Plus Friday and Saturday night, so he'll be there tonight. The same Greek guy, Valasi, owns them both. I'm sure he'll-"

"The phone, Mr. Bird?"

Papadoulis interrupted again, trying to bring him back to the point.

"He was the person who handed it to me, Michalis. For some reason now I remember that a lot more clearly than some of the rest of the evening. That's all a bit of a blur, an alcoholic blur I'm afraid."

"He handed it to you? When?"

"As Ken and me were leaving. Michalis stopped us on the way out and said one of the women we were with had left the phone on one of the tables. He said we should take it. I don't think he realised that we'd only met them that night and when we asked he said he didn't know which one of them the phone belonged to. So, I took it. When we ate some chips at Nikos just along from the club I tried to open it, but it was locked. Ken said if it was locked we couldn't even turn it off or find the number for it. So I took it, thinking I could call Memories hotel sometime today and ask about them, the three women, explain about the phone and get them to pass my number on to one of the women to get them to call me. The trouble was I was so hungover I'd not long got up and hadn't got around to doing it by the time you turned up. I presumed that in any case, failing that, they might be in the village tonight anyway. The problem was that because I couldn't turn it off it kept getting calls after I finally got into my bed, around six. For some reason, god knows why, I made the mistake in my drunken state of putting it on charge, so it just kept buzzing with calls. The trouble was I couldn't answer them anyway because it was locked, and the notifications that I saw coming up on the screen only had a name and no number, well some of them did, so I couldn't even call it back on my phone."

"What names?" Papadoulis asked firmly.

"Names?" In his hungover state Daniel Bird wasn't picking up on the questions easily.

"What names kept appearing on the screen, the names of the callers?" the Inspector asked again.

"Oh, err ... mostly 'Unknown caller' and then a few, a couple I think, from someone called 'Michael', but mostly 'Unknown number' ones. Again though, I was half-asleep for most of them and in a somewhat alcoholic induced haze."

The Inspector got up from his chair and told Bird, "Can you get the phone for us now please. We will need to take it and do some checks. We will also need to take your fingerprints. You need to come to Lindos Police Station in the next couple of hours please. I'll let the officer on the front desk there know and he'll take your prints. It won't take long."

"My-"

Papadoulis didn't let him finish.

"Yes, for elimination at this stage. We need to check who else may have handled the phone besides yourself and the victim. Did your friend Ken handle it at all?"

"No, no I don't think so. You can ask him, but I don't think so. Michalis did though."

"Ok, we will have to take his too, Michalis, and we'll check with this guy Ken when we locate him, see if he handled the phone at all."

Daniel Bird got up and went into the flat, then emerged a few seconds later with the phone. Georgiou held an evidence bag open and Bird dropped the phone in. As he did so Papadoulis asked, "You said you were here on holiday, but what do you do when you're not on holiday?"

"Sorry?" Bird looked confused again over the question.

"For work, what do you do for work?"

"Oh, I see, I'm a property developer."

"Here?"

"No, no, Inspector. I wished. That'd be nice, back in the U.K."

Bird wasn't the only one who looked a little confused over that question. The Sergeant also did.

"Ok Mr Bird, that'll be all for now. Don't forget to get the finger printing done," Papadoulis reminded him as he motioned to Georgiou that they could leave. The two policemen turned to make their way across the small courtyard. When they were almost at the doors to the alley the Inspector turned back towards him and couldn't resist asking one more question.

"Just one final thing for now, Mr. Bird. The victim, the woman, Kathleen, can you recall if at any time during the evening she might have introduced herself as Aileen or if you heard any of her two friends call her that? "

Georgiou discreetly rolled his eyes.

Bird again looked confused.

"No, not really. As I said, we had a lot to drink and I wasn't sure on the names before, but that is a bit of an unusual name. Irish is it?"

"Yes, it is, so?"

No, no, I'm sure I would have remembered that, that name, bit unusual. Can't recall hearing any of her two friends use it either, calling her that. You could ask Ken if you locate him, although he was about as drunk as me."

"We will, Mr. Bird, we will," the Inspector told him as he opened one of the doors as they left.

6

The Village House restaurant and the Courtyard Bar

As the two policemen stepped into the alley outside the courtyard to Daniel Bird's flat Georgiou asked, "Where now, sir?"

The Inspector glanced at his watch.

"Just after six, let's make a start on checking those places the three women visited last night, seeing if any of the staff remembers anything odd, starting with the restaurant. Then we'll check out the two bars and have a word with the manager of that club to see if Bird's story about the phone checks out. First though we need to drop the phone into the station here and get one of the officers to take it to Rhodes Town straightaway for fingerprint checks and get it unlocked. Bird should turn up at the station in the next couple of hours, so they can send his to Rhodes too. Then we should know if there are any others on it besides his and O'Mara's. Give the tech guys at Rhodes station a call now to let them know the phone's on its way and that we need the fingerprint checks urgently, plus tell them to get the phone unlocked and get O'Mara's phone records as soon as possible, particularly for any calls Friday night and early Saturday morning."

As they walked down the alley turned right and then left to head up the slight hill to the station the Sergeant made the call to the Rhodes Town station. While he arranged back at the station for an officer to take the phone to Rhodes Papadoulis called Alison Lees and Suzanne Carmichael to ask if they knew Ken's full name by any chance; if he told them last night when they met or at the club possibly? When Georgiou came into the station back office having despatched the phone to Rhodes the Inspector told him, "Neither Carmichael and Lees knew this guy Ken's full name. He just introduced himself as Ken they said, and they said they couldn't say about O'Mara's phone being left in the club as they never knew she'd lost it till we asked about it when we saw them at the hotel this morning."

"That's logical, I suppose, sir, about the phone I mean.

"Yes, and they both said the only people who knew where they were staying in Lindos was close family. They are both divorced, so just brothers and sisters, and then Bird and the guy Ken last night after they told them. They couldn't be sure about who O'Mara may have told. They said basically they didn't know for sure about her family, but they both thought she said at one point that she didn't have any left alive."

The Inspector wandered over to look at the Incident Board for a moment and then picked up one of the markers and wrote the name 'DANIEL BIRD' on it, followed by 'KEN?' He scratched the back of his head briefly then told his Sergeant, "Right, let's go and check out that restaurant. It's been a long day and I'm quite hungry, but unfortunately we won't have time to eat, even though I bet the food is good."

Georgiou smiled and nodded as they made their way out of the office and the station, and down through the village alleyways.

The Lindos hot July sun had cooled and would soon be retiring for the night to be replaced by a growing twilight and eventual looming darkness that would shroud the village, illuminated only by the lights from the many restaurant rooftops and a large bright full moon which towered over the Acropolis like some ancient Greek god. The village alleyways were already filling up with the multitude of tourists heading for their pre-dinner drinks in the still warm air outside the many bars or just directly to the rooftop of one of the restaurants. It was that time of the evening when the beach and sun worshipping amongst the tourists gave way to the good Greek cuisine and alcohol appreciation. Soon the many restaurants would be full, followed shortly after by the bars as the pre-dinner drinks and then food were supplanted by the enjoyment of alcohol and music, including traditional Greek music in some of the bars.

This was the first real season when the picturesque tourist village could claim to have fully recovered from the effects of the Covid pandemic, and returned to its familiar tourist popularity.

Over many centuries Lindos had been occupied and fortified by the Romans, Byzantines, and The Knights of St. John when they were defeated and expelled from Jerusalem, as well as by the Ottomans and, of course, the Greeks. The village, which the Acropolis loomed over, divided two bays - Lindos Bay and the even more beautiful St Pauls Bay. Parts of the Acropolis dated from the fourth century BC.

The valley leading down to Lindos Bay housed the main part of the village, with the fine beaches in the bay surrounding the clear blue sea – the small Pallas Beach and the larger Main Beach. Lindos was a labyrinth of narrow alleyways running between white-washed houses and apartments. Shops stocked with souvenir t-shirts, bags, linen and the obligatory soft toy donkeys lined the alleyways in its centre. It was famous for its donkeys, or Lindos taxis as many of the donkey owners referred to them. There were plenty of the Lindos taxis available. At times they gave some of the alleys a very distinctive odour as the donkeys left their deposits in the hot sun, soon to be scooped up by a guy whose profession it was.. An endless stream of donkeys with their owners did a good trade ferrying the tourists from the Main Square down to the small scenic Pallas Beach at one end of the bay or up to the ancient Acropolis above the village. Cars, or any other vehicles, were prohibited in the village. The only exceptions were the small trucks which squeezed through the narrow alleyways in order to make deliveries to the bars, cafes and supermarkets, often scraping the walls on each side. Some residents regularly joked that you could always tell if you'd had too much to drink the night before if you woke up with whitewash dust on your arms from bouncing off of some of the walls of the narrower alleyways on your way back to your apartment.

Together with the shops, houses and apartments there was a myriad of restaurants and bars in the village. Each had its own particular characteristic, as well as its own characters that frequented, worked in, or owned them. Most of their staff were summer season workers. Peculiarly a good many of those were Albanian. In previous summers there had been quite a few young Brit workers. However, Brexit, and the consequent restrictions now as non-EU nationals which ruled that they could only spend ninety out of every one-hundred-and-eighty days in the EU, had severely reduced their number, such that there were only a couple by the summer of 2022. Although, there were still a good number of older Brit ex-pats who lived in and nearby the village.

All of the staff in the restaurants and bars had the Greek way of friendly service. Instantly you felt you were their friend. No doubt because of that, and the charm of the village itself, people regularly returned year after year for holidays.

The Village House restaurant was no exception. It was in a parallel alley just off the main alleyway through the village. A Lindian stone archway framed the entrance into a small courtyard with a few tables set for dinner. To the left of the courtyard a wrought iron flight of stairs led up to the rooftop terrace and more dining tables. The place was busy with evening diners. At the top of the stairs the two policemen were greeted by a quite tall, dark haired man in his late thirties, dressed in a white shirt with the sleeves rolled up, a pair of black jeans and black trainers. There were around ten tables on the terraces either side of the staircase, plus another four on a further terrace up a few steps. All of them were occupied.

"Sorry, gentlemen, we are full at the moment, but if you can wait fifteen minutes I should have a table for you," the man told them.

Glancing quickly at some of the tables Papadoulis was actually remembering how hungry he was, and thinking that the food looked delicious. In particular he was eyeing up a mezze of Greek dishes on the table of a couple near to the top of the stairs, including a prawn saganaki and a range of Greek dips with pitta bread. He could feel his stomach rumbling and was sure his mouth was watering. However, he simply produced his police badge and introduced the two policemen, followed by, "And you are?"

"The owner, Ari. What can I do for you? Is this an official visit? My staff have all the necessary papers, including employment papers."

He looked confused and a little concerned. He was actually from Albania originally, but had lived in Greece for many years. As well as his native Albanian, in addition to Greek and English he could speak parts of at least five other languages.

"No, well yes it is official, but not in that way," the Inspector informed him, followed by, "Can we go somewhere more private for a moment, downstairs in a part of the courtyard perhaps?"

The owner pointed down to a discrete corner of the courtyard below. "Sure Inspector, there should be ok."

As they reached the courtyard corner Papadoulis produced a photograph of Kathleen O'Mara, asking, "Do you remember this woman? We understand she was here last evening with two other women."

Ari took the photo and nodded slightly.

"Yes, I remember them. Good fun, they seem to be enjoying themselves. A fair bit of wine and they said they loved the food. She was Irish I think, but the other two sounded English. Is there a problem?"

"The Irish one, Kathleen O'Mara, was found murdered in Gennadi this morning."

Ari frowned.

The Inspector assumed it was simply an element of shock. He wasn't completely wrong, but his assumption wasn't completely accurate.

"Are you sure?" the owner asked.

Papadoulis looked surprised at such a strange question. Before he could answer though Georgiou did.

"Definitely, but that seems an odd thing to ask. Why do you ask that?"

Ari shook his head slightly at the confusion.

"No, no, I didn't mean are you sure she is dead. It was the identity of the one found murdered?"

The two policemen exchanged a brief glance before the owner continued.

"I had a feeling one of them, the Irish one, the one you said was found murdered, had been here before. I am quite good with my customers and usually remember them if they've been to the restaurant before. I didn't actually get their names last night, the three of them. In the end I didn't ask if they'd been before. I couldn't be completely sure, but I thought I remembered the Irish one. She looked familiar. Maybe it was because she was Irish and the other two weren't. Anyway, I don't recall the name of the woman I thought she was, but I'm pretty sure her name wasn't Kathleen. It was a much more Irish sounding name, unusual, I think, to me anyway. So, that's why I asked if you were sure the woman in the photo's name was Kathleen, that's all."

"When was that?" Papadoulis asked.

"When was what?"

"When was she here, the woman you thought it was?"

Ari rubbed the back of his head.

"Difficult to say exactly. It was pre-Covid and the pandemic. I'm sure of that. So, before summer 2020 I suppose, probably a couple of years before that."

"2016, summer of 2016?" the Inspector snapped back.

Ari puffed out his cheeks and shrugged before telling him, "It could have been, but I couldn't really be sure, couldn't say for certain. I just remember her because of the unusual Irish name."

Papadoulis glanced at his Sergeant once more. Georgiou was blank faced and not impressed. He was determined not to show any sort of facial expression, even though in his mind he knew exactly where the Inspector was headed with his questions. Before the Inspector could continue down that path though, Ari took hold of the photograph once more, stared at it for a few seconds, and then shaking his head said, "No, no, perhaps I'm mistaken. The woman I'm thinking of wasn't a blonde. I'm sure of that, and her hair was much longer."

The Inspector wasn't giving up, however.

"Aileen? The name of the woman you were thinking of, was it Aileen. That's Irish."

Ari was shaking his head again.

"Could have been, Inspector, but I really couldn't be sure. Admittedly that's an unusual name, being Irish, but I couldn't say for certain. Maybe I'm confused. The woman in the photo's hair is much different, and if you say her name is Kathleen then I guess you must have checked so ..."

Georgiou had noticed the rest of the restaurant staff were rushed off their feet and no doubt the owner would need to get back to helping soon. So, he decided to try and move the questions on from what he was seeing as his Inspector's growing obsession.

"What about the three of them last night? Did anyone join them by any chance or did they eat alone all the time they were here? Did you or any of your staff talk to them much while they were eating?"

"I did, just a short conversation after they asked for the bill and I brought it. But I don't think any of my staff had much of a conversation with them, except when they took their order. And it was just them, no one joined them."

Papadoulis threw a disparaging look in the direction of his Sergeant then asked, "What about their phones? Did you happen to notice if they had their phones, all of them?"

"I couldn't say all of them for sure, but one of them, or perhaps two, I think, were taking photos, you know, of the food and each other, and of the Acropolis all lit up. And after they paid the bill they got me to take one of the three of them, but I couldn't say whose phone it was."

He briefly glanced upstairs at one of his staff beckoning him up and added, "But if that's all, Inspector, we're very busy and I really should get back to the customers and my staff."

"Of course, yes that's all for now, but if you think of that woman's name at all for sure, the one who was here before, please let us know."

The Inspector handed Ari his card and the two policemen left.

As the two men made their way through the many tourists in the now very busy alley Georgiou couldn't resist asking, "So, you think that guy Ari could be right, sir? About remembering her and that the dead woman isn't who we think she is? You still think you could be right and she's that woman Aileen Regan"

"Yes, maybe, maybe, Sergeant, but that's for us to find out. I'm not ruling out the idea though, or anything, like why would that be? Why would the woman have two identities? Maybe that's what we should be concentrating on, focusing on, or at least thinking about. In the meantime, let's go to the first bar the women say they went to after they left the restaurant, the Courtyard, and see if anyone there, owner or staff, remembers any of the women, particularly the victim, and not just from last night."

They weaved their way through the tourists in the alley to the left of the Village House restaurant and then manoeuvred to the alley to the right through a group of a dozen people waiting outside the Dionysos Restaurant for tables to become free for their evening meals. After a further thirty metres and then the same sort of distance up another alley they climbed the few steps up and into the Courtyard Bar.

It was an old style traditional Lindian bar with the usual fair share of dark polished wood. The bar itself ran all along the length of the back wall, except for a few feet at the end for a doorway and narrow steps down to the toilets. At the opposite end were the music console and a larger and wider area with some tables and chairs and room for dancing, as well as a flight of stairs up to the roof terrace.

As they entered the bar the Inspector remembered it and the owner, Jack Constantino, from the investigation of the 2016 case. Constantino hadn't been involved, but the police enquiries in that case had included interviewing some of the bar owners in the village.

Jack Constantino was a very convivial friendly host and bar owner. Many Courtyard Bar customers were repeat ones who returned to Lindos, and particularly the Courtyard Bar, year after year, in many cases two or three times each summer. They spent a lot of time in his welcoming bar. It was particularly popular with families, not only because of its host but also because of the courtyard, which was perfect for them to sit outside the bar through the warm evenings and yet still be able hear the music drifting through the open doors of the bar. On some evenings, usually Sundays, there was live Greek music and dancing as Jack himself entertained the customers with his considerable various musical instrumental skills. He was a stocky, dark-haired, quite tall man in his late forties. Born and bred in Lindos, he would relate many stories from his youth in the village in entertaining his customers. He'd also spent some time in America a few years before he married back in Lindos. Besides his bar, or maybe as well as is a better way of putting it, his passion was his music and he was a great fan of Cat Stevens, or Yusuf Islam as he was now called . Jack regularly entertained his customers with renditions on his guitar or bouzouki of the songs of his favourite musician.

Outside in the courtyard from which the bar got its name only a couple of tables were occupied when the two policemen arrived. It was still early and inside the bar was empty. Later it would usually be much busier. As Papadoulis and Georgiou approached it Jack Constantino was busy restocking one of the middle shelves behind the long bar with bottles of the Greek beer, Mythos. At the other end Dimitris, one of the barmen, was also restocking some shelves with bottles of another beer from a green crate on the floor.

As the owner looked up Papadoulis produced his police credentials, introduced himself and the Sergeant, and then produced Kathleen O'Mara's photo from his inside jacket pocket while asking, "Was this woman in here last evening, with two other women?"

"Yes, three of them, around ten, I think. Tourists, was their first time in Lindos, they said. Just had the one drink and left. Is there a problem, Inspector?"

"Did anyone join them here, or talk to them? A couple of English guys perhaps?"

"No, no one joined them, and I didn't see them even talking to anyone in the bar. We were busy, but no, I didn't notice them getting into any conversations with the other customers. They kept themselves to themselves sat over there at the table in the corner at the end."

He pointed to a small alcove type area to the right at the end of the bar, near the doorway to the stairs down to the toilets, before adding again, "Is there a problem?"

"No, no problem, ok thanks," Papadoulis replied and then indicated with a slight nod to Georgiou that they should leave. Halfway across the bar towards the door though he turned around and asked, "Did you get their names by any chance?"

The Sergeant discreetly rolled his eyes slightly. He knew why his Inspector was asking that.

"Dimi would have done. He made and served them their cocktails. He usually gets the names of the women he serves. He's good at that," Constantino replied, ending with a slight smile.

The two policemen returned to the bar as Dimitris joined the owner at that end of it having overheard the last part of the conversation.

"Suzanne, Ali and ... erm ... oh yeah, the Irish one was Kathleen," the barman told them. "The other two had the same cocktail, but I remember she was Irish because she wanted an Irish Manhattan, a new one on me, but she told me it was the same ingredients as usual plus Jameson Irish whisky."

"Not Aileen, the Irish one's name wasn't Aileen by any chance?"

Constantino looked puzzled. Before Dimitris could answer he asked the Inspector, "Why do you think that?"

Papadoulis didn't answer, but instead just repeated his question to the barman.

"Was it by any chance, Aileen I mean? You didn't hear any of them use that name at all?"

"No, it was definitely Kathleen, I'm certain now, and I never heard any of them mention that name."

"So, why Inspector-"

Constantino started to ask again, but Papadoulis interrupted as he rubbed the back of his neck with the palm of his right hand.

"Her face, this woman Kathleen's, just looked familiar to me, like someone I came across here in a case six years ago. Her name was Aileen, Aileen Regan, but I must be mistaken. Anyway, thanks."

The two policemen turned away once again to head towards the doorway. Before they'd taken two paces Constantino said,

"Me too, Inspector, and I remember her, Aileen Regan, from six years ago."

Papadoulis turned around again, asking him, "You do?"

"Yes, I did think she looked familiar too, or at least I did at first when they came in last night, but then they all said they had never been here before, that it was their first time in Lindos. We get a lot of tourists in here though, and I guess sometimes people can look a bit the same in some ways, so ..."

He hesitated for a second or two then added, "Her face looked familiar, but then I remembered Aileen Regan had much longer hair and dark, very dark black. The woman who's photo you just showed me had short blonde hair."

The Inspector propped himself down onto one of the nearby bar stools and indicated to Georgiou to do the same. The Sergeant took that to mean Papadoulis wasn't going to let the Aileen Regan question drop easily this time.

"But the Irish woman Aileen Regan, has she been back to Lindos, and in the bar here at all since six years ago?"

Constantino shook his head.

"No, no, at least if she has she's not been in the bar. I've not seen her, and I'm sure she'd come in if she came back to Lindos because I helped her, helped her a lot, along with my mother, when she was here in 2016. She was trying to trace some of her relatives, her father to be exact. She said her mother was here working as a tour rep in the mid-seventies and got pregnant. Apparently on her birth certificate it stated 'Father unknown', and her mother would never tell her who he was before she died. She was sure he was Greek though, and my mother remembered the woman, Aileen's mother, from when she worked here, told her all about her and some of the people in the village at the time."

"Did she find him, her father, find out who he was?" Georgiou asked. It seemed even he was now getting increasingly interested in the mysterious Aileen Regan.

"Not sure, but if she did she never stayed around. In fact, it was all a bit odd, strange, how she just left."

"How do you mean?" the Inspector asked.

"When she was here that time she was in here quite a lot, August 2016 it was, and as I said I introduced her to my mother.

She spent a few afternoons talking with my mother at her place about the nineteen-seventies. From what my mother told her it turned out that her mother's mother, her grandmother, the woman Regan's grandmother, had also been here on Rhodes and in Lindos during the war fighting with the partisans against the Nazis. But after all that, spending a few evenings in here and afternoons with my mother she just left without even saying goodbye. That just seemed a bit odd to me."

"You have any idea where she went from here?"

"Not really. I didn't even know she was leaving. I assumed she went back to Ireland or England maybe as she left with an English guy. Cris, one of my sons who works here behind the bar, saw her and the guy getting into a taxi in the Main Square with their bags one morning. That must have been the day they left because the two of them never came in the bar again after that."

"Who was that, the guy? Did your son recognise him?" the Sergeant asked. He was definitely interested now.

"Martin, it was Martin Cleverley. She left with him. They seemed to get on very well when they were in the bar, if you know what I mean, Inspector."

Constantino tilted his head slightly as he revealed that observation. Papadoulis thought he also saw a slight wink. He knew quite well what the owner meant.

"Anyway, Martin was a regular in Lindos and in the bar, used to come here regularly. He and this Irish woman, Aileen, actually met in here for the first time earlier that summer, in June I think. They got on really well I seem to remember. She was here with another woman then. Sandra I think her name was-"

"Sandra what?"

"Oh, no, no I'm sorry I can't remember that, Inspector. Not sure I even actually got it at the time. No need to really. There's quite a few of our customers who've been coming here for years and I only know them by their first names."

Dimitris nodded in agreement before adding, "Her husband, the woman Sandra's husband, turned up the second week they were here. I remember that because he was a real prat. Not a nice guy at all."

"Do you remember his name?" Georgiou asked.

"Richard, but I couldn't tell you his second name either. He wasn't friendly at all. He seemed a very angry man, at least towards his wife, Sandra. The two women changed completely that second week as soon as he turned up. The first week they were both great. Laughing and enjoying themselves. The atmosphere between the three of them changed totally after he got here. I definitely had the feeling they didn't want him to come, both of them, the two women, not just his wife. If anything the Aileen woman seemed to resent him being here even more. Whenever the three of them were in here there was a clear tension between them."

"Hmm ... sounds like there might have been something going on between the three of them, something that was obviously making him angry. What about this guy Cleverley? Was he ever in here with the three of them? Any tension there, such as with Richard?"

Jack Constantino looked at Dimitris briefly and they both shook their heads slightly, followed by him telling the policemen, "No, I don't think so, but then I can't really remember Martin being in here at the same time as the husband was here. Do you Dimitris?"

"No, I can't either."

Papadoulis changed the focus of his questions more on to Martin Cleverley.

"Used to?" Papadoulis asked. "You said he used to come to Lindos regularly, but not recently, not this summer? Martin Cleverley hasn't been here this summer?"

Constantino shook his head slightly again before he answered.

"No, he used to come every summer for about seven or eight years I guess, sometimes two or three times each summer or even for the whole summer from May to October, but he's not been back since that summer of 2016 when he left with the Regan woman, or we assumed he left with her. At least if he has been back to Lindos he's not been in the bar, and if he's been in Lindos I'm sure he would have come in."

"What did he do work-wise to be able to come so regularly and stay for so long?" Georgiou asked.

"He said he was a writer. Said he'd had a couple of novels published, but I wouldn't know for certain, can't say I checked. Cris did and he said it was right, Martin had a couple of novels published. He also said Martin had posted a couple of things about them, the novels, on one of the Facebook Lindos sites. There are a few. I think he said it was on the Lindos Bars site. A couple of years or so ago Cris said he saw that Martin had posted a few photos of Crete on there, which was a bit odd, to post photos of Crete on a Lindos site. We assumed that was because that was where he was then and had given up coming to Lindos."

"Would you guys like a drink?" Constantino added as he reached for a glass to pour himself one. "On the house."

"No, no, it's ok, thanks," the Inspector told him, answering for both of them, adding, "Not on duty. Did your son happen to say if there was any mention or indication in those Facebook site postings if the woman, Aileen Regan, was with him then on Crete?"

At that point Constantino's son Cris turned up in the bar for his evening shift. His father beckoned him over to them and asked, "That stuff you saw on Facebook about Martin Cleverley and his novels and the photos of Crete was there any indication he was living there or holidaying there, and with anyone, a woman? The Inspector here was asking about him and Aileen Regan, if you remember them."

"Yep, I remember them. I saw them leaving that morning in the square, but no, there was no indication he was with her. I just assumed from the photos on there that he was in Crete. It did say over one of them something like, what a great place to live, but there was no mention of her. I just assumed he was living there then and alone."

"Do you remember when that was you saw the photos? When they were posted?" Papadoulis asked.

"Must have been a couple of years ago I saw them, but I can't remember looking to see when they were posted. I assumed they were recent. You could check back on the Lindos Bars site, I guess."

"Ok thanks, that's helpful," the Inspector told him.

When he hadn't been asking the odd question the Sergeant had been furiously scribbling down notes on all they'd heard in his police notebook. As he finished writing the last one about Martin Cleverley the Inspector commented, "Seems like we have quite a bit to check on, quite a few people to check up on now. Thanks Mr. Constantino. We will let you and your staff get back to work now. That's very helpful."

"Ok, but what's this woman Kathleen actually done? You never said," the bar owner asked.

"She's dead. Her body was found early this morning in Gennadi."

Constantino frowned a little as he asked, "Oh, how, how did she die?"

"We can't really say anything more at the moment. We are obviously still conducting our investigation, and as I said, what you've told us has been very helpful. There is just one more thing you can help us with, however. Arches Plus nightclub, where exactly can we find it in the village?"

"It won't be open yet. It's only just coming up to eight and it doesn't open until very late, midnight or one o'clock I think," Constantino informed him.

"That's ok. We just need to check something for our investigation. with the owner and the manager. I assume they'll be setting up for the evening at the moment."

"I expect so. The manager will be there, but I'm not sure the owner, Valasi, will be there yet. It's across the Main Square, down the road to the right, and it's at the end of that on the left. There are large white walls and inside is an open air space. You can't miss it."

With that the Inspector got down from the bar stool, followed by his Sergeant, thanked Jack Constantino again, and this time the two men headed out through the doorway and into the now busier courtyard.

7

Pal's Bar, Ken and the Arches Plus Club

Outside the Courtyard Bar there were two steps, then a further two to the left of those down to the alleyway that led to Pal's Bar about thirty metres further. Halfway down the alley on the right was the popular Kalypso Restaurant and then almost opposite Pal's Bar on both sides were Crepe Bars, always popular spots with tourists for late night crepe or wrap snacks to soak up the alcohol consumption of the evening.

As they reached the bottom of the second set of steps Papadoulis stopped to tell his Sergeant, "We need to do some thorough background checks on all these characters now. I told Kyriakopoulis back at Rhodes earlier to get checking on the ones we knew about then, Lees, Carmichael, O'Mara and Regan. Now we need to add Daniel Bird to that, plus the ones Constantino has just told us about, this guy Martin Cleverley, and if we can somehow find their full names, the guy Ken and the married couple, Sandra and Richard whoever. And we need to try and check whether Cleverley is still on Crete. If we can find him we can see what he can tell us about Aileen Regan, as we know she left here with him back in 2016."

He was shaking his head slightly once again as he added, "I've got a feeling Sergeant that there is more to this case than meets the eye, more than just a simple straightforward murder. We need to do some serious digging into all these characters."

"We've already got Rhodes working on O'Mara's phone records, sir, as they'll have her phone by now. I'll give Kyriakopoulis a call and tell him to get a team working with him on all that stuff for all those people, social media, plus any phone records we can legally get access to for Lees,

Carmichael, O'Mara and ... err ... Regan, and that we will be into the Rhodes Station later to start going through some of it?"

He was more than a little surprised at the Inspector's response, or at least some of it.

"Yes, tell him to get a team of officers started on it straightaway, tonight. But tell him we'll be in the station in the morning at eight to see what they've found so far, not tonight."

"Not tonight, sir?"

"Err ... no ... not tonight, Sergeant. Tomorrow morning will give them more time to check some of that stuff."

He hesitated for a few seconds before going on.

"It's been a long day. We need a clear head to start going through some of it, making sense of it, so first thing tomorrow will be better."

He glanced at the Sergeant out of the corner of his eyes, checking his reaction before adding, "And get one of our cars from the station here to run you back to Rhodes and home after we've been to see what we can find out in this next bar and from the Arches Plus club manager. I'll hang on to our car here and go over some of what we've got so far, update the Incident Board, for an hour before I head home to Rhodes."

"I can stay too for an hour or so, sir. I don't mind," Georgiou suggested, but Papadoulis insisted.

"No, no, that's ok, Sergeant. I'll just go through a few things here. Sometimes I can think things through easier and more clearly on my own for an hour or so. You just call Rhodes now and get them started checking on all those people, especially Regan and Cleverley. Get them to check on Regan and Cleverley's social media stuff if there's anybody with the first names Sandra and Richard"

He didn't wait for any more response.

As the Sergeant finished his call to the Rhodes station Papadoulis told him, "Right, let's go and see what we can find, if anything, in this other bar the three women went into last night."

With that he started to walk towards Pal's Bar. It was approaching eight o'clock, still quite early for Lindos tourist drinkers. Most of them would still be in the restaurants enjoying their rooftop evening meals in the warm evening air. One couple was sat at one of the two tables in the alleyway outside Pal's and only half-a-dozen people were inside, all of which looked like tourists and were middle-aged. At the front of the bar, sat on the low concrete bench with cushions, were another couple.

Pal's position was ideal for attracting tourists. Situated on the corner of the main alleyway through the village it was the first bar they would encounter after entering the village from the Main Square. It was a small, but very popular bar, with two sets of double folding doors on each side through which some customers spilled out into the alleys with their drinks. The bar itself ran along one wall, with a very small area and large window at one end. At the opposite end was the music console with the resident DJ, and a winding wrought iron, not easy to navigate, set of steps up to the toilets. Pal's clientele varied, mostly tourists, but with some Greek and Brit ex-pat regulars from time to time, as well as Greek nearby restaurant workers after they finished their shifts. The tourist customers tended to be middle-aged or even older. It was very popular with British holiday couples who returned to the village year after year. There was usually never much room inside the small bar once the evening wore on and it became busy. The music was often loud and even though it was still early, and far from packed inside, this evening was no exception. It still boomed out as the two policemen approached.

Once inside one of the two barmen came to serve them as they reached the bar. The Inspector again produced his police credentials and introduced the two of them, followed by, "And you are?"

The barman looked somewhat apprehensive as he replied, "Stelios, the manager."

Police officers turning up in the bars in Lindos usually meant they were checking work permits or tax documents, hence the barman's apprehension, even though he was certain everything was in order in terms of the required documents for him, the other barman and the Albanian guy, Leli, who basically took orders from customers seated outside and generally collected glasses. Stelios was Greek, from Athens, and came to Lindos every summer to work at Pal's. In his mid to late thirties he'd been doing that for many years, along with working in Athens during the winter months from November to March. His swept back jet black hair gave him a typical Greek look. He was very good at what he did in the bar. Drinking in Pal's while Stelios was serving was an evening's entertainment all by itself. He knew precisely how to get those in the crowded bar going with his constant antics to the continuous music. By the end of the evening when the music stopped at one o'clock, as per the local Lindos by-laws, he could usually be seen to be completely exhausted. For six months from May to October every summer he worked continuously every night from six or seven until past one o'clock, and sometimes way beyond that, serving drinks to regular customers until three or so. The bright energetic Stelios of the early summer of May and June was somewhat different to the clearly exhausted Stelios of October, even though he never let that affect his work and entertainment for the customers towards the end of summer and into the autumn.

Trying to make himself heard above the loud music the Inspector produced the photo of Kathleen O'Mara and asked him, "Do you remember this woman being in here last evening, with two other women?"

"Sure, they came in quite late. She was Irish, but the other two were English."

"Did you notice them talking to anyone in here?"

"Yeah, Ken over there."

He pointed to a guy who looked in his early fifties and was sat on one of the bar stools at the far end of the bar nursing a beer, then continued, "And Daniel, him and Daniel. They're regulars, come every year, not together, but like a lot of our regulars they just seem to be here at the same time. They, the three women, went off to Arches Plus with Ken and Daniel, quite late on. Must have been approaching two o'clock as the music had stopped and we were just serving a few people a few more drinks, including the three women and Ken and Daniel till they left."

Papadoulis turned around immediately to head towards the guy as he told Stelios, "Thanks."

Once more he produced his police credentials and identified the two policemen then asked, "Ken is it?"

The English guy looked circumspect.

"Yes, it is, Inspector. Is there a problem?"

"No, no problem, Mr?"

"Bradshaw, Ken Bradshaw, but what's this about. I haven't done-"

It had been a long day and Papadoulis was determined to get all this over with quickly now. He had other things he wanted to do that evening, other things on his mind. He didn't let the guy finish, nor even bother to offer him an explanation. Instead he produced Kathleen O'Mara's photo once again.

"The manager just told us you were drinking with this woman and her two friends, two other women, last night."

Ken glanced at the photo and immediately replied, "Yes, Kathleen, Ali and Suzanne, that's right. We, Daniel and I, took them to Arches Plus club. Must have been nearly two. It was their first night here, first time in Lindos they said, and they wanted to make a night of it, so asked me and Daniel where they could go to carry on drinking with some music. So, we took them to the club. Daniel's like me, a regular Lindos visitor. Not sure where he's staying this time, but Stelios might know, if you want to talk to him. But what's-"

This time Georgiou didn't let him finish his obvious question. He could sense the Inspector's growing irritation and impatience.

"What time did the women and you two guys leave the club?

Ken rubbed his chin with the palm of his right hand and then replied, "Oh … err …must have been around four when the women left. Can't be sure of that though as we'd all had a fair bit to drink by then. Been drinking shots, well most of us anyway. One of the women, the Irish one, Kathleen, wasn't so keen on them, kept declining. Thought it was a bit odd, what with her being Irish, still … Daniel wanted to stay at the club for one more, so probably gone five when we left and then we went to get some food from the all night place, Nikos, just along from the club."

Papadoulis was about to ask about the phone, but he didn't need to. Ken volunteered the information.

"But just as we were leaving Michalis, the club Manager, caught us at the door and told Daniel that one of the women had left her phone on one of the tables, so he gave it to him. It was one of the tables in the raised part of the club, the VIP area they call it. We both know the owner, Valasi as well as Michalis, so they-"

"Yes, yes." The Inspector didn't let him finish his description of the layout and architecture of the club, or of his friendship with the owner. Instead he asked, "Did you handle the phone at all or just Daniel and the Manager?"

"No, no, I never touched it. I'm sure, because Daniel said he'd try and unlock it, but he couldn't and I'm useless with phones, so I told him there was no way I'd know how to, plus I said I didn't see how unlocking it would help. It wasn't as though we could call the woman. We had her phone"

He let out a small chuckle, then continued. "We didn't even know which of the three women the phone belonged to. Daniel said he knew where they were staying. One of them, Ali, had told him Lindos Memories. So, he said he'd take it and call the hotel in the morning, probably in the afternoon I'm guessing, as he'd had a skinful of booze and no doubt would have a raging hangover. Anyway he said he'd tell the hotel reception to let the women know he had one of their phones. I told him I reckoned they'd be back in here tonight anyway so he would be able to give it to whoever out of the three of them it belonged to then. They'll be back in later I bet. They seemed to enjoy it here. So, what's this all-"

Yet again Papadoulis didn't let him finish. He guessed what he was about to ask and anyway wasn't about to tell him in an increasingly busy Lindos bar that he was wrong about them coming in the bar later as one of the women had been murdered. Instead he just told him, "Thank you, Mr. Bradshaw. That's very helpful."

Ken frowned. He wasn't at all sure what he'd been helpful with, but before he could ask again the Sergeant asked, "Where are you staying, sir, and for how much longer are you here in Lindos, just in case we need to speak to you again."

He was still frowning and looking confused as he answered, "Lindos Horizon, for another 10 nights."

"Thanks, enjoy your evening," Papadoulis wished him and the two men quickly turned to leave, thanking Stelios once again on their way out.

"Right, down towards the Main Square and the road off to the right to the Arches Plus Club at the end now, Sergeant, to speak to the Manager and then you're done for the evening," Papadoulis said as they made their way down the alley past the Crepe shop. "So far though, it's beginning to look like Daniel Bird's story about the phone checks out, if we believe that guy Ken. Let's see if the club Manager also corroborates it. He should be there setting up for the evening now."

Arches Plus Club was a quite large open air roofless area inside surrounding high white walls on the left of the road winding on down to eventually reach one end of the Main Beach. At the time in the evening the two policemen walked inside the club staff was busy setting up and stocking bars for opening later in the evening. Later, after one o'clock, it would be packed, largely with young Greeks from all over the island, but also some tourists. Now it was completely empty, except for the staff. It felt strange, bare, soul-less, and almost desolate when devoid of masses of people.

They had barely got inside when they were approached by a tall, dark haired Greek man wearing a black t-shirt with an Arches name on the left side of the chest.

"Can I help you," he asked.

Again the Inspector produced his police credentials and introduced himself and Georgiou, followed by, "Is the Manager, Michalis, around?"

"That's me, what can I do for you?" he replied.

Papadoulis produced the photo of Kathleen O'Mara once more and asked, "Do you remember this woman being here last night with two other women and two guys?"

"Yes, the three women came with Daniel and Ken, was their first time."

The Inspector didn't even have to ask his next question as Michalis continued, telling him straightaway, "One of them, one of the women, left their phone here when they left before the guys, so I gave it to Daniel. Is there a-"

The Inspector had heard what he wanted to hear, and was now anxious to get away, so he simply told the Manager, "Ok, thanks. We'll just need you to come to Lindos Police Station for fingerprinting, just to eliminate your prints from the woman's phone. It'll only take a few minutes."

"Now? Why, what's this about?"

"It's a murder enquiry. The woman was murdered sometime after she left your club last night. So, yes, now please. You can be back here in half-an-hour or so. Surely there's one of your staff who can sort things for you while you are away?"

"Ermm ... yes, yes, of course, Inspector." He looked a little shocked as he added, "Just give me a minute to let Giorgos know I'm going to be away for a bit and what he needs to get on with while I am."

A few minutes later the two policemen, along with the club Manager, were heading through the village to Lindos Police Station. Georgiou couldn't help noticing the Inspector was constantly checking his watch. He seemed distracted. It was coming up to nine o'clock, so the Sergeant simply assumed Papadoulis was anxious to get their work finished for the evening, spend that hour alone at Lindos Station updating the Incident Board as he'd said earlier, and then get back to Rhodes Town and his wife for what would be left of their Saturday evening. However, he thought it better not to ask.

After they got to the station the two policemen made their way back to the office while another officer took Michalis off to take his fingerprints. Before he did so the officer informed the Inspector that Daniel Bird had been in the station to have his prints taken. As soon as they got into the office Papadoulis made his way over to the Incident Board and wrote on it MARTIN CLEVERLEY, SANDRA? and RICHARD? and also added the name BRADSHAW behind KEN which was already written there.

"I can't see Daniel Bird or this guy Bradshaw being our killer, sir," Georgiou ventured while pointing to their names on the board. "Neither of them seems the type to have access to cyanide to me, and especially as they are obviously regular visitors here from what we've been told, plus they both said they were really pissed, which looking at the state of Bird when we found him seems credible. Just doesn't seem to fit to me one of them being our killer."

"I think you're right, Sergeant." Papadoulis agreed whilst standing once again gazing at the now quite full board.

"If there's nothing else for tonight, sir I'll go and sort my lift to Rhodes with the front desk."

"Err … yes, sure, Sergeant. I'll hang on here for a bit longer to try and make some sense of all this. I'll see you at Rhodes station at eight in the morning."

As soon as the Sergeant had left the office Papadoulis reached for his mobile and made a call. When the person answered he told them, "Hi, it's me."

"I knew you would, knew you'd call."

"Did you now. You always were a cocky sod."

A small laugh came down the line, followed by a confident, "That's why you liked me so much, remember. That's what you told me back then. You policemen do like to be in control don't you, but with me you can't be, can you?"

He didn't bother rising to that, but instead simply said, "Ok, ok, look I haven't got much time at the moment. My Sergeant will be back here in a minute. I'm still in Lindos at the station. So, in half-an-hour, and where?"

"Same place in Lardos as before in 2016, living in the same apartment as then, Yiannis. I'm sure you remember the way. Was in Rhodes Town for a bit, but it's second time I've come back here. Can't keep away from the place. Just like you can't keep away from me, I suppose."

With that she rang off.

8

Sally Hardcastle

It started in August 2016 while he was in Lindos investigating that case of the death of an English man in one of the back alleys in the village late one night; the one in which he'd interviewed Aileen Regan. Sally Hardcastle was working in Café Melia then, just as she was now. Just as he'd done this time he regularly went in there to buy something for lunch to take back to the Lindos station while on the investigation, or even on some mornings to buy croissants for breakfast if he'd had to leave home in Rhodes Town early. There was an immediate spark between them back then, just as there had been earlier that day in the café over the feta and spinach pies for him and Georgiou. It was instantly clear back in 2016 that it was more than the usual banter she often engaged in with some male customers, usually British tourists. He wasn't one of those though. He was a Greek Police Inspector, and a married one with two children. That didn't seem to matter, or be a problem, for Sally Hardcastle.

A week after the first time he'd gone into the café that August she came straight out with it while they were bantering as usual over the feta pies and how good they were. There were hardly any other customers there, and certainly no one in earshot, when she confidently asked, "You going to take me for a drink one evening then? When you've finished catching all those criminals of course," she added with a wink and a slight tilt of her head.

"How did you-" he started to ask, deliberately not answering her question directly.

"That you're a police officer? It's a village, someone's died, everyone knows that, and you're new in Lindos, not seen you here before, and you obviously are not a tourist, so."

He smiled as he told her, "You'd make a good detective, err ..."

"Sally, it's Sally. You wanted to know my name, and yes, I would wouldn't I, make a good detective, detective."

Now she was smiling back at him.

"Yiannis, I'm Yiannis, and it's Inspector, Sally."

Another smile, this time a sarcastic one from her, "Oh, sorry, yes of course, Inspector. So are you?"

"An Inspector, yes, you want to see my badge?"

He hadn't picked up her sarcasm, or the meaning of her question.

She chuckled a little, enjoying his obvious discomfort revealed in his serious response.

"No, no, I meant what I originally asked, you going to take me for a drink?"

He had no idea why he responded the way he did, the way the words come out of his mouth. It was so totally out of character for him, the 'follow the rules', 'play it by the book', Inspector.

"Sure, why not? When?"

"Tonight, call me, here's my number," she told him as she scribbled it down on a piece of paper torn from a waitresses order book. It wasn't even a suggestion or a question, more a confident sort of order. He found that surprisingly he liked her confidence, something she soon picked up, and reminded him of six years later when he came into the café for the feta and spinach pies for him and Georgiou's lunch.

So, he called her at around seven that evening, drove over to Lardos later under what was an emerging big bright full moon, and followed the directions she'd given him on the phone. He found her waiting for him at eight-thirty nursing a glass of red wine at a table outside Yammas Bar in the busy Main Square. He was obviously uneasy as he sat at the table opposite her.

"Here's a bit public, bit too public for my liking."

She laughed a little.

"Are you worried? Do you think many people will know the great Inspector here? Have you even ever had to investigate a case here in Lardos?"

"No, I haven't but-"

He stopped as the waiter appeared and he ordered, "Just a coke please," explaining to her, "I'm driving and back to Rhodes Town later, so."

She picked up her glass and before taking a sip told him, "Well, don't worry so much. If anyone does ask, recognise you here, you can surely just tell them that you're interviewing me for the case in Lindos. I'm sure the guy who died must have come into the café at some point, so."

"Yes, I guess so."

He started to feel more at ease as the waiter brought his coke, but that only lasted a moment as she told him, "In any case, we can always go somewhere a bit more private when we've finished our drinks. My place is only a couple of minutes from here. Maybe that'll make you feel more relaxed?"

It didn't. Anything but.

Nevertheless, twenty minutes later they were in her small apartment, and in five more minutes in her bed. That was what she wanted all along, him in her bed, and that's what she got. She usually did, get what she wanted. After that first time he was filled with guilt as he drove back to Rhodes Town later that night, but over the next three months the guilt got easier, less, such that by the middle of November he was starting to think more and more what it was that she actually wanted. How she thought what was between them might develop. It started with him going to her place once a week, then twice, but rapidly escalated to three or four times a week. The Lindos case had been closed, so he had no real reason or excuse to go to there, but he regularly made the forty-five minute drive from Rhodes Town to her place in Lardos, always telling his wife that he was on police business on a case.

Sally surprised him once more. He'd quickly learned that she was good at unpredictable surprises. A month into their affair she told him she knew he had a wife and two kids. When he asked how she knew that she simply told him she couldn't remember, someone in the café must have mentioned it one time after he left, after he'd been in for some pies. That wasn't true of course, but he wasn't to know that. She seemed to know a lot of little things about him, and his life, but he just dismissed it as usual village gossip. She told him quite a few of the Lindos locals and Brit ex-pats frequented the café and were always gossiping. And he knew, from his own experience, that she liked to chat with the customers, although he assumed not in quite the same way as she'd initially done with him.

At first it all felt awkward for him, probably because of the guilt. They didn't actually do much talking the first few times; not about each other, not about her and her past, or even her work, and apart from that time she said she knew he had a wife and kids, not about him and his life. It was just sex. She seemed perfectly happy with that, just that. After all, it was good sex. But after the third or fourth time it got more relaxed between them. She started asking about his work, and particularly about the case he was on in Lindos at that time of the English guy who died in the back alley. She said she was just curious as she worked in the village and perhaps the guy had been into the café. He told her he couldn't really talk about the case. She seemed more than interested and regularly asked how it was going over the next couple of times they were together. She was asking about the victim, asking if they had identified him, telling Papadoulis again she was just curious if she'd met him, if he'd come into the café while she was working. She also told him everyone who came into the café since it happened was curious about what exactly did happen. He told her he really couldn't tell her about the victim, but it did look like an accident. He began to get increasingly baffled as to why she kept asking about it, but then a week or so later when she asked again he told her the case was closed and the verdict of the investigation was that it was an accident.

By the middle of that November in 2016 the thought of what she actually wanted in the long term was increasingly playing on his mind, such that his work was suffering. He found it more and more difficult to focus on cases he was working on, mostly low level crimes and certainly not anything as big as a possible murder, as had happened in Lindos that August. Perhaps that was the problem; the mundane day to day cases he was investigating weren't as important, or didn't appear to be, as anything like a murder case. Whether that was the case or not he just couldn't seem to avoid her popping into his head three or four times a day while he should have been focusing on his police work. Even some of his fellow officers at the Rhodes Town station noticed he appeared to be increasingly distracted. It got to the point where one of his senior officers mentioned it to him. That was when he decided he had to talk to her, Sally, about it, about what they were doing and where it was going. That was something they had both avoided during the three months of the affair, or at least he thought they both deliberately had..

So, after driving over to her place one cool November evening that had a feeling of the early dampness of winter in the air he asked her directly after they had sex what she wanted out of their relationship. Before she could answer he added that he thought she might want more, more than they had, and that he wasn't sure he could give that to her because of his wife and kids.

Yet again she surprised him. He wasn't sure whether he was relieved over what she replied or whether his ego was sorely bruised by the fact that she didn't seem in any way annoyed over what he'd said.

In an almost matter of fact way she got up out of the bed leaving him lying there, put on a large t-shirt and pants and then turned back briefly to tell him nonchalantly, "Just fun, Yiannis. I'm perfectly happy the way it is."

He was somewhat stunned by her lack of any semblance of emotion. She certainly wasn't upset.

She walked over to sit at what passed for a small dressing table and began to brush her hair. Then without even turning her head around to look back at him in her bed she added in an equally dispassionate tone, "I'm not looking for anything more. I wasn't looking for anything more when we started this"

A confused frown spread over his face. He was speechless, not only over what she'd said, but the completely casual way she'd said it. All he could get out of his mouth was a low, "Oh."

Before he could find the words to say anything more she hit him with even more startling revelations.

"You're a detective Yiannis, you figure it out. I thought you would have by now. I'm just not that sort of woman, obviously not the woman you think I am. I'm not one for long term plans. Is that what you thought? Us together here on Rhodes, a happy couple, me with the respectable Police Inspector? You doing your police thing and me being your partner, the little wife or whatever with her part-time job in a café or a bar here? Us living together happily ever after?"

He just sat up in her bed shaking his head slightly and mouth gaping open in disbelief at the unnecessary tinge of aggression in her words.

She wasn't finished. Still sat at the dressing table with her back to him she went on, "And anyway, to be honest, Yiannis, I don't even know how much longer I'll be on Rhodes through this winter, nor after that summer after summer. So, as I said, this is about fun. I was just determined to enjoy myself."

She turned around on the dressing table stool to look across at him as she raised her eyebrows slightly and told him, "Still am if that's what you want? Just fun?"

As he told her earlier that was the problem, he didn't actually know what he wanted, not then anyway. However, perhaps her attitude and casual, matter of fact response made up his mind for him, or maybe the guilt just got too much for him. He was usually a well organised, disciplined, professional detective. He'd seen first-hand what the break-up of his marriage and the affair he started with a police pathologist, Crisa Tsagroni, had done to his former, now deceased, boss, Dimitris Karagoulis, his personal life and his career. Karagoulis was never the most organised of Inspectors. It was his way of approaching and solving crimes, including murders, but when he started his affair with the woman pathologist and his marriage collapsed so too did his whole life, descending almost into chaos.

When he dwelt on that over the next couple of days, and on Sally's almost couldn't care less attitude, plus the fact that things were getting increasingly difficult at home between him and his wife, he finally decided he couldn't destroy his marriage and let all of this affect his professional career. As a result, eventually at the end of that November he stopped it, told Sally they had to stop.

By that time, given her attitude a week or so before, he was hardly surprised when she simply agreed with another dispassionate, "Fine."

So it did stop, but now though it had started again, at her initiation, and this time, for now at least, he wasn't even giving a second thought to what she might want, what they both might want out of it this time.

It was just gone nine-thirty by the time she opened the door to her small apartment in Lardos to him that July Saturday evening in 2022. She'd changed out of her work clothes from when they met earlier and was now wearing a loose fitting large t-shirt type bright green top and tight white fitting shorts that were very short and very tight, along with flip flops. He noticed straightaway that she looked bright and fresh, a lot more so than when they'd met at Café Melia earlier that day and told him to call her. That was obviously the result of a shower after work and some make up she'd applied, no doubt for his benefit. Her bobbed dirty blonde hair had obviously been washed, obviously in the shower, and then dried and brushed into an appealing shape highlighting her cheek bones. Her legs were slim, tanned and nicely shaped, perfectly highlighted by the very short shorts. Certain he would come that evening she'd made an effort after work, although had been careful not to go overboard and be too overstated in what she chose to wear. What she did choose she knew would be easily enough, and revealing enough, to hold his interest. He'd told her many times six years ago that she had, as he put it, "great legs".

Her eyes were sparkling and her smile broad as she told him again in a confident tone, "I knew you'd call, knew you'd come."

He simply smiled back and raised his eyebrows a little.

"Glad you did, it was always good to see you, Yiannis, remember?"

She was confident, cocky, sure of herself and of his attraction to her. He wasn't anywhere near so, nowhere near as assured and confident, even though as an experienced Police Inspector he'd been trained to be just that. Just like that first time six years ago he was nervous, completely unsure if what he was doing, was about to do he guessed, was the right thing to do, was wise. Somehow though he couldn't resist it or her, and she knew that perfectly well. In a strange sort of way that was something that actually appealed to him, attracted him to her, her assuredness and confidence.

As she'd told him on the phone earlier the flat was the same one as six years ago where they'd spent many evenings in bed together over a three month period. It wasn't large, but there was a separate bedroom with a reasonably sized double bed. In one corner of the other room was a small kitchenette area with a two ring hob and sink, as well as a sofa and coffee table in the other part of the room. Off the bedroom was the shower room and toilet. The place was very clean and had clearly been recently redecorated. It was best described as functional, as was its position, just a few minutes from Lardos Main Square.

He sat down on the sofa and asked, "So, you never thought of moving from here then, to Lindos, easier for work?"

She could easily read the nervousness in his voice and attempt at small talk. That drew a little chuckle from her as she stood over him and initially ignored his question, asking instead, "You want some wine?"

"Oh, I'm driving, so better not."

She leaned down to place each hand on the side of his cheeks and kiss him gently, then told him, "Oh come on, Yiannis. A glass or two won't hurt will it?"

She didn't wait for his reply. Instead she disappeared into the kitchen and a few moments later appeared with two glasses of red wine, handing one to him as she sat alongside him on the sofa.

He took a sip and as he placed his glass on the coffee table in front of them he asked again, "So, did you, think of moving to Lindos?"

She smiled slightly again. His small talk attempt was amusing her. She, on the other hand, knew precisely what she wanted, and it didn't involve small talk. However, she decided to humour him and play along with it for a while.

"No, places there are more expensive to rent than here because of the tourist trade, and there are far less available for long term lets. They want, the owners, they want the tourists, that gives them more money, even though it's only for five or six months in the summer. Lardos is better, not just rent-wise, but less tourists. I go into Lindos at night sometimes, not that often, but sometimes to meet friends, Greeks and ex-pats, and that's fine, but if I was there every night I think I'd get a bit bored with the place. I've got a car, nothing grand of course, just a small Fiat Uno, and it only takes fifteen minutes or so to get from here to the café for work. I did go and live in Rhodes Town for a couple of winters, November to early April. That wasn't so expensive at that time as it is in the summer, but I preferred it back here, so I stayed here in Lardos for the other winters. There were a couple of bars and restaurants open, and a few Brit ex-pats, so there were worse places to be."

"How long you been on the island now then?" he asked.

"Oh, erm ... must be seven or eight years now."

"What about family back home though? Don't you miss them? Not even want to go back for a visit?"

"My parents are both dead. I have a brother from Kilkenny, like my parents. They moved to Manchester before I was born. My brother came to visit a few years ago. Not long after we err ... well you know ..."

She looked into his face with a small grin before continuing, "Well, you know ... so, that must have been almost six years ago now."

"You not seen him since?"

"Ermm ... no ... no ... I ... err," she stopped to clear her throat slightly, pick up her glass from the table and take a gulp of the wine. "Sorry, no I haven't seen or heard from him."

"Oh, I'm sorry, does that upset you, talking about him, the fact that you've lost touch."

She seemed much more composed now as she answered, "No, no it's fine, Yiannis. We never kept in touch much anyway, and I have my own life here."

As she finished she leaned forward to pick up his glass and hand him his wine.

"Come on, Yiannis, relax."

He took a drink of the wine, quite a large gulp as he thought it might indeed make him more relaxed.

After he placed his glass back on the coffee table she swung her tanned left leg up and across him, twisted her body towards his, and told him softly, "Now come on, Yiannis, I'm thinking you don't have much time, will have to get back to Rhodes, so shall we stop with all the small talk and get on with what we both want. I know I do, and I'm sure you do."

Before he could answer she withdrew her leg from across him, stood up, took his hand and led him towards the bedroom. Within a minute they were both naked and exploring each other's body on her double bed. More accurately, it was her that did most of the initial exploring. However, he was soon also enjoying what they were doing. He was certainly more relaxed and doing what they'd done so many times together for almost three months six years previously. She knew he would. That was what she'd planned.

For the next hour or so his guilt completely evaporated. When he finally rolled off her and let his head sink into one of her soft deep pillows all he could do was puff out his cheeks and briefly blow air upwards out of his mouth into the room before simply saying, "Phew."

She giggled a little at that as she stretched her right arm across his chest and then raised her hand up to cup his cheek gently while letting out a soft sigh of satisfaction.

"I'd forgotten quite-"

She didn't let him finish and moved her index finger to his lips to indicate he shouldn't speak for a moment.

For a full long minute they both simply lay there wrapped into each other's body in silence. Eventually she said softly, "Forgotten quite how good it was between us, Yiannis?"

"Yes, that's what I was going to say."

Another couple of silent minutes passed before he broke it and said, "Can I ask you a question?"

That drew a small laugh from her, before she teased him with, "You just have, Yiannis. Do you want to ask another one?"

As she said that she turned her head slightly to look into his face, opened her deep brown eyes widely, and raised her eyebrows a little, enjoying teasing him. Before he could say anything more she added, "Of course you can, Yiannis, of course you can ask another question."

"So, have you not been with anyone for the past six years?"

As she let out a little laugh again he knew she couldn't resist playing her game but added, "And?"

"And yes, of course I have."

She allowed another small smile to cross her lips while actually thinking was this a hint of jealousy he was exposing, and could she use it in some way, before she added, "I've had some, what can I call them, what do people call them, episodes. Is that the right word, moments maybe is better, or even events?"

Her delicate smile returned and she tilted her head slightly on the pillow as she continued, "Anyway, whatever the right word is, yes some, with a few men in Lindos, mostly Brit ex-pats, but definitely no tourists. That's not my way, my style, and definitely not here in Lardos. That would be a bit too close to deal with."

"British ex-pats? They still around? Is that a problem?"

She leaned over and stroked his cheek once again.

"No, Yiannis, not a problem at all. They were generally one night things after the clubs or late bars in Lindos, and always at their place, never here. That was my rule to myself."

She turned her head to look him straight in the eyes with a widening smile before telling him, "Fun, Yiannis. They were just fun. Remember, that's me, and always will be."

"Oh yeah, fun, Sally, you're favourite word I remember."

"I think one of them may still be around in Lindos, one of the ex-pats, but I haven't seen him there, or even in the café for six months or more I reckon, and as I said it was a one night thing anyway."

"No others still around though?"

She let out a chuckle bordering on a full blooded laugh.

"Jesus, Yiannis, I almost forgot you're a serious policeman. How many do you think there's been? It was three I guess, but no, only one of them is still around in Lindos I think, but I couldn't be sure as I haven't seen him in and around the village for quite some time, and definitely not this summer at all."

He just lay back in silence, not sure whether to be completely assured or not. But she wasn't quite finished.

"I know one of them left about four years ago, before the pandemic, and the other one, well ... the other one had to leave, if you know what I mean?"

"Had to leave?" He obviously didn't know what she meant.

"I'll not say much more, except to say that he had a bit of a reputation with relations with women in the village, got found out over a couple of those situations at one point and didn't really have much choice other than to leave Lindos. I heard that was made pretty clear to him by some in the village, and not just the Brit ex-pats. That was all way after I had a one night thing with him, just for fun, as I said."

He sat up, pulling the pillow up behind his back, then nodded slightly.

She did the same and asked, "Why are you so interested in all that? You're not a bit jealous are you, Inspector? After all, you've got your wife, haven't you?"

Was she teasing him again, or just probing? Before he could reply she added another probing question.

"So, tell me, Yiannis, what really made you come to the café today, besides the pies of course? They were just an excuse weren't they?"

Her cocky side had returned.

"Yes, of course, it was for the pies."

Now it was his turn to let out a small chuckle while he stared straight ahead into the space in front of him and the blank white wall at the foot of the bed.

"It was the 2016 case. I requested the file for that and of course it prompted me remembering us, and all that happened that late summer and autumn between us. So, as you used to do before, you popped into my head, and as before I couldn't get you out of it."

"Popped into your head? Really, just like that? Oh, come on, Yiannis."

"Ok, ok, I'd been thinking about you since as soon as I knew we, this case, would be based in Lindos. Just wanted an excuse to see if you still worked in the café. I didn't know if you would still be there, but we, my Sergeant and I, needed some food, some lunch, so what better than the pies. I could have sent my Sergeant I suppose, but in the end I couldn't resist coming to see if you were still there. And you were. I was very glad I came for the pies."

"So, I have to thank that 2016 case then, Yiannis, and the pies. Don't forget the pies."

"Guess so."

"Did you ask for that file because you think the 2016 case is connected to the current one? It's a woman isn't it? Found dead in Gennadi? That's a bit away from Lindos though."

"Wow! News certainly does travel fast here doesn't it, Sally. We only found the body early this morning."

"I overheard a couple of women talking about it in the supermarket in the square here earlier after I finished work. Anyway, indirectly that's your fault. I only went in there to get that bottle of wine you were drinking."

She was grinning over at him, trying to lighten the conversation it appeared. She soon changed back to a more serious side, however.

"Any leads yet, or do you think it was an accident, just like the 2016 one with the guy in the Lindos back alley?"

He shook his head a little.

"No, this was definitely not an accident, but I shouldn't say anything more. We've only just started the investigation, but it's already looking a bit complicated."

"Ooo … interesting, now I'm intrigued. How do you mean complicated? Now you have to tell me more."

He glanced at her sideways out of the corners of his eyes and then told her, "I don't think that'd be a good idea, Sally. I'd be in deep trouble if any of it got out, and I've probably already told you more than I should. Plus, it's not really the type of pillow talk I had in mind when I called you earlier."

She smiled as he glanced at his watch and added, "Look, I should go. It's nearly midnight and it'll take me the best part of an hour to get back to Rhodes Town."

"Sure, but don't you think you'd better take a quick shower first. You don't want to get home still smelling of me do you? That wouldn't be very clever at all would it? You know where it is. I'll get you a towel."

She got out of the bed, pulled a t-shirt over her head and put on a pair of pants while he headed off to the shower.

Fifteen minutes later she gave him a deep, soft lingering kiss and then sent him on his way home. He had almost an hour's drive to Rhodes Town to contemplate, and go over and over things in his mind. But not about the case, about Sally Hardcastle and what he'd just done, started again.

9

Ημέρα δεύτερη (Day 2)
Sunday July 3rd 2022

His wife was in bed asleep when he finally got home to their apartment in Rhodes Town at just gone one in the morning. She stirred slightly as he slipped into bed and told him in a quiet drowsy tone, "You're late."

"Crazy murder case. Lots of loose ends, and I have to leave early in the morning too. Go back to sleep," he whispered as he kissed her on the back of the neck. However, guilt was sweeping over him and he found it difficult to get off to sleep quickly, even after a busy day in Lindos and an equally busy, if different, evening in Lardos. But it wasn't the murder case, it was getting Sally and what he'd just done out of his head for now that was keeping his brain ticking over and preventing him drifting off into a welcoming and needed sleep.

Dimitra Papadoulis and Yiannis met when they were both training at the Hellenic Police Officers School. She was a very Greek looking woman in her late forties with long dark hair which she usually wore up in a ponytail, and striking high cheek bones. She was shorter than him, but not by much, and had retained much of her relatively slim figure, even after giving birth to their two children, now teenagers. Like her husband she was from Rhodes Town, a local woman. They married twenty one years ago and as soon as she became pregnant three years later she gave up her career in the police force. These days she had a part-time job in an office dealing in and marketing computer software. For many years before that following the birth of their first child she devoted her life to Yiannis and the two children. Her focus was her family, Having trained as a police officer she fully understood the pressures and demands of the job on her husband's time, particularly after he was promoted to Inspector, something she regularly told him.

He eventually managed to get some sleep, but was awake and up at six-thirty on Sunday morning. As he emerged from the shower his again drowsy, wife surprised him by asking, "Had you been drinking last night? I thought I could smell alcohol when you got into bed and kissed my neck."

"No, of course not," he told her. "You were half asleep when I got into bed. Maybe you were dreaming."

"Hmmm ... maybe ... must have been a nice dream then, but I don't remember any more of it. Shall I make you some coffee?"

"No, no, it's Sunday remember. I didn't mean to wake you. I can't hear the kids stirring so why don't you have a bit of a lie in, another hour or so. It's only just coming up to seven, but I have to go soon because of this bloody murder case, first to the station here and then probably back to Lindos."

He leaned down to kiss her on the cheek as she sunk her head deep into the pillow accompanied by a small contented moan.

"Got to go, I'll call you later, probably after lunch, and let you know when I think I'll make it home. Have a good day. Go to the beach. It's July, summer, and get the kids to go with you."

"Hmm ...," she uttered softly and drifted off into a comforting sleep.

When he reached the Rhodes Police Station at just after seven-thirty he was surprised to see Georgiou and Sergeant Kyriakopoulis already at their desks. Hot and humid July blazed its way into Rhodes Town in the same fashion every year. At that time even the Greek waiters working in the many restaurants on the island found their shirts heavily marked with sweat, attaching them irritatingly to their bodies as they weaved their way between tables, balancing trays of food for the tourist customers. In July of 2022 the heat felt even fiercer. It delivered intensity and humidity that usually only arrived in August. Consequently, in the big open plan second floor office of the three storey Rhodes Town main police station the air-conditioning units high up on the walls at each end of the room were operating at their maximum capacity, even though at just past seven-thirty it was early morning.

"You're even earlier than I said," the Inspector told the two Sergeants as he passed their desks on his way across to his glass and plasterboard encased small office in one corner.

"Thought it better to get here before everywhere gets too hot, sir, even with the aircon, even though some of us were here till almost midnight last night," Kyriakopoulis commented.

He was a stout, shortish, balding man, who's waistline clearly betrayed his obvious love of the Greek cuisine, particularly the lunchtime gyros he was so fond of and the evening moussaka. His wife was obviously an excellent cook.

Like many open plan offices the room was bland and functional, with a dozen plain grey metal desks arranged in an orderly fashion. Most of them were covered in various documents and papers. That particular Sunday morning the overwhelming majority of them were empty, with only the two Sergeants and two other officers seated at them. On one wall, opposite the windows, was a large white Incident Board, partly covered with papers and photos stuck to it, some relating to the Gennadi case, as well various marker pen scribbled notes. The large windows running the full length of two sides of the office would certainly have magnified the heat, making the place more akin to a Greek bread oven, if it weren't for the blinds that were pulled down fully in each of them shutting out the anticipated soon blistering sun, along with the cooling effect of the air conditioning.

"Find anything interesting last night," Papadoulis asked as he emerged back out of his office and approached the desks of the two Sergeants.

"The door to door in the holiday accommodation complex on the lane down to Gennadi beach, near where the body was found, didn't turn up anything, sir. Nothing unusual, no one even heard a vehicle or anything, although given that it would have been the early hours, after four in the morning, hardly surprising. And not really much positive yet on the social media checks. Just a few things that were not unusual at all about some of the people you asked us to do background checks on."

"Nothing useful or interesting on Carmichael, Lees, Bird or Bradshaw anywhere on social media, sir," Kyriakopoulis added as the Inspector propped himself on one corner of his desk. "Just the usual holiday and family photos and stuff. But we couldn't find anything on any social media for O'Mara or the other woman you asked us to check on, Aileen Regan."

"Nothing at all for those two names?"

"There are obviously quite a few women's social media accounts in the names of O'Mara and Regan. They are common Irish names, I suppose, and there are a few specifically in the names of Kathleen O'Mara and Aileen Regan, although much fewer in the Regan case. None of them look as though they are the two women we're interested in however, sir, and even the ones there are in those names don't have anything that could be of interest for us on them."

Papadoulis scratched the back of his head very briefly as he told the two Sergeants, "Hmm ... well I suppose the very fact that there doesn't seem to be anything on those two anywhere on social media could be interesting in itself. So, presumably no luck trying to find anything on the married couple Constantino told us about from 2016, Richard and Sandra? We don't have their surname. Constantino said he didn't know it, but I was hoping we might be able to find them on Aileen Regan's list of friends on social media as Constantino said they were here with her then."

"No, sir, as I said, no social media at all for the Aileen Regan we're interested in, so no chance of finding that married couple there."

"What about Lees and Carmichael's social media, anything on there from the last few days?" the Inspector asked. "Not even any photos of the three of them, those two and O'Mara, at the airport setting off for their holiday break or out in Lindos on Friday night?"

"There are some posts on both Lees and Carmichael's about them being at the airport in London and flying to Rhodes, but just comments, no photos, and no photos from Friday night in Lindos. There are a few comments from social media friends and family of theirs under those, but just generally saying have a good time and stuff like that. They don't look like they are from anyone suspicious."

"What about Bird and Bradshaw?" the Inspector asked.

"Just the same sort of general stuff, plus a couple of check-ins for Lindos bars by both of the men on Friday night. One for Pal's Bar and one later for the Arches Plus club, both of which tie up with the sort of times they told us they were there with the three women."

Papadoulis eased himself off the corner of Kyriakopoulis' desk and turned to face Georgiou's as he asked him, "What about the phone? Anything on any prints yet?"

"Only Bird's, O'Mara's and the Manager of the Arches Plus Club, Michalis' on it, sir. It doesn't look like the phone is actually as important to the investigation as we thought it might be."

"Maybe, Sergeant, but there's still the phone records, perhaps they'll tell us more. Where are we with them, Kyriakopoulis?"

"Still waiting on them, but the tech guys did manage to get the phone unlocked. Daniel Bird was right when he said there were some calls through Friday night, early Saturday morning while he was sleeping. The missed calls record in the phone confirmed that."

The Sergeant clicked on his computer keyboard and pulled up the tech report on Kathleen O'Mara's phone.

"Two calls came from an unknown number, unknown caller, at or just before midnight, obviously the caller was not in O'Mara's phone contacts, but-"

"Perhaps a burner phone, sir?" Georgiou suggested, interrupting.

Kyriakopoulis passed a sceptical glance at him across their desks before continuing.

"But there were four calls later, none of which it appears she answered, no doubt because by the time some of them were made Bird had the phone and was sleeping, although he couldn't have answered it anyway as it was locked. All the calls showed as missed, including the two at or just before midnight. Another of the unknown number ones was made just before one o'clock and then there was another of those much later, at seven-thirty. Two later ones at six-fifteen and six-thirty-five came from someone in her phone contacts just as Michael, and no surname."

"So somebody, or some people, including this guy Michael, was obviously desperate to get hold off her between midnight on Friday and seven-thirty Saturday morning," the Inspector said as he started to wander a few paces away from the desks and across the office.

"But according to Christof's report, sir, O'Mara was killed between four and five Saturday morning, and we know from the hotel room key card that she returned to her room from the women's night out in Lindos at twelve minutes past four, plus there is hotel CCTV pictures of two people, possibly one being her, going towards a vehicle in the hotel car park at four-twenty."

"And, Sergeant? What's your point?"

The Inspector's voice betrayed his impatience with what he saw as Georgiou's convoluted attempt at getting his argument out. Lack of sleep the night before was having its affect.

"Well that means whoever was calling her from the unknown number at seven-thirty couldn't have known she was dead could they, likewise the guy Michael who called at six-fifteen and six-thirty-five. Of course, they could have been the same person, Michael, maybe also using a burner phone," Georgiou repeated his earlier suggestion.

Papadoulis nodded slightly, finally acknowledging the logic of his Sergeant's point.

"They could have indeed been the same person, Michael, calling her from two different phones, and the calls at those times do certainly suggest the caller or callers didn't know she was dead."

He walked back to prop himself once again on the corner of Kyriakopoulis' desk as he asked him, "Now the phone is unlocked have you tried the number, this guy Michael's number from her list of missed calls? He may not have known she was dead, but he might be able to help us with some things, like why did he feel the need to call her twice so early on Saturday morning."

"No luck I'm afraid. It's unobtainable, sir. Tried it four times, always get the same 'this number is unobtainable' message."

"Weird. So, we have his name and number in her phone on Friday and obviously on Saturday morning and he calls her from it early twice, but twenty-four hours later the number is unobtainable. Why would you do that, particularly if you don't know she's dead? And then there's the other calls from the unknown number."

"There could be a simple explanation, sir, like this guy Michael lost his phone between making the calls and now, or it got damaged," Kyriakopoulis suggested.

"Or he could be her boyfriend. She wasn't married and Carmichael and Lees said she had no family still alive as far as they knew. So, Michael can't be her brother," Georgiou interjected.

"No, surely Carmichael and Lees would have said if she had a boyfriend. To let him know she's dead, surely."

As he finished saying that the Inspector moved off the desk once more. He started to pace back and forth across the open plan office and muttered, "So, who the bloody hell is this Michael guy?"

"There is a voice message from him on her phone though, sir, or at least from his number. It's from the call he made at six-thirty-five. Doesn't tell us much but-"

Before Kyriakopoulis could finish the Inspector spun around on his heels exclaiming loudly, "What? A voice message? You didn't think to tell me that earlier, Sergeant?"

His tired impatience was back.

"I was about to, sir, but I thought you wanted to know about the missed calls first."

"You got it downloaded on your computer, the voice message?"

"Err ... yes, sir. I'll play it now."

The Sergeant tapped away at his computer keyboard and the message from O'Mara's phone began to play.

"Be careful Kathleen. Is it done?" a male voice said.

Papadoulis slumped down into a chair by a nearby desk.

"Is what done? Assuming that's the mysterious Michael, what does he mean? And 'Be careful Kathleen'? Be careful of what? Is he just a friend or is it something more sinister? It sounds like an Irish accent, so maybe it is just a friend and something to do with her birthday? Carmichael and Lees said that's why they were here, to celebrate her birthday. And is he someone on the island, in Lindos perhaps?"

"We could ask some of the bar and restaurant owners and staff we interviewed in Lindos if they know of anyone by that name in the village, sir," Georgiou suggested.

Papadoulis rubbed his chin with his right hand for a few seconds.

"This bloody case gets more and more complicated every minute," he began. After a few more seconds hesitation he told Georgiou, "Right, yes, let's go to back to Lindos and do that. The Courtyard Bar and Pal's Bar won't be open till around six or seven, but that restaurant, The Village House, might be open for lunch so we can ask the owner there if he knows anyone Irish called Michael in the village. It's a long shot, but he seemed to know Lindos, and the locals and some of the tourists, quite well when we spoke to him yesterday. And we can ask around some of the other cafes and bars to see if anyone knows this guy Michael. While we're there Kyriakopoulis chase up all those phone records, plus call the UK police in London and see if they've got anything in their files, on record on Bird, Bradshaw, Carmichael and Lees, as well as Martin Cleverley, O'Mara and Aileen Regan. Georgiou, while I'm updating the Incident Board in Lindos with what we've got from O'Mara's phone you can make a start on the social media check on Cleverley, including that Lindos Bars site Jack Constantino's son told us he saw Cleverley had posted some stuff on about Crete, as well as some photos. Plus, there's his two novels Constantino's son also said Cleverley had published. Perhaps you can find some stuff on him through those on social media. Leave Cleverley's social media checks to Georgiou, Kyriakopoulis. You concentrate on his phone stuff and seeing if the U.K. police have anything on him and the others."

Georgiou raised his eyes slightly in the direction of Kyriakopoulis at the Inspector's inclusion of the name Aileen Regan yet again in their investigations.

10

Sunday afternoon: heat and a typical Lindos rainstorm

Papadoulis and Georgiou parked at the top of Lindos village by the Atmosphere Bar and Lindos Reception. The heat in the middle of the day was sweltering, an oppressive suffocating heat like a very thick heavy blanket lying over the island. Even for July it was unusually hot. Even the two policemen were beginning to sweat in the instant contrast between that heat and their car's cool air-conditioning. As they walked down the slope and around the small bend at the bottom towards the alleyway on the right where Lindos Police Station was located dark threatening clouds were increasingly gathering overhead, blocking out the midday sun, but not the humid air.

"Looks like there is going to be a storm," Georgiou commented. "Unusual on the island for July."

Seconds later there was a huge clap of thunder. As they reached the courtyard in front of station the first few large splodges of rain hit the flagstones accompanied by a sudden wind. The two men quickened their step. No sooner had they made it inside than the heavens opened with heavy incessant piercing rain and more thunder, this time accompanied by large long lightning streaks shattering the now startling dark Lindos sky.

"Looks like you two have upset the Lindos gods," the desk officer joked as the Inspector and his Sergeant made their way quickly across the reception area towards the short hallway leading to their office.

"These sort of storms don't usually last long here. There was one when we were working on that case here in 2016," Papadoulis started to say as he sat down at his desk.

"If I remember correctly that only lasted about fifteen minutes or so. That was enough to flood the alleyways, however. Torrents of angry water, a foot deep in places, swept through the village down the slopes of the alleys and paths from the top of it to the bottom towards the Main Square. I was halfway down the main alley through the village when it started, not far from here, and managed to find a piece of wall outside Socrates Bar to seek sanctuary from the water. It was quite a spectacle. In less than an hour though, the water from the storm, as well as the wind and rain, had gone. The Lindos air was still once again. It was late afternoon when that happened and the peculiar damp smell throughout the village lingered through the evening and into the night, all through until the returning heat of the next morning. The paths through the alleyways were completely dry a couple of hours after the rainstorm, which was just as well as they can be tricky in parts even when dry, and more so when wet. The flagstones were worn shiny in places. I suppose from the millions of tourist footsteps over the years."

They could hear the rain continuing to heavily hammer on the police station roof as the Inspector finished reminiscing, and what Georgiou thought as his weather report. In fact, although he was talking about a storm in Lindos in the late summer of 2016 he was really thinking about a similar heavy storm which arrived suddenly and equally as dramatically, even later that summer while he was in Sally Hardcastle's bed in Lardos one evening.

That prompted him to add, "Give it half-an-hour or so and the alleyways will dry out, and I'll go and get us a couple more of those delicious feta and spinach homemade pies. Meanwhile, I'll update the Incident Board with what we got from Rhodes Town on the missed calls on O'Mara's phone and the Michael voice message, and you can start looking for that social media stuff on Cleverley which Jack Constantino's son told us about."

"What about the restaurant owner, The Village House one, and asking him if he knows anything about Michael, sir, and some of the cafes and bars in the village?"

"We'll have to do that a bit later now. The restaurant won't be open now with the rain. There's no cover. So, we'll do that later, early evening, and ask in some of the bars."

As he finished adding the O'Mara phone stuff to the board Papadoulis stepped back a couple of paces and stood staring at it for a good full minute. Eventually he rubbed his chin briefly with his left hand and then shook his head slightly once.

"Why would someone who appears to be just an innocent woman holidaymaker have use for contact and phone calls from someone with a burner phone? And there was no sign at all of another phone in her hotel room, not a burner phone she may have had."

It wasn't a real question. He was simply thinking aloud.

As he suggested earlier, the storm and the rain only lasted about fifteen minutes, and now he could hear it had stopped. Before the Sergeant could comment on the phone calls to O'Mara the Inspector asked a real question.

"Are you hungry? I am. I expect the sun and the heat have returned. The alleys should be getting dry out there now so I'll go and get some of those pies."

However, it wasn't just the feta and spinach pies he was heading to Café Melia for, as good as they were. He was hoping to see Sally Hardcastle. He was disappointed. Not with the pies. They were fresh, freshly made and warm, but she wasn't there and he didn't want to ask the other two women serving about her, where she was. That might have drawn attention to him and he didn't want to risk that in the village and provide some gossip. So, he settled for just getting the pies he liked so much.

Papadoulis came through the door to the small station office saying, "Bloody baking hot out there again already, and mostly the paths and alleys are almost dry."

Georgiou's response was simply, "Got him, sir. Cleverley, I think I've found him."

He went straight over to his own desk and pulled his chair over to the Sergeant's to peer at his computer screen.

"I checked that Lindos Bars social media site for the photos of Crete Constantino's son told us Cleverley had posted on it. It took a while, that was a couple of years ago, 2020, but eventually I found them. They were just a couple of photos of what Cleverley wrote in the post was the main square of a place called Neapoli. I did a search for that. It's a small town about eleven kilometres west of Agios Nikolaos on Crete and about forty-five from Heraklion."

"But a couple of years ago, how-"

"How do we know he's still there, sir?" Georgiou interrupted "Yes, well I did a search for him on that Lindos site, and Constantino's son was right. Cleverley has had a couple of novels published, and one of them, 'Greek Sun', was published at the end of 2018. And look at this."

The Sergeant clicked on his computer screen and scrolled down to some text headed 'Greek Sun', then began to read from it.

"It says that book is a fictional love story based on Crete between a Greek man and a woman." Georgiou leaned back from the computer screen and added with some emphasis in his voice, "and guess what, sir, an Irish woman."

He looked up at the Inspector and tilted his head slightly in a questioning sort of manner saying, "Could she be based on Kathleen O'Mara, sir?"

"Hmm … or Aileen Regan, Sergeant, one and the same person it seems. But how does that mean he's still there, on Crete?"

"There's more, sir. On that Lindos bars site more recently, just a couple of months ago in early May, there's a post from Cleverley which sort of obviously advertises his two novels. For 'summer and Greek beach reading', he wrote, and there's a link to his personal website for the novels. On there it says he lives on Crete in that place, Neapoli."

"Good work, Sergeant, but how do we know his website is up to date. How-"

"Do we know he's still there," Georgiou finished his question for him again before adding, "It gives the name of his publisher in London on the website. So, I called them, explained who I was and what this was about, and they confirmed he's still living in Neapoli. Working on a new novel, they said."

He let out a small chuckle before continuing, "They actually said all this sounds like a very good plot for a novel."

Papadoulis glared down at him.

"Yes, yes, Sergeant, but did you get any contact details for him?"

"There's an email address for him on his website, for anyone wanting to contact him about his novels, but after I told the publisher what this was about, and after a lot of persuading, I managed to get his mobile number from them."

"Well, you've certainly earned your pie, Sergeant."

With that Papadoulis walked over to the Incident Board and wrote under Cleverley's name the words 'Crete' and 'novel Greek Sun'.

After a minute staring at the board contemplating what they'd, or rather Georgiou, had discovered, he told the Sergeant, "Looks like a trip to Crete to see Mr. Cleverley is needed, and as soon as possible I think. There's obviously a lot more to this case than we at first thought, and it's expanding all the time. Let's see what Cleverley can tell us about O'Mara or Aileen Regan if, as Constantino said, she left with him from here to Crete six years ago. I'll call the high-ups at Rhodes Town to get the ok for it and then check out some flights to Crete and back for tomorrow. When I get it sorted we better let the Crete police know I'm coming and why."

Having made the call to the Rhodes Town station to request permission for the expenditure for the flights the Inspector instructed Georgiou, "Right, let's go and see what, if anything, any of the café and bar owners can tell us about the mysterious Irish Michael, and then we'll check with the owner of the Village House restaurant later to see if he can help us, and then Jack Constantino at the Courtyard Bar."

As Papadoulis said the alleyways were virtually dry as the two policemen stepped out of the station courtyard. Just an hour or less before the ones through the centre of the village had been covered in rushing torrents of water. The baking hot overhead mid-afternoon Lindos sun had regained its prime position in the cloudless clear blue sky with a vengeance, and had done its work to good effect in drying the flagstones and paths. The rain, even though torrential, had also freshened up the beautiful bright pink overhanging bougainvillea plants in some of the alleyways, particularly the one they passed beneath a few metres down from the turning into the police station off the main alleyway through the village.

As they reached the centre of the village further down the slope with the little square and the large tree surrounded by a low white wall it was already beginning to fill up again with tourists, the ones who had no doubt been driven off the beaches earlier by the rainstorm. Bars and cafes, like Yannis, had removed their temporary plastic sheeting shields against the rain and were now doing a busy afternoon trade from people sat with coffees or glasses of beer happily watching the steady flow of other tourists passing by.

Opposite Yannis Bar, on the slight bend in the alley path, the remaining small front façade of an old chapel, Greek Orthodox obviously, with none of the existing structure remaining behind, looked down on the pleasant tourist scene, the Greek rain gods having obviously vented their anger for the day. As they turned the slight bend to continue along the main alley through the village they encountered even more crowds of tourists peering into the little shops. That part of the village drew the largest number of them throughout the day and into the evening, whether they were tourists staying in and around Lindos or the multitude of day trippers from Rhodes Town. Throughout the day a large number of coaches arrived from there bringing tourists from off the huge cruise ships which docked in Rhodes. Not being allowed to, or even able to enter the village with its narrow pedestrianised alleyways, nor the Main Square, the coaches lined up in rows parked at the top of one end of the village in Krana.

The two policemen weaved their way through the tourist crowds past the Red Rose Bar to the right with its elevated equally busy outside seating and the Odyssia Restaurant on the left.

Eventually Georgiou asked, "Where exactly are we headed, sir? Where do you think is a good place to start asking about this Irish guy, Michael?"

Just at that point they reached the end of that small stretch of alley by the, at that time of day closed, Pal's Bar. Papadoulis pointed to his right and a small café bar about twenty metres or so away, adding, "There, I think, Sergeant. Giorgos. That looks central enough. Let's try there. Maybe even a small beer?"

The café looked ideal for sitting at one of the few small tables outside to enjoy their beer whilst taking in the general bustle of the village and its tourism, but also more importantly for asking the staff and the owner if they knew an Irish man called Michael in the village.

They made their way to the only vacant small circular table outside. In addition, there were a couple of occupied small white square tables, each with a couple of chairs, as well as a couple of slightly larger ones either side of the doorway into the cafe bar with bench type stone seats and cushions to one side against the bar wall, also occupied. Above the outside area was a loose iron looking trellis work, partly covered in green plant trailing branches and leaves.

Shortly after they sat at the table a very slim young woman waitress, probably in her late twenties, with long straight dark hair dressed in a black t-shirt with the small logo Giorgos on it, a short black skirt and black trainers, arrived at their table, handing them a menu accompanied with, "Kalimera." She obviously realised immediately from their appearance that the two men were Greek, or at the very least assumed they were. From her accent, however, she didn't appear to be. The Inspector's accent confirmed her assumption as he told her, "Just a couple of small Mythos beers, please."

As the waitress started to turn to get their beers Papadoulis asked, "Are you from Lindos?"

She smiled as she replied, "No, Slovakia."

Papadoulis followed up with, "Have you worked here long or just this summer?"

"Erm ... yes, this is my eighth season working here, but I stay most of the year now, even in the winter."

She looked a little confused by his questions, and just a bit more concerned when he added, "Is the owner around by any chance?"

"Yes, he's inside serving tables there. I'll get him to bring your beers."

While they waited for their beers, and for the owner to appear, the Inspector took the opportunity to cast an eye over the customers seated at the other tables, as well as watch the people passing by on their way through the village. It appeared that all the fellow customers were foreigners, tourists from what sounded from their language and accents like France, Germany and Britain. There were no obvious Irish accents to be heard. Similarly, most of the passers-by appeared to be tourists, either staying in the village or visiting Lindos on a day trip from other parts of the island, including Rhodes Town. Very occasionally he guessed there was what looked like the odd local from the village, or a seasonal young worker, who passed the café bar, but mostly it was clearly tourists - younger, older and middle-aged couples, groups of three or four, or even more, younger men and women tourists strolling through the village on their way now in the hot sun to one of the beaches for a late afternoon swim or simply sunbathe. By now the bright shimmering white of the walls of the buildings opposite where they were sitting were fully reflecting the returned savage heat of the day.

A few minutes later a middle-aged Greek man with dark curly hair wearing a black t-shirt, black jeans and a long dark apron appeared with their small beers and introduced himself as, "Tsamis, the owner. Is there a problem, gentlemen?"

Papadoulis asked him the same initial question.

"Are you from Lindos?"

"Yes."

Now he looked confused. That disappeared as Papadoulis produced his police credentials and quietly introduced the two of them, adding to try and allay the owner's concern, "But no there's not any problem at all. We just thought you might be able to help us with something. You're café bar seems pretty popular. Are your customers mostly tourists? Any locals, Greek or British or Irish ex-pats who live in or near the village?"

"It's a mixture, mainly tourists, but some Greek locals and a few Brit ex-pats. Can't think of any Irish ones though."

"What about the tourists though?" Georgiou asked. "Many Irish ones?"

"Some, yeah, but not that many, and mostly from the north, around Belfast and that part."

"Ever come across an Irish guy called Michael by any chance, tourist maybe, especially recently?"

Tsamis shook his head slightly.

"We get a lot of tourists who come here regularly, come back year after year, especially families. I know quite a lot of them by name because of that. Some are called Michael, but I can't recall anyone of those who are Irish, Inspector. Do you know he comes in here?"

"No, no, just a shot in the dark really. Thanks anyway," Papadoulis told him as he reached to take a sip of his beer.

As Tsamis disappeared through the open doorway back inside the bar Georgiou commented, "No luck there, sir, although you said it would be a long shot asking in the bars."

"Yes, well at least we got a chance to have a beer, Sergeant."

He glanced at his watch before adding, "Let's just enjoy the beer here in the sun, watch the world go by for a bit, relax from this frantic investigation a while, and then see if we have any different luck on Michael with the Village House restaurant owner and Jack Constantino in the Courtyard Bar when they are open later."

Georgiou nodded his agreement as he reached for his cool beer, although the condensation was already beginning to gather on the outside of the glass from the heat of the warm Lindos air.

Half-an-hour later they walked through the stone arch entrance to an empty Village House restaurant in which the staff were busy setting up tables and preparing for the evening's customers and opening at six. They had no better luck there on their quest for Irish Michael, however. Once again the owner, Ari, told them he knew quite a lot of his customers well, and like Tsamis in Giorgos many of them returned to the restaurant year on year, plus yes some of them were called Michael, usually in couples, but he couldn't recall any of those being Irish.

They got the same answer from Jack Constantino when the Inspector asked him the same question in the Courtyard Bar shortly after, as he and his staff were also setting up for the opening that evening. Constantino's son, Cris, did ask if it's was connected to what they were asking before about Aileen Regan, her being Irish. Papadoulis diverted from answering that by telling him, "Thanks for the tip about Martin Cleverley and the Lindos Bars site postings."

"Did you find him," Jack asked. "Is he still on Crete?"

Again though Papadoulis was non-committal and just replied with, "Yes, we found him. Thanks again for that. We better let you get on setting up for the evening."

With that they left and made their way back towards the station, still none the wiser about the elusive Michael. As they walked back through the village Georgiou suggested they give it a try in a few more bars. They went into Antika Bar on the right in in the centre of the village in an old traditional Lindian stone high fronted building. Again that was empty as it was still early and the staff were also setting up for the evening. They asked the same questions of Ledi, the Head Barman, but got similar answers. No Irish Michael.

A few minutes later they tried the Crazy Moon cocktail bar. It was nearer the end of the village where the police station was located, through the small square with the tree in the centre surrounded by the low white wall, to the right of Bar404, and thirty metres or so up the slightly inclined part of the slope out of the village and then down a narrow alleyway to the right opposite a small supermarket. Crazy Moon was one of the relatively newer bars in Lindos, at least it was in its latest incarnation. It had been a few different bars previously. Through another Lindian stone arched entrance it had a very pleasant garden courtyard outside the bar with a number of tables and chairs. Inside, the small bar was nicely decorated with some great photos of various music icons on the walls. The bar itself was against the back wall with a few stools in front of it. There were two couples at the tables in the courtyard, but no one inside. Again, it was early still in terms of Lindos nightlife and the bar and the outside courtyard would be much busier later.

Once again the two policemen approached the bar and asked the young barman if the owner was around. He directed them to a curly haired man in his late twenties sat in the corner at the far end of the bar looking at his laptop. When they reached him they could see he was, in fact, selecting the music being played. As in the other bars Papadoulis produced his credentials and introduced the two policemen, then asked the same question as previously about the Irish man, Michael. As in the other bars he got the same negative response from the owner, along with the similar, "We have regulars, tourists who come year after year, as well as some Brit ex-pats who live in and around the village, but no Irish guy called Michael I can recall."

After they thanked him and left Crazy Moon to walk down the narrow alley to the main one again Georgiou appeared keener on continuing to check some of the bars and suggested one last one, the Lindian House Bar. It was another thirty metres or so to the right further up the slope towards the police station and on the left in another impressive high Lindian stone fronted building. It had an inside bar, a garden outside, reached through that inner bar, with a number of high-backed wicker chairs and tables, and an upper roof terrace with more tables and chairs. The inner bar, with the entrance, had an area for dancing, some stools at the bar that stretched all along one side, some short padded wall benches and a couple of tables. In one corner opposite the bar was the small DJ area and console The Lindian House inside bar had a magnificent wooden Lindian carved ceiling. Later in the evening the inner bar would usually be packed, with some people trying to dance and other groups just standing and talking. However, at this time there were only a couple of solitary drinkers sat at the bar. A tourist couple finishing a pre-dinner drink perhaps.

When the two policemen reached the bar a young dark haired Greek guy behind it, probably in his mid-twenties and with a thin close to chin beard, came and asked them what he could get them to drink. Once again the Inspector produced his police credentials and introduced the two of them, followed by asking for the manager.

"That's me, Giwrgos," the guy informed them, followed by the usual, "Is there a problem?"

"No, no problem. Have you ever come across a customer in here called Michael, Irish guy?"

The guy grimaced.

"We have our regulars, Inspector, and I know quite a few of them, know their names, who return every year, but there are a lot of customers who maybe only come in a couple of times or so while they are in the village on holiday and I don't get their names, especially when the bar is busy. We don't usually have much time to talk to the customers then."

"But any Michael's amongst your regulars, Irish?" Papadoulis pushed him.

"No ... no, can't say I know of any, sorry Inspector."

"Ok, thanks anyway"

With that the two policemen headed for the doorway and back out into the slightly sloping alleyway, then up it to the left towards the station.

11

Three phone calls and the 2016 case file

"Well, it was a long shot I suppose. Thinking we might turn up who this Irish guy Michael is from some of the bar and restaurant owners," Papadoulis commented as he once again stood in front of the Incident Board in the Lindos station office.

"We could get a couple of officers checking with some of the other bar owners in the village, sir," Georgiou suggested as he made his way to turn on the kettle on the small table in the corner adding, "Coffee?"

"Ok, Sergeant, yes to both those suggestions. I suppose a couple of local officers might have a better idea of the rest of the bars to check. I don't hold out much hope though. It's a long shot. We don't even know where this guy Michael was calling from. We don't know that he was even ever in Lindos."

He hesitated for a few seconds, rubbing the back of his neck before agreeing.

"Ok, yes. Tell the officer on the front desk to get a couple on it tonight. And maybe coffee will get my brain cells working on it, and this case in general."

He turned away from the board and walked back over to his desk and computer saying, "Right, let's take a look at that 2016 case file. See if that can add anything to our investigation."

Before he could start to go through the file, however, the office phone rang.

When he finished the call he told Georgiou, "So, I'm off on a little trip to Crete tomorrow now, Sergeant. Rhodes Town has given the go-ahead and I've got an early start. Have to go via Athens. So they've booked me on a six-thirty flight to there, then one at ten to Heraklion. Back on the eighteen-forty-five from there tomorrow night to Athens and from there into

123

Rhodes at nine-thirty. Looks like it's going to be a busy day. Now I better give Mr. Cleverley a call to tell him he needs to make himself available for interview at mid-day tomorrow and find out his exact location, where he's living. While I do that give Crete police a call and let them know I'm coming, plus ask them to arrange a car to pick me up at Heraklion airport to take me to Cleverley's and then take me back to the airport after I've interviewed him. My flight is scheduled to land at Heraklion at ten-fifty."

While Georgiou did that the Inspector looked across at the Incident Board and the phone number written on it under Martin Cleverley's name that the Sergeant had got from his publisher and began to dial it.

When a male voice answered he asked, "Is that Martin Cleverley?"

"Yes, who's this?"

"My name is Inspector Papadoulis of the Rhodes police."

"Oh, I see, what's this about, Inspector?"

"I prefer not to go into it in detail over the phone. I would like to interview you tomorrow concerning a case we are investigating."

"A case? What sort of case?"

"As I said, sir, I'd prefer not to go into it over the phone. You are in Crete I believe? Neapoli?"

"Yes I am, but-"

"Tomorrow, sir, at about twelve, would that be convenient for you?"

"Err ... yes ... but can't you at least give me some idea what this is about? What you need to speak to me about that is so important that you are going to come here from Rhodes, and it can't be done on the phone?"

"I think it's best if I come to see you, sir. We'd prefer that in this case. Where exactly are you living in Neapoli? Can you give me your address there please?"

Cleverley obviously seemed confused, unable to think what it could be the Rhodes police would want to interview him about.

"But I haven't even been on Rhodes for, it must be six years or so, Inspector."

124

Papadoulis ignored that comment.

"Your address please, sir?"

"Err ... yes, it's on the street Ioannoi Sergaki, not far from the main square and just about a hundred metres along that road from the Hotel Neapolis. It's the old stone house on the left past the hotel. It doesn't actually have a number, but everyone knows it. You can't miss it. If you want I can meet you in the square and bring you here?"

"No, that won't be necessary Mr. Cleverley. I'm sure the local officers will know it."

"Local officers? What's it got to-"

"Just courtesy, sir. We have to inform them when we are coming to interview someone in their region, and they would have to do the same if it was the other way round. They will pick me up with a car from Heraklion airport."

Martin Cleverley's confusion was just starting to change into frustrated annoyance. He raised his voice a little as he said, "Look, Inspector, I need to know something of what exactly this is about at least don't you think?"

There was a short ten second silence as Papadoulis considered how to reply and what to tell him, how much.

"Inspector? Inspector?"

"Ok, Mr. Cleverley. It's about someone you met in Lindos on Rhodes six years ago, a woman, Aileen Regan."

"Aileen?"

He hesitated for a few seconds. He hadn't heard anyone call her by that name for six years.

"But I haven't seen her for four years, what could-"

Papadoulis didn't let him finish his question and he didn't want to tell him at that point, on the phone, that she was dead. He preferred to see and gauge his reaction in person when he did tell him. It was pretty obvious from Cleverley's reaction and comment over the phone though that he didn't know she was dead. Perhaps that meant he wasn't the killer, was what the Inspector was considering, or maybe he was just a good actor and hid it well. He'd have a better idea when he told him face to face.

125

"As I said a few minutes ago, I prefer not to go into it any more over the phone. I will explain fully when we meet tomorrow and see what you can tell me, sir."

"But, about Aileen, I also knew her as-"

"Tomorrow, Mr. Cleverley. We can go into it all tomorrow. I will see you at twelve at your house. Thank you."

With that the Inspector rang off.

Martin Cleverley was actually about to tell him that he also eventually knew Aileen as Kathleen O'Mara, which would, of course, have finally completely confirmed Papadoulis' suspicion. That would have to wait until they met now.

As soon as he came off his call to Martin Cleverley Georgiou told him, "It's all arranged with the Crete police, sir. They'll meet you with a car at the airport and then bring you back when you've finished interviewing Cleverley, Apparently they have an officer who is from Neapoli and he'll go with you. What did Cleverley say? I gather from what I heard you didn't want to give him too much information at this stage."

"Not much, although he did say he hadn't seen Aileen Regan for four years. She obviously left him. Hopefully I'll find out why tomorrow, and it seemed like he didn't know she was dead, been murdered."

"So, he's not our killer then?"

"Maybe not, unless he's a good actor. I'll get a better idea tomorrow. In the meantime get on to Kyriakopoulis at Rhodes, give him Cleverley's number and get him to add that to the other phone records he's chasing for all the others. Now, I really need to have a look at this 2016 case file before I see him tomorrow."

No sooner had he opened the file though than his phone rang again.

"Am I going to see you tonight, Yiannis, what with last night being so good, if you know what I mean? Are you coming over?" Sally Hardcastle asked when he answered it.

"Oh ... err ..."

He sounded and looked flustered.

"No, I don't think that will be possible."

He got up from his desk and headed quickly towards the office door as he continued, "Too much to sort on the case at the moment. It's gone crazy and now I have to go to Crete early tomorrow morning."

"I went to the café earlier, but you weren't there," he added as he reached the courtyard in front of the station.

"Did you miss me then? Are you?"

"What?"

"Missing me? I'm missing you, Yiannis, now we've connected again after all this time."

He was thinking this wasn't like her at all, telling him something like that. It wasn't her usual cocky confident self at all.

He didn't answer, so she explained, "I had a day off. I usually get one every two weeks. Did you ask anyone there where I was?"

"Err ... no, thought it best not to, gossip and the village and all that you know."

"Yes, I suppose so. That's disappointing though, Yiannis."

"Disappointing that I didn't ask where you were?"

He heard her let out a short small laugh at the other end of the line before she told him, "No, disappointing that you can't come over tonight. What about tomorrow night?"

"I don't get back to Rhodes airport till nine-thirty, so I don't think that's going to be possible either, Sally."

So, why?"

"Why what? Why it's not going to be possible for me to come over tomorrow night? I just said."

"No, why do you have to go to Crete tomorrow? Is it for the case?"

He hesitated for a few seconds.

"Yiannis? Crete, is it for the case?"

"You know I can't tell you that, Sally, don't you."

"Hmm ... that means it is then."

He couldn't see, but she was grinning as she said that followed by a quizzical, "Interesting, so what is-"

He decided he should stop the conversation at that point. He knew Lindos and Lardos were hotbeds of rumour and gossip. Although he believed he could trust her, and he knew he had done six years previously over their affair and she hadn't betrayed that trust, he didn't want to take a chance that

127

something would get out in the villages about the case that could only have come from him. Professionally for his career that wouldn't be good at all.

He interrupted her question with one of his own that he thought he could ask without betraying something related to the case.

"I don't suppose you know of anyone in Lindos, or who comes into the café, by the name of Michael who's Irish?"

"Michael who? What's his other name?"

"We don't have his full name, just Michael and he's Irish."

"From the north or the south?"

"What?"

"Northern Ireland, or as my grandmother used to insist on calling it, the north of Ireland, or from the south, the Republic?"

"Not sure."

"Well if you ever find him, Yiannis, you'll understand and see the difference in the accents."

"Right, I see, so no then, no one you know of in Lindos?"

"There's a few Michael's, or some who like to be called Mick, in Lindos, but no, no one I know is Irish. A couple of Brit ex-pats, and plenty of the Greeks, Michalis, of course."

"Okay, just thought I'd ask."

"Even more interesting, Yiannis. Can't wait to hear more when I get to see you again. I'll call you in a couple of days and hopefully you'll be less busy and we can fix something. Be good to see you. Enjoy Crete."

She rang off and he headed back into the station to join Georgiou in the office and finally get round to the 2016 case file.

The Sergeant had heard the start of the phone conversation before Papadoulis left the office to go into the courtyard and assumed it was his wife.

"Not happy with the late nights, sir, and you being off to Crete early tomorrow?"

As he was crossing the office to his desk from the doorway the Inspector spun around on his heels to face him. Looking a little uneasy he asked, "What, Sergeant?"

"Your wife, not happy?"

He wanted to tell him it was none of his business, but he settled for a compromising, "Oh, yes, well you know, this case is keeping us busy." He continued with, "Now, this bloody 2016 case file, and hopefully no more interruptions."

He made himself a coffee, offered one to Georgiou who declined, and then settled down at his desk to study the case file.

Most of what was in it he recognised as he'd been the officer in charge who'd recorded it, except for the pathologist's report of course. There were various photos of the body of the dead man and the place where the body was found; in a narrow alley leading from the alleyway that ran all along the back of Lindos village down to the main alleyway through it. After he'd looked at those he began to read what he'd written in the report back in the summer of 2016, both the official report and his various miscellaneous case notes.

He'd recorded that the dead man had no means of identification on him, nothing that indicated where he was staying in the village, or even on Rhodes. Papadoulis had written the assumption was he was a tourist on holiday. Various attempts were made to ascertain his identity, including officers from Lindos and Rhodes Town going around the village bars and restaurants with a photo of him. Although the only photo they had of him was the one taken at the scene by the pathologist team. The investigating officers hoped that might help identify him and his movements in the village on the Saturday night of his death, if anyone working in the bars and restaurants remembered him. The British police said they had nothing on record that matched his finger prints or DNA.

Papadoulis paused from reading the case notes to take another drink of his coffee. At which point Georgiou asked, "Anything jump out, sir?"

"Not yet, Sergeant. Nothing obvious, just the usual stuff so far. I'll have a look at my notes from what I got and recorded from interviewing Regan."

He continued by reading out some of the things in the file so that Georgiou could be aware of what was in it, even though the Sergeant still retained some degree of scepticism about Aileen Regan and Kathleen O'Mara being one and the same person,

129

and over why Regan was continuing to be so important in the case for his Inspector.

"Pathologist's report put the victim's time of death at sometime between one and four or five on that Sunday morning that the body was found. Erm ... a broken nose caused by a blow to the face, possibly from a fall into the wall by the deceased ... cause of death a head trauma, a fracture to the skull from a blow to the head by a blunt object ... err ... probably the relatively large stone that was found at the scene covered in blood, which had been detached from the path slab previously, presumably by wear and tear on the path ... most likely scenario is that the large stone inflicted the initial, eventually fatal, injury from a fall by the male, who then attempted to get up dazed, stumbled down the steps and fell again hitting the front of the skull against wall ... err ... led to profuse bleeding, concussion, and substantial eventual blood loss while the deceased lost consciousness."

"Drunk, sir?" Georgiou interjected.

"Err ... no it doesn't seem like it. The report says there was alcohol in the victim's blood stream, but nothing excessive."

"Just lost his footing on the rough path in the dark then?"

Papadoulis seemed a little detached as he carried on reading the file, before he agreed. "Err ... yes, that's the way it seemed, and if I remember it is quite dark up there in those back alleys, not much lighting, so ..."

He went back to studying the file again, and in particular his notes, then told Georgiou "Regan told me she lived in Boston in the U.S., had an American passport, and worked for herself as a freelance, security adviser."

He looked up from the file and rubbed his chin.

"Yes, I remember now, the passport, the American passport thing."

"What about it, sir?"

"The American Embassy in Athens said they had no record of any American passport in the name of Aileen Regan."

"Oh yes, I remember that now. Odd, sir."

"Very odd, Sergeant. Even more odd than that though was, if you recall, the number two U.S Embassy diplomat in Athens called us back over what appeared to be a quite innocuous enquiry by us about a supposed American passport holder? I remember wondering at the time why we got a call back from someone who held a senior position connected to the U.S. Department of Homeland Security"

"And we never got the chance to ask Regan about that stuff on the passport later did we?"

"That's right, not long after that call I got the call from the Lieutenant General Chief of the Hellenic Police ordering me to release the body to the British Vice-Consul in Rhodes Town to be returned to England, and ordering the end of our investigation, case closed as an accident."

Papadoulis went back to scanning the file and reading bits out for Georgiou's benefit.

"Says she, Regan, said she was here trying to trace her family history, including her birth father ... staff in Courtyard Bar and Pal's Bar remembered the dead guy being in their bars the night before the body was found. One of the staff in Pal's Bar said he was asking about an Irish woman being in the village, and thought he might have meant Regan. But Regan said she'd never met the dead guy, and I remember she brushed that off when I interviewed her by saying there were plenty of Irish female tourists in Lindos regularly, and particularly at that time. The Pal's barman said he pointed the guy out to Regan across the bar that night he died. When I put that to her she said the guy had his back to her at the other end of the bar, so all she saw was the back of his head and couldn't recognise him from the photo I showed her. She just repeated that in any case he could have been looking for any Irish female in the village, not her. Consequently, she never went over to see him in Pal's, she told me, as it was late and she was about to leave to meet some people about tracing her family stuff."

Papadoulis looked up and scratched the back of his head briefly, then continued.

"I do remember though that when I put all that to her about the guy asking about an Irish woman in Pal's she eventually got a bit agitated. She said no one she knew even knew she was in Lindos, so why would she think the guy was looking for her, especially when she never recognised him, even if it was only from behind. She assumed it could have been anyone, any Irish woman he was looking for, not her. She told me why would she think otherwise."

He looked down at the file again.

"My notes here say that when I asked if she went back to her apartment after Pal's that night she said she went to the Glow club and then to the Crazy Moon cocktail bar around two. Also here it says we checked that out and the partner of one of the owners of Crazy Moon, Emily, remembered her. Then later that night she went to the club in the centre of the village, Arches, to meet a tourist couple who she met earlier in Pal's, James and Katy. The doorman at the club, Cris, remembered her and confirmed that she arrived at around three then left at just after four, saying it was too crowded. She said she went back to her apartment and bed after that."

Georgiou shook his head slightly.

Papadoulis looked across the desk at him. Reading Georgiou's mind he commented, "Yes, that's what I remember thinking at the time, Sergeant. It was all a bit too neat, almost rehearsed. I would have liked to have got a sample from her for DNA testing to see if, by any chance, any of hers was on the guy's body at all and there was any connection. But before we could even think about approaching her for that, and I'm not sure she would have cooperated, she didn't have to, I got that call from the Chief in Athens and then it was case closed."

He got up from his desk and wandered over to the Incident Board staring at the names Aileen Regan and Martin Cleverley written there.

"I do remember her asking at one point towards the end of the interview with her whether I thought the guy's death was anything other than an accident. I thought at the time that was a bit of an odd thing to ask."

"Just curious perhaps, sir?"

"Maybe, Sergeant, maybe, but one thing's for sure, we know her death, Aileen Regan or Kathleen O'Mara, whoever she was, wasn't an accident."

He turned his head slightly to focus on the name Martin Cleverley in silence for a short time. Then he tilted it slightly to one side and said, "Hmm ... you know what is odd, Georgiou? Very odd?"

It was a rhetorical question. He didn't wait for the Sergeant to respond.

He pointed to the board saying, "Where was he in all that 2016 investigation? Where was Martin Cleverley?"

"In Lindos, sir", Georgiou commented.

The Inspector glanced back over his shoulder with a bit of a disparaging look on his face.

"I meant where was he in our investigation? His name doesn't come up anywhere in the case files. Yes, we know he was in Lindos, and that he knew Aileen Regan, met her here, and they went off to Crete together later, within a few days of the guy's so-called accidental death here. Why didn't we interview him? And didn't Constantino tell us that Regan had met Cleverley earlier that summer in …?"

Georgiou checked his notes from interviewing Jack Constantino the day before in the Courtyard Bar.

"Yes, June that summer of 2016. That's when Constantino said they met and 'got on very well', as he put it."

"Yet Cleverley is not mentioned anywhere in the case file. She never mentioned him when I interviewed her. She couldn't have done or I'm sure we would have interviewed him. Was she with him at all that night of the guy's death perhaps? If so, why not mention it, mention him, especially seeing as 'they got on very well', according to Constantino. It would have been, could have been, an alibi for her if she was with him, but she never mentioned him. Looks like that's something else I'm going to have to ask Mr. Cleverley in Crete tomorrow. Where was he on that night on the so-called accident? Where did he think Regan was, and why weren't they together that night? They must have been pretty close for them to both go off to Crete together."

He walked back to his desk and scanned the case file again and his notes within it.

"Yes, here it is."

Georgiou looked mystified. What was his Inspector referring to now? Where what was? He was quickly enlightened.

"Regan told me she was going to be here for a few months, a couple of months at least she said according to my notes, in Lindos looking for her family history stuff, and trying to find out who was her birth father. Yet she disappeared with

Cleverley out of Lindos after a couple of weeks at the most, according to Constantino, off to Crete according to his son. That's got to be odd surely? You come to Lindos intending to research your family history, wanting to find out who your birth father is, and then after a couple of weeks you give that up and go off to Crete with a guy you only met a couple of months before."

"Yes, does seem somewhat odd, sir. But another thing that just occurred to me, what about Regan's friend Sandra and her husband, Richard, who Constantino told us she was here with earlier that summer in June. Are they not mentioned in the file? Did you not ask her about them when you interviewed her?"

"No, Sergeant, because we obviously didn't know about them when I interviewed her at that time in August six years ago, and she never mentioned them. In fact, I don't recall us talking at all about her previous visit to Lindos that June, or not very much at least.. There's nothing about that in the file."

He was quite dismissive of the Sergeant's question, but then checked himself and was easier on him when he added, "But it's definitely something I should ask Cleverley about tomorrow, and hopefully there's a chance he will know their full names."

The Inspector glanced at his watch.

"Ok, Sergeant, I've got an early start tomorrow morning for that six-thirty flight, so I think we'll call it a day for today and head back to Rhodes Town."

PART TWO

THE SUSPECTS AND HOMER'S ODYSSEY:
Hospitality, vengeance and loyalty

12

Τρίτη μέρα (Day 3)

Monday July 4th 2022: Martin Cleverley (hospitality)

Papadoulis was met by two Crete police officers as he came through arrivals at Heraklion Airport just after eleven on Monday morning. In the car outside one of them informed him that he was from Neapoli and knew the street, including the old stone house where Martin Cleverley was living.

Just over thirty minutes later they parked in the main square of the small Cretan town. The Inspector and the same officer emerged from the police car into the baking hot Crete mid-day sun to walk down the street off the square leading to Cleverley's house.

The town was located in a green valley with dense olive groves. It had the appearance of a sleepy, quiet town with beautiful buildings, nice gardens and old churches. Most of it, along with the attractive square, was dominated by a large church, the Church of the Megali Panaglia, the largest church in Eastern Crete.

As Martin Cleverley had told him, the house was just a hundred metres or so past the somewhat tired looking three star Hotel Neapolis. The house of traditional Cretan stone was a couple of storeys high, although not very wide and faced straight on to the road. As he rang the small bell the Inspector told the officer he should go in with him and make some notes of the interview.

Martin Cleverley was wearing dark blue shorts and a grey t-shirt with flip flops when he opened the door and Papadoulis showed him his police credentials, explaining that his fellow officer was from the Crete police. Cleverley was tall, six foot one, with short light brown hair that was just starting to show hints of grey flecks on the sides. His angular face with its wide cheekbones was clean shaven, producing a pronounced jawline. He was just beginning to display some unattractive bulges around his waist, no doubt as a result of the good life and food on the Greek island, as well as his fondness for the occasional Mythos Greek beer, sometimes more. Despite that he remained something of an attractive guy, and when he was younger would obviously have been even more so.

He showed the two police officers through to a basically furnished lounge with quite bare beige walls and just a couple of small cheap looking paintings of the Cretan coastline on them, a couch that had seen better days and a couple of dark green cloth covered armchairs. As the Inspector went to sit in one of the those Cleverley pointed through some large open glass sliding doors on one side of the lounge to a small shaded courtyard with a table and chairs, as well as a large parasol, and suggested they sit outside. He offered them a drink of coffee or tea or something cold, but they both declined.

Before Papadoulis could say anything as they sat at the table Cleverley asked, "You said this is about Aileen Regan and some case on Rhodes. You mean a recent one, Inspector, but as I told you I-?"

"You said on the phone that you haven't seen her for four years. Is that right?" the Inspector interrupted.

"Yes, that's when she left here to go back to England. Did she go back to Rhodes after that? So, is it a recent case?"

"Yes."

Papadoulis was deliberately telling him very little initially, letting him speak to see what he knew, if anything.

"But how is she involved?"

The Inspector was observing his reactions closely, trying to ascertain if Cleverley was putting on an act and knew all along that Aileen Regan was dead. He decided to test that to the full by eventually informing him bluntly, "She's the victim. She was murdered in the early hours of Saturday morning. Her body was found in a place called Gennadi on Rhodes, in the south of the island."

Cleverley did look genuinely shocked. So much so that while he sat in silence for a long minute Papadoulis asked if he was ok, and whether he wanted the other police officer to fetch him some water.

Eventually he responded with, "By who? Murdered by who?"

"We don't know that yet. That's why I wanted to speak to you to see if you could help us with anything that might assist our investigation."

Cleverley shook his head slightly in disbelief at what he'd just been told before replying, "But, as I said, I haven't seen her for four years."

"We were told you left Lindos together in 2016, late summer. Is that when you came here to Neapoli together?"

The Inspector was trying to go over and piece together the timeline of when Cleverley and Aileen Regan were together, including their movements.

"Err … dead, really …err, sorry yes … yes, that's right, Inspector. We came here to Crete and found this place in Neapoli, this house."

"Why did you leave Rhodes at that time and why come here, Crete? We've been told that you planned to be there for the whole summer writing and that she also planned to be there for a few months tracing her family history, or part of it."

Cleverley looked a little confused. He wasn't sure why he was being asked those types of questions about something six years ago.

"Erm … well … yes I did, did plan to be there for the whole summer. I'd been in Lindos for most of the first part of that summer. I was writing a novel."

"Yes we saw from your website that you're a writer. That's how we found you, through your publisher. That wasn't your first though was it? What did you do before you became a writer?"

"No, it was my second one. I was a Professor of Greek Mythology at King's College London before."

Papadoulis grinned slightly before explaining.

"My former boss, Inspector Karagoulis, would have loved to have met you. It was his hobby, some said obsession, Greek Mythology. He even applied some of it to his investigations, even got me a little interested in it eventually. Erm ... yes, sorry, Aileen Regan, she planned to be there in Lindos for a few months too, so why did you both leave and why here to Crete?"

"She did, but suddenly in the middle of August I think it was, she said she'd found out all she could about her family history, mainly about who her birth father was. On her birth certificate it said 'Father unknown' apparently, and her mother, who'd recently died, refused to divulge who he was. She told me she was born in 1978 and from her Mother's belongings after she died Aileen found that she'd worked in Lindos as a Tour Rep for two summers before that. Consequently, she guessed that her birth father was Greek and from Lindos, or nearby, so she decided to go there and see what she could find."

Papadoulis knew some of that from what Jack Constantino had told him in the Courtyard Bar in Lindos, but he thought it best to let Cleverley talk, before asking once again, "So, why did you both leave at that time and why here?"

Cleverley shook his head briefly once again.

"Well yes, Inspector, that was the odd thing. She'd disappeared once before earlier that summer, left me when we were together briefly back in England, but this time she was very keen that we left together. And it was quite sudden. She asked me to go with her and then wanted us to leave within a day or so. I wanted to be with her, and I could write anywhere, so I agreed. It seemed she didn't really have a place that we should go to in mind initially. Then she suggested Crete, so I agreed."

"So why do you think she suggested Crete?" The Inspector asked again.

"Not sure really."

"It was just her random choice then?"

"Not really just, only, her choice, Inspector."

He was sounding vague and unsure.

"Sure, she suggested it once we'd decided to leave together, leave Lindos, leave Rhodes, but I agreed, was happy to go anywhere with her and, as I said, what I do now, did then, write novels, I can do that anywhere these days," he repeated.

"And anyway, because of my Greek Mythology stuff I'd always been interested in Crete and knew quite a bit about the place historically. It was the birthplace of the Minoan civilisation five thousand years ago you know, the first advanced civilisation in Europe, and the birthplace of Zeus who, with his consort the Phoenician Princess Europa, produced Minos, the King of Crete, the founder of the Minoan civilisation. So-"

He was rambling on about Greek Mythology and Crete. Papadoulis was trying to hide a small smile as it instantly reminded him again of his former boss, Dimitris Karagoulis, and the way he would go on about Greek Mythology when they were involved in a case together and going over the evidence. Eventually he interrupted and brought him back to his question.

"So, she suggested Crete, but you haven't got any idea why? She never said?"

"Not directly. Perhaps it had some connection to what she'd found out about her family? I seem to recall she did say something at one point about one of her family leaving Rhodes for Crete years ago, but as far as I remember she never made any attempt to find them once we got here. I just got the impression that she'd decided, and quite suddenly really, that she wanted to leave Lindos, leave Rhodes, and could have gone anywhere as long as it was away from there."

"Why do you think that was, her suddenly being desperate to get away from Lindos?"

His reply surprised Papadoulis.

"She was scared of something or someone, Inspector. She didn't tell me that when she suggested we leave, or even later while we were here. I asked her a few times, what she was so afraid of, but she just shrugged it off and said I must be imagining things. When we got here though, and as time went on, I was more and more convinced I was right."

The Inspector leaned forward in his chair, thinking that Cleverley was finally getting to something that would be of interest in the case.

"Like what, what made you think that, that she was scared?"

"Nothing clear or major, just little things. As I said, when I asked her she just shrugged off my questions, but it was, for example, when she suggested we come to Crete she added that it was a large island so there would be plenty of places to live away from the tourist spots. At first I just thought she meant a place to rent to live would be cheaper away from the tourist areas and quieter, but as time went on and she got increasingly what I saw as paranoid, I began to wonder if she meant because of the size of the island it would be a place that it was easy to disappear on. Plus, she was suddenly desperate to get away from Rhodes. I'm surprised that she went back. I never thought she would. Maybe her murder shows why she was so desperate suddenly to leave there?"

Papadoulis quickly looked over to the Crete officer to ensure he was making notes of all this. He was.

"She was there this time on a short holiday with two women friends from her work in London, Alison Lees and Suzanne Carmichael. Do you know them at all?"

"No, no, not at all, Inspector. I've had no contact with Alison since she left here four years ago. I didn't even know she was working in London now."

"You thought she was scared of someone on Rhodes, in Lindos perhaps, and that was why she was so desperate to get away that August. Do you know if she'd been to Lindos at all before that summer? Made some enemies there perhaps?"

"She never said, but thinking about it I'm sure when I first met her on the plane to Rhodes that June, we were sat next to each other, she said it was her first time. That's how I got to know her. Offered to show her and her friend, Sandra, around as I'd been quite a few times, and then I met her for a drink one night in the Courtyard Bar."

"Her friend, Sandra, did you met her in Lindos with Aileen while they were there? We were told she was there with her husband, Richard."

"Oh god, yep, he was a right prat, a real pain in the arse. An angry man for sure. He turned up for their second week that June. Not long after he did Aileen and I left for London and then Brighton. Thinking about it now it was Aileen who wanted to suddenly leave Lindos that time as well."

"You two, you and this Richard guy, didn't get on then?"

"No one got on with that man, although I quickly got the impression he had a bit of a thing about Aileen."

"And she with him?"

Cleverley was shaking his head slightly as he replied.

"Not really, Inspector, but it's a bit more complicated than that. There's a lot more to it than just that, the relationships between Aileen and Richard and Sandra Weston, as she eventually told me just before we left Lindos that August in 2016. A lot more, believe me."

He puffed out his cheeks and then said, "But I definitely need a drink before I tell you all she told me. Are you sure you two don't want one."

As he got up Papadoulis said, "Weston, so that was their surname?"

"Yes, Inspector."

"No drinks for us, thanks again," Papadoulis replied for both of them as Cleverley disappeared off to the kitchen and returned with a long glass telling the Inspector, "I need a cold vodka and orange to tell this story. I was shocked at the time when she told me and wasn't sure I believed it then but-"

He stopped for a moment to take a gulp of his drink.

"Aileen told me that Sandra was her best friend. They'd been good friends since university. Richard Weston just thought he was god's gift to all women."

"Do you think that he may have had enough of a thing about Aileen to kill her, or maybe his wife, Sandra, could have out of jealousy?"

"No idea if he's your killer, Inspector, but I can tell you for sure Sandra Weston isn't."

"What makes you say that?"

Papadoulis was leaning forward once again in curiosity.

"Because she's dead. When I asked about Sandra and her vile husband after I met Aileen again back in Lindos that August she told me that she'd heard that Sandra had been killed earlier that month."

"Killed? How, by who?"

"She said she didn't know how or by who, but she said that she knew Sandra was depressed after their holiday in Lindos in

June as she'd lost her own photographic agency and had split up with her husband. Aileen also told me that she'd actually had an affair with Richard previous to her coming to Lindos in that June with Sandra, and then Richard Weston joining them in their second week. Explains why he had a bit of a thing for Aileen, their affair, as I thought."

"Affair? When, how?" Papadoulis was throwing out all sorts of questions that were now popping into his brain.

Cleverley took another drink and then sat back in his chair saying, "Ok, Inspector, let me tell you all that Aileen told me on that last night we spent together in Lindos that August six years ago before we left to come here. Why she did it, had the affair, and what she told me about her real past. She was a woman with a lot of secrets."

Papadoulis leaned forward in his chair once again wondering just what Aileen Regan's big secret was.

"She started by telling me adamantly that night that I could never repeat any of what she was about to tell me, to anyone. She said that if I did we, her and me, would both be in deep, deep trouble. More than I could imagine. But as she's now dead I guess I can tell you. I could see from that, and the way she was at the time, that she was torn about telling me and that it wasn't easy to do so. Then I was really, really shocked, Inspector, by what she said next, believe me. I had no idea. She just came straight out and bluntly said she had been an agent in the British Security Services, MI6, for almost twenty years. I can never forget just sitting there on her bed in blank faced bewilderment at that and as she added more. She said MI6 had given her a false identity as Aileen Regan, a legend she said they called it. It was not just a false name, but a whole invented past personal history and documentation; a passport and the whole works, including a false birth certificate. Not the one that said 'Father unknown' on it obviously. That was her real one for Kathleen O'Mara. I knew-"

The Inspector couldn't contain himself or stop himself interrupting.

"I was right then. When I saw her body at the murder scene I thought Aileen Regan and Kathleen O'Mara was the same person because I interviewed her as Aileen back in Lindos in that August of 2016 after the body of a man was found one night in one of the Lindos back alleys. Her hair was different now from back in 2016, shorter and blonde, but I was convinced it was the same woman. But I never knew you were involved with her back then. She never mentioned you when I interviewed her. Did she ever tell you anything about that case?"

Cleverley looked a bit bemused and not exactly happy at being interrupted.

"No, nothing, I didn't think she was involved in that at all. I do remember the guy being found dead, but it was a few days after that happened that I bumped into her again for the first time since that June. It was in the Courtyard Bar one night. I think I recall her telling me one time in passing later, a few days later possibly, that she'd been interviewed by the police about it. Something about because they thought an Irish woman might be involved, and obviously she was Irish, but she never said anything more to me about it, except that it was an accident," he said quite sharply before continuing.

"But when she told me about her double identity on that last night we had in Lindos in August of 2016 I already knew about it and I told her so, and how I found out."

"How, how did you find out?" Papadoulis interrupted again. His impatience was getting the better of him.

Cleverley sighed a little at the Inspector's impatience and interruptions, then continued.

"We left Lindos together the first time suddenly in June that year, again at her insistence a few days after the prat Richard Weston turned up there. We flew to London and then went to live in Brighton, again her idea, even though she'd told me she was working in London. She used to go off there, to London, for work she said, when we first got to Brighton. Richard Weston had told me some pretty nasty things about Aileen and him, that they'd had a relationship, and also claimed she'd told him some not very flattering things about me, which quite frankly I didn't believe. Stupidly though I couldn't get them out of my head. That was precisely what he wanted of course. I couldn't stop myself and just as stupidly I asked Aileen about them while we were living in Brighton. I still knew her only as

Aileen Regan at that time. As a result we had a huge argument early one evening over what he'd taunted me with and later that night while I was in the shower she just left without telling me she was going, disappeared without trace. I was in agony searching Brighton and London for her for three days, but with no luck. When I finally went to the office of the company she told me she worked at in London was when I discovered that she wasn't who she said she was, or who I thought she was. From a photo on my phone of us both in Lindos that I showed to a Human Resources Manager there, after she was adamant there was no Aileen Regan on their payroll, purely by chance I discovered that they knew her there as Kathleen O'Mara, not Aileen Regan. But, the HR Manager told me Kathleen O'Mara left the company three weeks previously, which was before she came to Lindos in June with Sandra Weston and we met."

He stopped briefly to reach for his glass and take another drink.

"Apparently Sandra Weston was Aileen's boss in MI6, well, one of them, she said. Sandra was quite high up in the organisation. Aileen also told me on that last night before we left Lindos in August 2016 that MI6 had a lead from an informer inside the Russian Secret Service, the FSB, what used to be the KGB, that Sandra's husband Richard was spying for them. They, MI6, were told that was why he'd married Sandra years ago, knowing her position in MI6 and to get close to her, and he'd been feeding sensitive stuff that he'd picked up from her back to Moscow for years. What MI6 weren't sure about, however, was whether he'd actually turned her, persuaded Sandra to work for them, or whether it was all just him spying on her, somehow gathering sensitive information which she had access to without her knowledge and feeding it back to Moscow. Aileen told me that Sandra wasn't even supposed to tell him that she worked for MI6, because in the agency, as she called it, they weren't supposed to tell partners in case it compromised them. And apparently that would have contravened the Official Secrets Act, which they all had to sign. Aileen said the agency gave her a meaningless bureaucratic title for her supposed work in the Ministry of Defence. That was all part of her legend. She told me that in Sandra's case she had a freelance fashion photography business which operated as perfect cover for her. It gave her access undercover to loads of fashion shows in perfect locations for MI6 missions, lots of cities across the world."

Now it was the Inspector's turn to be shocked, trying to take in all he was being told. He shook his head slightly from side to side once again in astonishment at what he was hearing.

Seeing the shocked look on the Inspector's face, and his shake of the head, Cleverley continued. "There's more, Inspector, and it's even more bizarre."

"Aileen said the information MI6 got from their Russian informer was about how quite a bit of sensitive stuff that could only have gone across Sandra Weston's desk, through her department, was ending up with the FSB in Moscow. The word was that it was coming from Richard. So, Aileen was re-assigned to another section in the agency for what Sandra was told was a small promotion, so she wouldn't get suspicious. It wasn't of course, and Aileen said she was presented with a job, a mission, and told she had no choice and had to accept it. The Section Head even tried to dress it up as her chance to prove Sandra innocent. The job, the plan, was for her to get close to Richard, seduce him and have an affair with him. To try to find out anything that would confirm him and Sandra were working for the Russians, that she'd been turned. To find out whether she was passing the information on to him, or whether he was acting alone and somehow gathering information which she had access to. Aileen said the Section Head told her she'd actually been selected for the mission, the job, because she was best placed as Sandra's best friend to get really close to them both. So, it was hardly very difficult to seduce him, get in his boxers. She told me that was so bloody easy actually, no fun at all. You can imagine, Inspector, hearing that from Aileen wasn't exactly fun for me either. She said that, according to the briefing MI6 provided her with, Richard Weston had a bit of a reputation for it anyway, extra-marital affairs. And she knew he'd been caught out by Sandra one time having an affair with his secretary. The agency, MI6, placed her in another department of the company he worked for, in a different part of London. He was a Senior Global Project Executive, but Aileen's position was as a P.A to the company's International Legal Director. The plan was for her to seduce him at the Christmas Party for all the departments in a hotel in Central London, and that's exactly what she did. He was staying the night and had a room in the hotel. She said that's when it started, their affair. They met up a few more times after that, for the sex, as well as to try and find out as much as she could about what, if anything, him and Sandra had been up to for the Russians. However, she said she didn't get anywhere in terms of that. He wouldn't even talk about it most of the time, him and Sandra, their relationship. All he said was that they'd had their problems at times. So, after a few months she wasn't getting anywhere and there was no progress on her investigation, not even the slightest indication of her discovering if even he was working for the Russians, let alone Sandra. Soon after that she said she came to the conclusion he wasn't, and that most probably meant Sandra wasn't either."

"Quite an explosive situation all round," Papadoulis commented.

"You definitely could say that Inspector," Cleverley replied as he reached for his glass and the last drops of his drink.

"But it didn't end there, and in fact things got much more difficult between the three of them, her, Sandra and Richard Weston, according to Aileen, especially when the unsuspecting Sandra, unsuspecting in terms of not knowing about Aileen and Richard's affair at that point, was determined to persuade Aileen to go on holiday with her to Lindos. Before that Aileen had reported to her agency Section Head that her investigation into Richard and Sandra had turned up nothing and was going nowhere. Consequently, the operation was pulled and her Section Head ordered Aileen to end her affair with Richard. The problem was that there were two people involved in the affair and one of them was Richard Weston. He wouldn't, didn't want to end it. He was a man who was used to getting his own way, being in control. I saw that for myself when he turned up in Lindos for the second week of their holiday, despite, she told me, Aileen telling him not to. She said when she told him she wanted to stop it, the affair, he got very angry. That didn't happen to him, the woman stopping their affair. From the Section briefing info Aileen got before their affair started she knew that he'd had plenty of affairs, but he was always the one to end them and go back to Sandra. A woman ending it wasn't in his playbook at all. But Aileen did, and refused to see him again. Then, she said, he kept sending her endless bloody text messages, which she ignored. Eventually she replied threatening to tell Sandra everything and he stopped for a while. Aileen told me that by then she was simply tired of it all, the deceit, the lies, and the half-truths. She said that's when she quit the agency, MI6. She also said it was quite ironic that when she informed Sandra she was quitting Sandra told her that no one who quits is ever really free of them though. She never told Sandra about her and Richard, of course. She said she just told her, and her Section Head, that she had grown tired of it all after nearly twenty years; the secret life, the double lives, and she wanted a new life of her own. When Aileen told me all this on that last night we had in Lindos in that August of 2016 she ended by saying that what she'd told her Section Head as the reason for her quitting was actually true. Obviously I found the affair she had with that prat Richard Weston difficult to take. He was a nasty angry man when he turned up in Lindos on the second week of Aileen and Sandra's holiday that June and I met him. Of course I didn't know that at the time, but no doubt it was because of Aileen ending their affair. And to be honest, Inspector, his wife wasn't much better either. Sandra Weston and him were well suited. I never told Aileen, but one night on Aileen and Sandra's June Lindos holiday a very drunk Sandra offered to have sex with me. Thankfully I declined."

Cleverley puffed out his cheeks again and sat back in his chair. Papadoulis sat in silence for a few moments trying to take in all he had just heard. Meanwhile, the Crete police officer had been scribbling away in his notebook trying to get it all down.

"So, it was Sandra Weston whose idea it was for her and Aileen to go on holiday together and purely by chance to Lindos. I suppose I should be grateful to her for that or Aileen and I would never have met," Cleverley added in a somewhat resigned tone.

"I believed her you see, Inspector. I believed Aileen, or the woman I came to know as Kathleen O'Mara, when she told me she'd grown tired of her secret life in MI6 and that she wanted a new life of her own. She swore to me that it was true. She said she'd told her MI6 Section Head that, but at that time in August 2016 there was a bit more to add to it now because she'd met me. She wanted her new life to be with me, and that's why she wanted us to leave Lindos together, and eventually for here. She even said that ironically she had something to be thankful to Sandra for, for persuading her to come to Lindos on holiday with her, because luckily she met me."

He stared ahead ruefully in another few moments silence contemplating that and then grimaced a little as he added, "She did tell me at that time, when she said she wanted us to be together, that I should be aware that it wouldn't always be easy, not for the both of us now. She said she could never be sure that her past wouldn't suddenly pop up to haunt her, or rather someone from her past. I wasn't entirely sure at all what she meant by that. Maybe she was simply referring to what Sandra Weston had said to her about never being free of MI6? There were a couple of other odd things I remember now though, Inspector. She insisted we didn't tell anyone we were leaving Lindos or that we were coming here, not even Jack Constantino from the Courtyard Bar who'd helped her a lot in tracing her family past. Also, she was adamant that she didn't want us to fly to Crete from Rhodes. She said the ferry would be better. So that's what we took. I thought both of those things were odd at the time, but just went along with whatever she wanted because I just wanted to be with her."

He never commented, but what Papadoulis was thinking was that if she actually thought someone was looking for her, like MI6, then she would obviously be much less conspicuous there at the ferry ports, less likely to be spotted, rather than at the airports, at Rhodes and landing on Crete. She probably thought, or even would have known, that MI6 could have their agents and paid informers placed anywhere. Perhaps they did have some informers at Rhodes or Crete airports, but anyway she wasn't going to take that chance. Presumably she thought they would be much less likely to have any at the internal Greek ferry ports.

Instead of voicing his opinion on that, however, the Inspector told him, "You must have thought a lot of her to go with her to here after she told you all that about her past life in MI6, as well as her affair with Richard Weston, despite the fact that was only in her position as an agent for them, something she said she was ordered to do?"

"I did, yes I did, Inspector. So much so that I wanted to help her, go with her, when she suddenly said she was leaving Lindos that August in 2016. She wanted me to go with her, asked me to. And after she told me all that stuff about her past and MI6, as well as Richard and Sandra Weston, I thought I was supporting her, and not just financially, protecting her in some way by going with her."

He hesitated for a few seconds, frowned a little and then told Papadoulis, "I suppose the truth is I fell in love with her twice that summer of 2016. The first time in June before she disappeared on me in Brighton after we came back from Lindos, but then I fell in love with her all over again that August in Lindos after I met her by chance that night in the Courtyard Bar. When I told her that while we were here together on Crete, that I loved her, each time she would always reply that loving someone makes you vulnerable. I thought it was just her way of making light of it, that I loved her, but now it seems maybe she was right."

He rubbed the back of his neck as if it was aching from thinking about it all.

"She was a very attractive woman back then, Inspector. Still was too when she left me here four years ago."

He hesitated once again for a moment. There was a vacant look on his face, as though his mind was elsewhere.

"She also used to say quite a few times, Inspector, that we all have secrets. I remember one particular time she said something else, something more, which made me more concerned. She said we all have secrets, but that nothing stays buried forever. Truth and secrets will always surface in the end. Seems that she was right on that as well."

He hesitated for a few seconds again before shaking his head slightly once and adding, "I guess sometimes people's lives run parallel and close together, but at different speeds. That was me and Kathleen. As I said, I loved her, helped her that time in August 2016 and for two more years here after we left Lindos."

Maybe it was the effect of the large vodka, but he was beginning to ramble and sound a bit morose. Papadoulis attempted to bring him back to what he wanted to know about her.

"In what ways? In what ways did you help her? Financially or?"

Cleverley looked across the table at him and said, "As I said before, Inspector, she was scared. After we came here to Crete I could see that in her every day over those two years. Besides what she told me on that last night in Lindos, shortly after we got here she also told me she'd done some terrible things in MI6, but she wouldn't tell me what or even who she was scared off. So, it wasn't financially that I helped her, not at first at least. She had money which she'd accumulated doing whatever she did over the years before we met, in MI6 presumably, but eventually after two years even that began to run out. I didn't mind, and I told her that. I looked after her financially. As I said, I was in love with her, no matter what she'd done. So, to answer your question, Inspector, I looked after her not just financially, but mentally. She was a mess, lost mentally, screwed up by her past life of the previous twenty years, and as I said, very scared someone would come looking for her. That's what she kept saying, but when I tried to talk to her about it, tried to get her to tell me more, she would never say who, just that she was scared someone would come looking for her. So, I gave her what support I could, including love, and I suppose you might say hospitality eventually when she'd almost run out of money. I didn't mind. I just wanted to give her somewhere to stay with me here and make sure she was safe, but ..."

He stopped for a moment and swallowed hard. The Inspector thought he even detected some moisture in his eyes before he continued.

"But I guess that was never enough, not enough reassurance for her. I thought that in some way, some small way, I was protecting her, although I knew that if she was right and someone did come looking for her from her past there was very little I would be able to do in that respect. Basically she obviously wasn't comfortable at all staying in one place. She was desperate to get away from Lindos in August 2016, then two years later desperate to get away from here. Eventually she manufactured, at least that's what I thought, she manufactured a huge argument between us and left, left me again."

"So that was 2018? What was the argument over?"

Cleverley brushed some of the moisture away from one of his eyes with his right hand before he answered.

"Yes, end of November 2018. She was bored and getting more and more anxious about being safe. I was writing. That's what I came to Lindos to do in 2016. That's what I wanted to do here. She seemed happy with that at first. I'd write for hours on end once I got going. All through the night sometimes,. But more and more she wasn't actually doing anything, except going to one of the beaches, sunbathing and swimming. In the winter months she couldn't even do that. At least I had my writing to occupy me during that time. Then increasingly she didn't even want to go out in the town here at night to restaurants or bars in Neapoli. Increasingly it was as if she was constantly looking over her shoulder, checking if anyone was following her, had come to find her. Finally, we had the huge argument. It was over what I was writing, had written. I suppose that's what was the final straw, or at least she used it that way. Like I said, manufactured the argument. Looking back at it now I guess she had her reasons and thought they were valid, fuelled as they were by what I thought was her paranoia. For some reason, I don't know why, maybe out of boredom, one day she checked some of my stuff, some of the stuff I'd written for my new novel, and she recognised that I'd based one of the characters in it on her."

"'Greek Sun', a fictional love story based on Crete between a Greek man and a woman, an Irish woman?" Papadoulis interjected.

"Yes, that was it. It was about to be published at the end of 2018, was published eventually, and we had a huge row. She said she was worried that someone would pick up from the novel where she was. The novel is based on Crete, with large parts of it in Neapoli. She started screaming at me about it after she found out. She became uncontrollable and inconsolable. I'd never seen her like that. She was shouting that I was bloody stupid to do that, that I simply didn't understand how dangerous that was for her. She said I had to stop it being published. I tried to calm her down, but said it wouldn't be possible to stop publication because it was due in a few weeks. I had signed a contract with the publisher and my agent, had a sizeable advance, and there would already be thousands of copies printed which would have to be destroyed if it wasn't published, which would be costly, to the publisher and me."

"So, who was it she was so worried would pick up where she was from the novel? Papadoulis interrupted again."

"I wasn't entirely sure at first, Inspector. I couldn't be certain, but it definitely really freaked her out. From what she told me on that last night in Lindos I assumed she meant the British Security Services, MI6. I tried to tell her, convince her, surely that was all in the past, the MI6 stuff. But she wouldn't have it. She just kept saying that I really didn't understand. She said you never leave those sort of organisations. You think you have, but you never do. They never let you. Once they have their hooks into you that's it, you're hooked for life. She reminded me she'd told me before that was also what Sandra Weston told her when she quit MI6. So, she said she couldn't stay here then with the novel being published, and couldn't stay with me. She said it wouldn't be safe for either of us. Even when I said I really didn't think anyone would pick up that the character, the woman, was based on her, and tried to convince her of that, she said I really was naïve. She said that the novel was published in my name and was based on Crete, so the British Security Services would put two and two together and assume she was here with me. She said they would easily have picked up from the locals in Lindos that I left there with her, just as you did obviously, and even though none of the locals in Lindos, such as Jack Constantino, knew we were coming to Crete the novel would have given MI6 a big clue that we did. I just thought, and told her, that I was sure organisations like MI6 would have better things to do than check up on novels and characters in them. She just screamed at me again and said that I really didn't understand how they operated, MI6. She said there are people working for them, and other organisations, that never let a vendetta, a grudge, an old score to be settled drop and would go through the rest of their life wanting and seeking vengeance and retribution. To do that they would keep on searching and checking the smallest things."

He shook his head again once.

"I was really confused, Inspector, then and after when I thought about it, after she left. I just couldn't see the reason she was so scared someone would come looking for her here. Couldn't see the reason she thought MI6 would come looking. What reason would they have to do that? She told me she worked for them for twenty years, but she never said she'd done anything that would cause them to send someone looking for her, nothing that would give her reason to be so scared of that and what their agent might do to her."

"Kill her?" Papadoulis asked. "Did you ever manage to get her to tell you the reason why she thought that?"

"I tried a couple of times before she left, after we had the huge argument. The first time she said I just didn't understand. I hadn't been in the 'Service', as she called it, and I couldn't possibly know or understand."

"And the second time, did she tell you anything more the second time?"

"No, not really, she simply said a little bit more, but it was something quite odd. She said as I hadn't been in the 'Service' I couldn't possibly have any idea about their reasons to do anything, particularly when it came to, as she called it, eliminating people. Then she said, and I remember her exact words because I've gone over and over them in my head many times trying to figure out what she meant, what she was trying to tell me; she said, 'there is reason as logic, reason as motive, and reason as a way of life in terms of beliefs and ideology'."

"Hmmm ... what do you think she meant by all that? Did you ever come to any conclusion?"

"Well, maybe, sort of, Inspector. I'm still not sure really, but I think she was trying to say that the British Security Services, like MI6, can have all sorts of reasons for eliminating people, as she put it. Reasons they can justify to themselves on any of those grounds, logic, motive, and protecting a way of life, presumably a British way of life, whatever that is. I still never got out of her though which of those was likely to apply to them looking for her and why. I suppose I gave up in the end because the more I pressed her on it, the more she was determined to not tell me and just leave. So I-"

Papadoulis interrupted yet again, picking up on something Cleverley had said just a little earlier.

"Hang on, what other organisations?"

"Sorry, what, Inspector?"

"You said just now that in one of your arguments she said there are people working for them, and other organisations, that never let a vendetta, a grudge, an old score to be settled drop. By 'people working for them' I assume she meant MI6, but what do you think she meant by 'and other organisations'. Are you sure that's what she said? What do you think she meant? Who do you think she meant by 'other organisations'? Had she ever mentioned before any of these 'other organisations' she referred to, and working for them?"

"Cleverley looked confused, raised his eyebrows and then scratched the back of his head. "Ermm ... yes, yes, I'm sure that's what she said, or something very similar, but I simply assumed she meant some other parts of the British Security Services, that's all. I never really gave it a second thought. Eventually, pretty soon she just shut down completely. She refused to discuss it any more at all and just announced two days later she was leaving that afternoon. So she did, and was gone again, wouldn't even tell me where."

He struggled with a tortured half smile as he said, "You know it's funny, Inspector, one of the things she was very fond of saying, especially when we were leaving Lindos, was that there are no endings, only beginnings. She said it was a quote from Thomas Cromwell, who served as Chief Minister to the English King, Henry the Eighth. She used to tell me over and over she believed that was true. Yet she left me twice, ended it twice, once in Brighton and once here, two endings, and now she's dead there definitely will not be another beginning will there."

His voice tailed off quietly and a rueful look spread across his face.

"Did you hear from her after that at all, after she left here?" Papadoulis asked.

"No, not a word, nothing. I tried calling quite a few times, if only to check she was still safe, but she must have changed her number straightaway, as soon as she left, because it just came up as unobtainable each time as soon as I tried."

He shook his head slightly once again, then added, "She was very freaked out, Inspector. Well and truly freaked out. Very, very scared by the time she left."

He looked across the table at the policeman and then asked something somewhat off the track which surprised him, although as he was a writer perhaps it wasn't quite so surprising.

"Have you heard of the Irish author Sally Rooney, Inspector?"

As he answered, "No, can't say I have," the Inspector looked confused over why exactly he was bringing this up, where he was going with it?"

"There's a line in one of her novels that I always think of when I think of Aileen and me, or think of Kathleen and me as I eventually came to know her, think of what we had in that short time together, even with all her faults and crimes, many more than I even know about I'm sure. Sally Rooney wrote, 'We hate people for making mistakes so much more than we love them for doing good, so that the easiest way to live is to do nothing, say nothing, and love no one'. 'Love no one', that's the way I feel now after Kathleen. It's the easiest way, Inspector."

There was a deep sadness that filled his eyes as he finished.

"That's quite sad, sir, if you don't mind me saying, and I'm sorry but I do have to ask you this," the Inspector started to say. "Where were you last Friday night and early Saturday morning?"

Cleverley looked puzzled. "Early Saturday morning I was here in bed"

"Alone?"

"Yes, Inspector, alone."

"And on Friday night?"

"I was at a little bookshop here in Neapoli. Ironically Inspector, I was promoting my new novel, not the one Aileen got so pissed off about. It was just a small thing that the bookshop arranged for a few of the ex-pats here, a dozen people or so."

"What time would that have been?"

"It started at seven and was supposed to finish at nine, but it went on a bit and then the bookshop owner and a couple of the ex-pats and me went to a little bar nearby. I got back here at approaching midnight."

He got up and walked inside for a moment. Then a few seconds later emerged with what looked like a bookmark.

Handing it to the Inspector he told him, "The number of the bookshop is on here. You can give the owner a call to check, or, it's only just off the main square so you could call in after you leave here. Perhaps even buy one of my novels, Inspector?"

He grinned slightly as he finished.

"Thanks," Papadoulis told him, followed by, "Just one final thing, do you think there is any possibility at all that MI6, the British Security Services, could be behind her death? That perhaps she was right, and what she was so worried about in your novel would have triggered them finding her and killing her?"

Cleverley shook his head slightly and grinned again.

"That would make a good plot for a novel, Inspector, but I just think it's highly unlikely. The novel was published almost four years ago, and all that MI6 stuff with Richard Weston that she told me about was even longer ago, six years. What reason would MI6 have for killing her, and even now after all these years. Not really good for their 'business' and recruitment if it got out that they go around eliminating their ex-agents is it? Besides which I really wouldn't like to think the I through one of my novels played a part in her death, her murder. "

"Hmm ... yes ... I guess you're right about that, and as you said, what reason would they have to kill her, especially now after all this time?"

Papadoulis got up, thanked Martin Cleverley, adding, "If there's anything more we will be in touch, and if you think of anything more please call me," and then handed him his card.

13

Sally Hardcastle – again

While the Inspector was at Crete airport waiting for his flight to Athens for the connecting flight back to Rhodes he called Georgiou to update him on his interview with Cleverley.

As soon as the Sergeant answered his call Papadoulis told him, "We can rule Martin Cleverley out. He's not our killer. He was here on Crete all Friday night till very late doing a promotion at a bookshop for his latest novel. He said he was drinking after that with the bookshop owner and a couple of others till around midnight. He gave me the bookshop guy's number and I called him. It checked out. There's no way Cleverley could have been on Rhodes Friday night or even early Saturday morning, unless he had a helicopter or a private jet, which I'm pretty sure he hasn't looking at where he's living. Besides which I can't see any clear motive he'd have for killing her."

"Nothing from what he told you suggests he had any motive then, and there was nothing useful for our investigation?"

"Oh, there was plenty of stuff he told me that is definitely useful for our investigation of her murder, but nothing to suggest he had any motive to kill her, even though it seems she left him here on Crete at the end of 2018 because they fell out over that character in one of his novels you discovered. That doesn't stack up at all as a motive for him to kill her though, and his alibi says he didn't. Plenty of other stuff he said she told him about her past, as well as about those characters with her in Lindos in June of 2016, Richard and Sandra, and MI6, I'm sure has a bearing on the case, although I can't really figure out how yet. Weston by the way, that was their surname Cleverley said. I'll fill you in on all that tomorrow. I've got loads of notes of what Cleverley told me which a local Crete officer made while I interviewed him."

"So, I was right about the Irish woman character in his novel, "Greek Sun" then, sir?"

Georgiou was quite full of himself over that.

"Yes, you were, Sergeant. Cleverley said they fell out in a big way over that character in his novel, over him basing a character on her in it without telling her. He said she always seemed scared, paranoid, during the two years they were together on Crete. He wasn't sure of what though, just that someone could come looking for her here, find her from the fact that his novel is based on Crete and included an Irish woman character. She told him a lot about her past, that she worked for the British Security Services for twenty years. Cleverley also said she told him Sandra Weston was her boss at one point at MI6. He said he thought at one time that perhaps it was them, MI6, that she was scared would find her, although he had no idea why they'd come looking, what reason they'd have to do so. He said he asked her about it a number of times, what the reason would be, but she refused to tell him. He does think that was the reason she left after they argued, along with the fact that she was bored with doing nothing on Crete while he was busy writing. Anyway, if we're looking for a motive, I can't see that Cleverley would kill her over an argument over that, over him putting a character in one of his novels based on her. It's surely much more likely she'd kill him."

"Hmm ... you're right, there is quite a lot of stuff and information there," Georgiou agreed.

"Oh there's quite a bit more, much more in relation to her and Richard Weston, believe me Sergeant. It's quite mind blowing, although I'm not really clear yet how it's going to help us find the killer. But I'll fill you in on all the rest tomorrow. I'll pick you up in the morning at eight to go to Lindos and review where we're at with all of it."

"Before you go, sir, Kyriakopoulis said the phone records we requested came through, but there's nothing unusual, nothing that stands out, as far as he can see in Cleverley, Lees, Carmichael, Bird or Bradshaw's."

"Ok, tell him to add Sandra and Richard Weston's names to our police records requests to the British police."

"Will do, sir, see you in the morning."

As he rang off Papadoulis saw that they were showing boarding for his flight to Athens. The flight was only forty-five minutes, but for the whole time he couldn't get all the things Martin Cleverley had told him out of his head. He glanced through the Crete officer's notes and went over and over some of the things he'd heard. Nothing was making perfect sense, jumping out at him. At first he concentrated on Kathleen O'Mara's MI6 involvement as Aileen Regan, but he kept coming to the same conclusion as Martin Cleverley had expressed to him. Why would MI6 kill her? What reason would they have? And why now six years after her mission for them in connection with Richard Weston and him being a Russian spy, and her affair with him as part of that mission. None of it made sense. Almost as the flight was landing at Athens he realised eventually that the only gap in all of that was where was Richard Weston now? Sandra Weston was dead, according to what Cleverley said Aileen Regan told him in August 2016, but what about Richard Weston? Could he be the killer? Is that who they were missing from the investigation?

As soon as he got through arrivals and into the gate area for his Rhodes flight he called Georgiou again, much to his Sergeant's surprise.

"Are you still at Rhodes station?" he asked.

"Yes, sir, I was about to leave, but-"

"Is Kyriakopoulis still there?"

"Yes."

"Right, Sergeant, tell him to get on and try and trace Richard Weston. Where he is now. He's the one person we are missing in all this. Cleverley said Regan told him in August 2016 that she'd heard Sandra Weston had been killed in London, in early August he thought she said, but she didn't know how. But we need to find out if Richard Weston is still alive and where he is, plus more importantly, where he was last Friday night. Cleverley said that Regan told him that back in 2015 and 2016 Richard Weston was a Senior Global Project Executive for a large London based company. That's all she told him, so we don't know the company name. Hopefully the British police can give us some help on that. He may not still be working in the same company of course, but maybe the British police can help trace him if Kyriakopoulis informs them it's a murder enquiry. Tell him to get on to them tonight, straightaway."

Georgiou could tell from his Inspector's tone of voice that he thought they may have at last had a bit of a breakthrough and a possible suspect. He was somewhat more sceptical as he didn't at that point know everything that Cleverley had told his Inspector about Aileen Regan and Richard Weston. He decided to voice his scepticism.

"I will, sir, of course, but why do you think this Richard Weston guy has a motive for killing Regan?"

His Inspector's voice had a sharper edge to it as he replied, "They had an affair, Sergeant. It was part of a mission she was assigned by MI6, who suspected he was a Russian spy. I'll give you all the details tomorrow. Just get Kyriakopoulis on to seeing if we, or the British police, can find where Weston is now."

"Phew! Affair, MI6, you said Cleverley told you a lot of useful information, sir. Once again, there's definitely more to this case than we thought. So-"

"Sergeant!" Papadoulis interrupted with a raised voice. "Just get Kyriakopoulis on it right now. I'll see you in the morning"

He shook his head at Georgiou's seeming lack of urgency, and then sat back in his seat at the gate in Athens departures waiting for his flight, and trying to relax a little after a long day. He wasn't able to relax for long, however, as a few minutes later he heard and felt his phone buzzing in his pocket. As he reached to take it out he assumed it would be the Sergeant asking something more, which killed his attempt to relax. Glancing at the screen though he saw it was Sally Hardcastle.

When he answered she asked, "How was your trip today? Useful?"

"Some. Not back yet. Just waiting at Athens to board flight back to Rhodes."

"Busy day travelling then?"

"You could say that. Didn't even get a chance to get some food, and airport food here doesn't exactly look appetising."

"What time do land at Rhodes?"

"Nine-thirty."

"Come over, I'll feed you," she suggested.

That disorientated him somewhat. He wasn't even expecting to hear from her, let alone her suggesting going to see her in Lardos.

"Erm ... but it'll be late," was all he could think to say.

She chuckled slightly down the phone.

"I'll still be up, Yiannis. It won't be that late, and I'm not one for early nights. You should remember that."

"Yes, I do. But I've got an early start at Lindos on the case tomorrow too so-."

Interrupting, her reply to that surprised him even more.

"Stay over here then. Go straight to Lindos from here. It's closer after all."

"Oh ... erm ... I-"

She interrupted his hesitancy again with her usual cocky confidence.

"Come on, Yiannis, you know you want to."

This time her voice had softened persuasively. She knew exactly what she was doing.

"Erm ..."

He hesitated again. She was right. He did want to, but part of him was telling him it wasn't a totally good idea. She didn't wait for his reply. Instead she offered him an option, a delay in deciding.

"Look, call me when you land at Rhodes, Yiannis. Maybe you'll have made up your mind on the flight."

Her voice softened again as she added, "It'd be really, really good to see you, and for more than just an hour or two if you stayed over. As I said, I'll still be up." She added, with a deliberate, even more persuasive, softening voice, "I'll still be up, at least for a little while then."

Once again she didn't wait for his reply. She rang off. She was confident he'd call from Rhodes airport and that she'd see him later that evening in her apartment and in her bed.

However, when he landed at Rhodes she wasn't the first call he made. That was to Dimitra, his wife, lying, telling her he'd had to stay over in Crete for the case, and that he'd get an early flight to Rhodes via Athens in the morning, but then he'd have to go straight to the Lindos station. He ended the call by telling her he'd be home tomorrow evening.

The second call he made was to Sally, telling her he'd be at her place in about an hour.

All she said in her usual confident manner was, "I knew you would." No hint of a "Good," or "See you soon," just a simple, firm, "I knew you would," and with that she rang off immediately.

Finally he texted Georgiou telling him there was a change of plan and that he'd meet him at Lindos police station at eight-thirty tomorrow morning, so he'd have to make his own way there in his car.

After his call to Dimitra he felts pangs of guilt starting to sweep over him on his drive to Lardos. Things between them hadn't been good for a while, quite a while in fact. They'd drifted more and more apart. Was it his work? That's what they both told themselves for a while. It was easier, more satisfying in a way, safer even, to think that. After all it could be a crazy job, crazy at times like now in the middle of an investigation. But was that the real reason behind their problems? In all relationships the newness, the excitement, declines over time, wears off, to be replaced in most cases by comfort and safety; a comfortable, safe relationship. In most cases couples are happy with that and just get on and live their lives that way. They tell themselves, convince themselves, that's normal, the normal way of things in relationships and marriages. In some cases, however, that comfort and safety is replaced by, and breeds, indifference, even in some cases leading to sheer repulsion bordering on hatred, and certainly a lack of any loving passion whatsoever between them. Passivity increases as each mundane comfortable day passes in the relationship.

That is what had happened between him and Dimitra. Telling themselves it was all down to his work and sometimes long hours they slipped into easily accepting the way it was now between them. For Yiannis though he'd found another outlet to counter his indifference and the lack of passion in his marriage – Sally Hardcastle again, and the exciting anticipation of his meetings with her, as well as the excitement of the time they spent together.

The further south he drove on the island the more the darkness of the night shrouded the dimly lit road. The lighting on the road gradually diminished. Much like what was happening in his life, which was once again becoming shrouded in gloom and doubt about his marriage. He knew that what he was doing yet again was crazy, madness, but he simply couldn't resist seeing her. They'd stopped once before, but now he really wasn't sure he could stop it again. He just felt that things had got so much worse, so much more mundane in his marriage. Sally Hardcastle could though. She could stop it any time she chose to, wanted to. He knew that full well. That's what she'd done before, six years ago. That was the way she was. She definitely had control, complete control, of what was between them. He was abdicating that to her, any responsibility for what they had between them. He knew it, and she definitely knew it. In fact, that's what she liked best about their relationship, about any relationships she had. That's what she always wanted, and was all she wanted. That meant it was fun for her. That's all, and that's what she'd told him before. Of course, for him her having the control in their relationship helped him convince himself that he could avoid having to make any decision about it, about their relationship and if and how it should continue. He knew she would do that for him. It was a totally different position for Yiannis Papadoulis; a totally different position for him to be in and to accept compared to his work, his job as a Detective Inspector. The creeping darkness of the road ahead as he got closer to Lardos, and closer to seeing her, helped him cope with, and in the end, ignore that.

That control Sally Hardcastle exerted in their relationship last time was there again. It was even evident when they were in bed together. When having sex during their previous affair she was fond of telling him to wait, wait for her to be fully satisfied first, which he always did. When they'd slept together again on that previous Saturday evening she hadn't changed in that respect. She didn't hold back from whispering to him passionately to wait, wait for her.

"Pizza, I got pizzas, hope that's ok? You said you were starving so I got a couple delivered ten minutes ago," she told him as she opened her Lardos apartment door at gone ten-thirty on that warm July Monday evening. All she was wearing was a long loose dark red t-shirt and flip flops. As she turned away from him to head for the kitchen to get the pizzas her t-shirt rode up slightly and he could see the lower part of her skimpy red panties at the top of her well suntanned shapely legs.

"Pizza will be fine," he said and followed her into the kitchen to put his arms around her from behind and kiss her on the neck while she placed the pizzas on a couple of plates.

"Long day?" Yiannis

"Very."

"Useful though, you said on the phone."

"Yes, very."

"So, you about to arrest your killer then? Your trip to Crete helped identify him?"

He followed as she took the two plates and a couple of knives through to the small table in the lounge, adding, "Some wine or beer."

"Beer with pizza, please."

Seconds later she emerged back out of the kitchen with a couple of cold cans of Mythos Greek beer. As she sat to join him at the table she asked again, "So, are you about to make an arrest?"

He puffed out his cheeks as he cut a piece of pizza.

"No, Crete was useful in finding out a few more things about the victim and eliminating a suspect, rather than identifying who the killer is."

"So you had a suspect then?"

He was chewing his piece of pizza. While she waited for him to swallow it before answering he was thinking why she was asking him about the case. Was it just her making small talk? It was an odd kind of small talk. He'd had enough of the case for one day, a very long day, going over and over parts of it in his head after meeting Martin Cleverley. It certainly wasn't what he'd come over to see her for, not to review the case. He had something different in mind, and he was certain from their phone conversation earlier so had she.

But she wasn't dropping the subject. Before he could answer her previous question about a suspect she asked another.

"I heard the victim was Irish?"

He was munching on another piece of his pizza, thinking how did she know that? Yet more Lindos gossip overheard at her work in Café Melia probably. All he did was gently nod and reach for his beer.

"She was then." She wasn't leaving it, didn't seem to want to leave it there. He did though, and what was more, professionally he knew he should.

She threw him one more 'curve ball' question based on what she seemed to know about the case.

"Was a guy you went to Crete to see was it?"

He looked up from his pizza and reached for his can of beer without answering. He was actually thinking did she know it was, and if so, how, or was that just a vague question out of curiosity? What she surprisingly said next resolved that dilemma for him.

"Martin Cleverley was it?"

He put down his beer, looked across at her and was thinking where was she getting all this information about the case from? He asked "What makes you think that?"

"The writer, Martin Cleverley, he was here with an Irish woman in the summer of 2016 I remember. Well, he met her here as I recall, in June, I think. Everyone in the village knew they were together again in the August here back then. One of the taxi drivers who came into the café regularly at that time said he took them to the airport together that August. People in the village knew he was a writer, and I saw that he posted some stuff on the Lindos Bars Facebook site a couple of years ago about a place on Crete, Neapoli. Some photos and stuff, plus there's a website about his novels. So, the victim was an Irish woman, you go to Crete, Martin Cleverley was here in 2016 a couple of times with an Irish woman and left with her that August, and he's on Crete. Two plus two, Yiannis? I'd make a good detective."

"Maybe, maybe you would, Sally," was all he would say about that, followed by a firm, "But I really didn't come over to talk about the case. My head's been full of it all day. I'd rather it was full of you now, if you know what I mean?" He added, with a slight smile, "I'd much prefer to finish my pizza and beer and then let you take me to your bed."

Now it was her who was smiling and nodding slightly. She changed the subject, but it was to another awkward question that he really didn't want to have to think about.

"Where are you then now, Yiannis?"

His answer started in an even firmer tone of voice.

"Look, Sally, on the case, I can't-"

She reached across to grip his hand briefly as she interrupted.

"No, Yiannis, not the case, sorry, I realise you shouldn't talk about that. I meant where does your wife think you are tonight?"

"Oh, right, yes, I told her I had to stay over on Crete for some more stuff on the case, but I really don't want to talk about her either tonight. Can we just eat this, drink the beer and go to bed. I've got another early start in the morning. I should leave here before eight, and I'm sure we've got plenty of things to do before I get some sleep. I'm sure you can think of a few."

He ended with a small smile and she reached across to take his hand again, telling him, "I certainly can, quite a few."

Ten minutes or so later they were in her bedroom and she was pulling her t-shirt up over her head to reveal what he'd suspected as he looked across at her while they were eating their pizzas. She was wearing no bra and only the skimpiest of tight panties. She drew him into her and began to unbutton his shirt and after removing it reached to unfasten the belt of his trousers and let them drop to the floor.

"No more talk about the case, I promise, Yiannis," she whispered softly in his ear, and then pulled him down on top of her on to the bed to kiss him passionately. Seconds later she added, again softly, "I want to feel you inside me."

Soon she did, as his hand caressed her hair and then his lips moved down to kiss her breasts. Her moans of excitement increased as they rolled across her bed, only interrupted by her usual soft, "Don't … just wait … wait for me."

As usual, he did just that, as she told him to, so that when her climax came she screamed loudly in ecstasy to him, "Now, now, Yiannis, now, for me now."

He did. She had a way of making his satisfaction seem longer and more fulfilling. He kissed her tenderly on the lips and then a minute or so later rolled off her to lie alongside. Suddenly he could feel the tiredness of the long day of his early start and trip to Crete beginning to sweep over him again.

However, she wasn't finished, wasn't satisfied by any means, and not just with the sex between them. After a few minutes of silence while she stared up at the ceiling she asked, "So, what do you want, Yiannis?"

He was a little confused by that question now. He turned his head on the soft pillow to look at her still gazing up at the ceiling.

"With us? I thought we had that conversation six years ago. You said then that you just wanted fun. If I remember rightly you said something like you weren't the sort of woman, obviously not the sort of woman, I thought you were. You weren't one for long term plans you said."

"Well, yes, but-" She interrupted, but he didn't wait for her to finish.

"I remember you got quite angry and asked if I thought I saw us together here on Rhodes? I think you even said, asked if I saw us in the future as a happy couple? Me as the respectable Police Inspector, me doing my police thing, and you being my partner? The little wife you called it, with her part-time job in a café or a bar here? Us living together happily ever after?"

She laughed and then continued to look up vacantly at the ceiling.

"Wow, you've got a good memory, Yiannis. I guess that's the detective in you. I'm not sure if I said those actual words, and whether or not in that way. Doesn't sound like me at all. But I wasn't actually asking what you want now with us. I've not changed what I want now from what I wanted back then six years ago. I'm still the same, want the same. Fun, yep, that's me. That's all I want. I actually meant what do you want in your life now here on Rhodes, and going forward, in the future?"

"Oh, I see, I … errm-"

She turned her head on the pillow to face him, placed her left hand tenderly on his cheek and then kissed him before he could continue.

"I mean, I suppose if you solve this case it would help a lot with your career, wouldn't it? Maybe a promotion, or even a transfer if you wanted it?"

"Erm ..."

He hesitated again and rubbed his chin before answering.

"It could do I suppose, a promotion I mean, but I'm not sure I'd want to leave Rhodes for somewhere like Athens or Thessaloniki, for example. From what my previous Inspector told me after he was transferred here from Athens, Karagoulis, it's a bit of a snake pit there, and not just because there's more crime."

"What else then? What else is a snake pit, as he put it?"

"Some of the police officers. He said he never trusted them, especially some of the more senior ones."

"Hmm ... that doesn't sound like it'd be a good move then, a good transfer. Maybe you'd be better off not solving this current case here."

She smiled and reached to kiss him again before adding, "So, are you?"

"Am I what?"

"Are you any nearer to solving it?"

His head was spinning. She was back on talking about the case, or attempting to get him to.

"Not great for the tourist trade in the height of summer having a tourist murdered on the island," she continued. "Is it simply a random attack do you think, a robbery maybe, or something premeditated? Where was the woman staying? The body was found in Gennadi I heard. Is that where she was staying?"

She was suddenly firing off questions to him about the case again like a machine gun barrage.

Yet again he was a little surprised why she was so interested. In the end though he put it down to the fact that the murder was an unusual occurrence on the island, particularly in Gennadi, and no doubt it would have been a high topic of conversation where she worked in Café Melia. He was careful with his answers, giving her a very limited answer.

"Yes, Gennadi, and she was a tourist, but she wasn't staying there."

"Not in Gennadi, and not a robbery then? Where then? Where was she staying? Do you know?"

He briefly looked sideways out of the corners of his eyes at her. He didn't want this topic of conversation to continue at all. It wasn't necessarily that he didn't trust her, but he always knew there would be plenty of gossip and rumours flying around in Lindos and Lardos.

He settled for a short non-committal, not exactly the truth about knowing where the victim was staying.

"No, not really."

Then he leaned over to kiss her before rolling on top of her once more and adding, "No more work, no more talking about work please. I have to leave early in the morning for the Lindos station and I have a much better idea of how we can use the time before I get some badly needed sleep after a long day's travelling."

"Me too, on both counts, Yiannis, that better idea for the use of our time, as well as leaving early for work in the café for me."

14

MI6 (vengeance) August 2016 and July 2022

"Can you come and have a look at this please, sir. From checking CCTV for some of the other areas of Oxford Circus underground station, besides the platform, I think I could have found who it was who killed Sandra Weston."

The MI6 technical analyst in their London Section was calling his supervisor at the beginning of the second week of August 2016 having been given the task of checking the background information available following the death of one of their former operatives. The official identification of the cause of death was suicide, but the death of any MI6 agent, current or past, was always subject to further investigation. Officially Sandra Weston had thrown herself under a train arriving at a very packed Oxford Circus London Underground platform during the rush hour just under a week before. She had recently lost her position in the Service following the disappearance of one of her key agents operating in her section, Aileen Regan. Regan was someone she'd personally recruited when they were together at university many years before, and who she believed to be a good friend. At around the same time her marriage to Richard had disintegrated following her discovery of the latest of his many affairs; this latest one being with her 'good friend' Aileen. As a result of those two things she had neglected her fashion photography business which went into rapid collapse, causing her financial difficulties. Those personal and professional disasters, ruining her cosy good life, had seemingly pushed Sandra over the edge and led her in growing despair to taking her own life.

For the Head of the London Section of MI6, Peter Sturridge, it was all a bit too neat, not least because of the disappearance of Aileen Regan just prior to Sandra Weston's dismissal and death. Officially Regan had quit, informing her supervisor and boss at the time Sandra Weston of that. However, the very next day she disappeared off the radar, never reported in to the Service or attended the department, as she was officially required to do for another month before leaving.

When the London Section Supervisor arrived at the technical analyst's desk in the large open plan office he was told, "I had another look at the CCTV for Oxford Circus Station on that day of Sandra Weston's death, 2nd of August, not just the stuff from the cameras on the platform but for the whole station, plus for an hour before."

"And?" Sturridge said impatiently.

"For most of it there's nothing, sir. But look, this is from one of the platform cameras, and check out the person in the black baseball cap pulled right down and black bomber jacket edging through the crowd on the platform into the area where Weston was standing."

The Supervisor leaned down to peer at the computer screen.

"Yes, we saw that, but there are plenty of people around Weston and we can only see the back of the head of the person in the baseball cap and the image is quite blurry at that."

Sturridge wasn't convinced by whatever he was supposed to be looking at.

"It looks like a plain cap, but if we zoom in on that person, sir, we can see a very small emblem on the side of it, looking like a very small Nike swoosh."

The Supervisor still looked perplexed over quite where the technical analyst was going with this, what point he was trying to make. He decided to remain silent and let the analyst carry on as he pulled up another section of CCTV footage.

"Now, this is the main station concourse by the ticket office windows and machines ten minutes before."

He pointed to the screen.

"There's Weston heading towards the ticket barriers."

He pointed to a figure not far behind her, also heading towards the barriers.

"And there's the same person in the black pulled down baseball cap and bomber jacket. This time we get a better look at the face, and if we zoom in we can pick out the small NIKE swoosh logo on the cap."

Sturridge straightened back up and with a large amount of scepticism in his voice commented, "Yes, so the same person maybe followed Weston, or more likely was just heading towards the same platform because they had to get the same train. What does that prove exactly? Why do you think they had anything to do with Weston's death?"

The analyst turned to look up at him and with some self-satisfaction announced, "It's Aileen Regan, sir."

"What? How can you-"

The analyst interrupted, "Be sure, sir, how can I be sure. Well, as sure as the computers are. I blew up a still frame of the face of the person in the baseball cap and took a chance in running it through some of our Digital Facial Recognition software on our operatives in our data base. Eventually it threw up Regan, almost a perfect match, sir, ninety-nine point five percent. It's her, I'm sure. So, she was there, eventually on the platform almost right behind Weston, and if we look closely at the CCTV for where Weston was on the platform in the seconds before the train arrives Regan is right behind her. I'd bet good money on the fact that Regan pushed her; a crowded platform, rush hour, easy enough to give Weston a slight nudge in the back. She was right on the platform edge. She killed her, sir. I'm sure, and that's why she completely disappeared off our radar, out of the Service, before and after she killed Weston. She pre-planned leaving and then killing her."

The Supervisor pulled up another chair and said, "Regan? Phew! But why, why would Regan kill Weston?"

"That's not my pay grade, sir, way above it. That's for you bods and your spooks to find out, figure out. Those of us down here at the new technology coal face just find and feed you the information."

Sturridge shook his head slightly before saying, "Yes, yes, a bit above my pay grade too, but anyway well done on this. Good work. I need to go and report this to the Section Head Director upstairs and they can take it from here. I guess the first thing they'll want to try and find out is where the bloody hell Regan is now."

The London Section Head Director was Pauline Ware; a no nonsense, straight talking, slim divorced woman in her mid-fifties. She was quite tall at five feet nine even in her moderately low heeled, quite expensive but not appearing so, functional work shoes. She was a woman of that certain age and some style who would not be out of place in well-heeled company at a Cotswold dinner party, or even at a weekend country shooting party in that part of the world. Always a well-dressed woman, in the office she would usually be seen in a dark business suit of skirt and jacket with high necked blouse. Despite the cool, calm, respectable exterior image her work wardrobe easily conveyed she had an edge to her, a ruthless one, which had served her well and got her to where she now was in the Service.

She'd been in it, the 'circus' as she liked to call it, for over twenty-five years and had risen through the ranks from being an agent in the field in the Middle East to a number of more desk bound positions in what MI6 agents referred to as the 'River House', officially Vauxhall Cross on London's Albert Embankment. No one in MI6 past or present actually really knew for certain the origin of the name 'the circus'. There were many stories and claims of where it came from. The most believed, and repeated, amongst people who worked there, in the field or in the building itself, was that, somewhat ironically, it came from fiction. Agents used to joke that was not unlike some of the information they received from the 'River House' regarding their missions and operations which was also fiction and often based on rumour, fabrications and assumptions. In his espionage novels, author John le Carré placed the headquarters of the fictionalised British intelligence service based on MI6 in buildings on Shaftesbury Avenue and Cambridge Circus in London. It was from this that Le Carré's nickname for the agency, "the circus", derived.

Peter Sturridge had called Pauline Ware's Personal Assistant on the next floor up in 'River House' and told her he needed to get in to see her boss urgently about a missing rogue agent. Five minutes later the P.A. called him back and told him he could see Ware briefly in twenty minutes. He knew from experience that he needed to be clear and concise about what his technical analyst had discovered, and what he believed they needed to do next, and quickly, concerning finding Aileen Regan. He thought he did that well when he got to see Pauline Ware. However, he'd temporarily forgotten that she didn't suffer fools gladly when it came to some things, especially allocating resources without specifically defined targets, particularly allocating hard pressed finances and funding.

She listened intently as he summarised what they had discovered in his section regarding Sandra Weston's death and what they believed was Aileen Regan's part in it. Her facial expression never changed throughout. Sturridge could ascertain no clear indication from it if she was going to support his further search to find Regan. There was not even a small acknowledging nod of her head at any point. She no doubt was a very good poker player, as she had to be in her position in the Service, and always had been in her rise through the ranks, something that undoubtedly contributed greatly to where she was now.

As he finished explaining there was an awkward silence for ten seconds or even slightly more. Eventually she got up out of her large leather chair and walked around her also very large polished dark wood desk to lean on it in front of, and almost hovering over, Sturridge.

"So, where?" she asked simply.

"Where, Mam?"

"Yes, where do you suggest we start this search for Regan? Any ideas, anything from what your people saw on the CCTV footage or anywhere else that suggests where we should start looking, get some of our operatives in the field looking?"

Sturridge shifted uneasily in his chair. He simply thought his section had done their bit, played their part, in identifying Aileen Regan, and that another section could take it from there, although he'd no idea how or a plan for where. Unfortunately for Sturridge his silence in response to her question betrayed that fully.

"No, I thought not," she told him firmly. "Look Sturridge, resources are tight. You know that. We can't just trawl the whole world looking for this one bloody rogue operative. We have to have some idea where to start. I seriously doubt she will still be in London, don't you?"

"Erm ... I suppose not, Mam."

She offered him a 'bone', a lifeline.

"Although we could check with the current Head of the Section she was operating in here and see what her log tells us about her missions and movements for us over the past year. It'll all be there, even where she spent her holidays. She would have had to register and record them. We should check Sandra Weston's as well, if you're right, Sturridge, and Regan did kill her. In the end I'd be very surprised if this was our baby. As I said, I very much doubt that she's still going to be in our section, London. If that's right we can hand it over to whoever's it is and maybe they can find her. At least that will save my Section's budget. I'll get my P.A. to find out which Section Regan was operating in and get the Head to call you so you can fill them in."

The following afternoon Sturridge got a call from the Irish Section Head Director, Brian Rogers, asking him to go and see him straightaway to fill him in on what he'd found on Aileen Regan, and to his surprise, Sandra Weston. Sturridge was even more surprised to learn during their meeting that Sandra Weston had been Aileen Regan's boss in the Irish Section, her controller, before they both left the service, as well as that they had been good friends since university. Yet it didn't appear difficult for Sturridge to convince Rogers that he was sure Regan had killed her good friend. There was obviously more that Sturridge was not privy to. He knew better than to ask. Rogers was a straight 'up and down' old school tie public school man. He wasn't going to give away any more than he thought necessary, especially to someone like Sturridge, whom he clearly recognised as junior to him.

Rogers also told him that one of the final things recorded on both Regan's and Weston's files was a request granted for permission for them to go on holiday together to Rhodes in June earlier that summer of 2016. However, he never told Sturridge about the mission on their files that Aileen Regan undertook in relation to Sandra Weston's husband Richard's possible

Russian spying activities, or indeed, her affair with him for that purpose.

"I could have a word with the Mediterranean Section Head Director I suppose old chap. See if they've got anything on the two of them, Regan and Weston. Why they chose Rhodes perhaps, or anything a bit odd they got up to while they were there. I know him pretty well, Tom Fortescue, went to school together at Winchester. He owes me a favour or two. Last time I had a few drinks with him, a couple of months ago now, I seem to remember something he dropped into the conversation about them having a 'sleeper' agent somewhere in that part of the Med who they needed to reactivate. From memory don't think it was Rhodes though, maybe another island, Crete maybe, or even on the mainland in Athens, somewhere in that part of the world anyway."

"Thanks. Hopefully we can track her down and deal with her for Weston's death, sir."

"Yes, can't have people going around bumping off our agents now can we, or even former agents, Weston having left the Service by then. I'll let Pauline know if we turn anything up, sorry, your Section Head Director, must remember to be more formal these days, what with all the regulations and HR. Nice woman though, very competent."

"Err .. yes." Sturridge didn't really know the appropriate old school way to reply to that. So he simply settled for a, "Thank you," got up and left.

It was out of his hands now, now way above his pay grade. One of the Section Head Director's would deal with it. Probably the one who's Section Aileen Regan has been operating in. As it turned out, as it often turned out, it was not entirely clear who should deal with it, which section. The first reaction and interest in it though came from Tom Fortescue's Mediterranean Section and his call to Pauline Ware the following midday.

"Pauline, Tom, just to update you, keep you in the loop if you want to be. Brian Rogers saw that chap of yours, Sturridge, yesterday about the Regan and Weston business and called me after to see if we had anything that might be of help in locating Regan. I've informed Brian that we think we've got some movement on it. By the way, bloody good job that tech analyst of yours did identifying Regan from that CCTV."

"Yes, yes, Tom, so what is it?"

She was someone who didn't do pleasantries easily, if at all.

"Well, we took a long shot and put some feelers out overnight with some of our contacts in Athens and Rhodes. We got lucky. One of our people in our Athens Embassy Section has a quite high up friendly contact in the Greek Border Services. They got them to check British and Irish passport arrivals in Regan's name since Weston's death on 2nd August. As a said, just a long shot, but as her and Weston were on Rhodes a couple of months ago we thought that maybe-"

"Yes, so, Tom, what did they find?"

Her impatience wasn't abating. It was always heightened when talking with her public school male colleagues

"Incredible really, Pauline."

There was an audible sigh down the line. Her exasperation was building rapidly, but she wasn't one to lose her cool easily, if at all. From her training she knew better than to do that. That wasn't to say she couldn't be quite viciously ruthless though when she wanted to be, or felt she needed to be.

"What is, Tom?"

"Regan, she used her Irish passport in that name when she arrived on Rhodes yesterday, on a flight from Athens. Who'd have thought it? Either felt very confident she'd got away without being recognised over Weston's supposed suicide or-"

"Or bloody arrogant, Tom," she interrupted firmly and added, "So, what are we going to do about her now? If she's still on Rhodes she's obviously in your Section. So, your show isn't it?"

"Yes, we've got a 'sleeper' asset in Athens. We've instructed him to get on a plane to Rhodes as soon as, preferably tonight. It's only a forty-five minute flight or so. He should be able to start looking for her there tomorrow. Find her and do what's necessary. My people in the Section here say he's been inactive for a year or so, but pretty experienced, so it should be a quite straightforward job. He's been briefed that her and Weston stayed in a little tourist village called Lindos in June when they were there earlier this year, supposedly on holiday, but who knows with those two. He's been instructed to start looking there."

"Good, all yours then, Tom, can't have people going around bumping off our agents, even past ones. Keep me in the loop about how it goes, particularly if you think there's anything I need to know concerning Regan and my Section."

"Ok, Pauline, will do."

However, what Tom Fortescue told Pauline Ware in their telephone conversation was wrong. He'd been wrongly informed of the situation by people in his Section. They did have a 'sleeper' agent in Athens, and through their contact in the Greek Border Services in Athens Aileen Regan had been discovered to have arrived in Rhodes on a flight from Athens using a passport in that name on the 9th of August, but their 'sleeper' agent wasn't ready to fly to Rhodes immediately. He was no longer officially a 'sleeper'. He had been activated and was currently engaged on another operation in Athens. It was winding down, but he couldn't leave it at that point so wouldn't be able to fly to Rhodes for another couple of days. Fortescue was livid when he was told. He certainly didn't want to tell Pauline Ware that. It would reflect very badly on his Section, and him. So, he didn't do so, didn't "keep her in the loop" straightaway as he'd promised.

The MI6 agent from Athens actually arrived on Rhodes two days later, on the 12th of August. Based on his briefing, and what it contained about her and Sandra Weston visiting Lindos in June of that year, he was instructed that was the best place to start looking for Regan. That evening of the twelfth he started asking, he thought quite discreetly, some of the staff in some of the bars, about an Irish woman on holiday in the village. He had a photograph of Regan on his phone from the briefing. However, he thought that to show that around the village might spook her if she was told about it by any of the bar staff he'd showed it to and she might disappear on him, away from the village and eventually Rhodes. The answers he got on that first evening were pretty general, mainly that there were quite a few Irish women in Lindos at that time as it was the height of the tourist season and it always attracted a large number of visitors from both Northern Ireland and the Republic, especially

Northern Ireland. Throughout that evening he kept checking in various bars, but there was no sign of her.

He began to think that perhaps she hadn't come back to Lindos after all. Maybe she had gone to another part of the island, but there was no way he could check all the places on it. On the second evening, Saturday the 13th, he got lucky however. He again asked about an Irish woman, this time of one of the bar staff in Pal's Bar. Initially, he got the same answer as in other bars, but while sat outside later having decided he'd earned a few Gin and Tonics he spotted her inside through the large window on one side of the bar. Pal's Bar had two entrances. One faced the alley in which he was sat, while the other was slightly around the corner of the bar and faced another alley that ran at right angles to one he was in. She must have entered the bar by that one after he'd taken his drink to the seat outside. He watched her discreetly through the window as she appeared to be chatting with, and drinking shots with, the two barmen and a couple who were customers. There was no chance she would recognise him, of course, but he decided he'd have to obviously wait for somewhere much more private before confronting her. Unbeknown to him though one of the Pal's Bar staff had told her an English guy had been asking about an Irish woman, and then pointed him out to her sat outside through the large bar window.

Aileen Regan had seen, and even worked with, plenty of MI6 operatives over the past twenty years. She could spot them from a mile away, smell them almost, like a sixth sense she'd developed. Black polo shirt and chinos, slicked back short hair, all that was standard supposed undercover MI6 uniform. She was sure what he was and that he was looking for her, had no doubt about it.

For over an hour she stayed inside the bar, chatting to the English couple she'd had shots with, James and Katy, but occasionally, as discreetly as possible, glancing across the bar and through the window to check he was still there. She was obviously trying to think through just what to do about him, how to deal with him.

Just before twelve-thirty he moved, left to go up the alleyway and wait in the darkness up some steps alongside the

Courtyard Bar where he could still observe anyone leaving from one of the doors into the alley from Pal's Bar. At shortly after one o'clock he saw her emerge from the bar and head up the alley towards where he was hiding. The music in Pal's had finished so it was relatively easy for him to hear her tell the Pal's bar staff as she was leaving that she was, "Off to Glow."

Glow was only seconds from Pal's, up the alley and a few steps, and to the right just past the Courtyard Bar. As she got to the few steps leading up to the Courtyard Bar she nearly saw him. She actually stopped, thinking for a brief moment that she glimpsed someone - a figure in the darkness further up the steps towards the top alley – peering down at her from out of the shadows. However, when she looked again she could see no one there. She thought that she was obviously now just getting paranoid. He waited back in the darkness as she went into Glow. She never stayed there long though. Just for one drink. Saturday night appeared to be the night when local young Greeks went out clubbing and she felt decidedly old, almost ancient compared to the overwhelming majority of young Greek men and women in the club. She had the one drink and then decided to make her way to Arches Club which was up another alleyway in the centre of the village.

Approaching one-thirty he saw her leaving Glow. For some reason she chose to make her way up the few steps immediately opposite Glow towards the top alleyway that ran behind the Courtyard Bar. She could then cut down one of the alleys running off it to the left that led down to the entrance to Arches. Maybe she thought it was the shortest and quickest route or perhaps just because it had the advantage of avoiding the main alleyway through the village and its probable groups of drunken tourists, especially any groups of young British guys who might suddenly decide in their drunken state that they want to stop and try to chat her up.

That choice which took her into one of the darkest and poorly lit parts of the village was perfect for what he intended. To do what he was sent to do and eliminate her. The path was a little uneven, but she wasn't actually paying much attention to her earthly surroundings as she made her way along the alley, preferring to gaze up at the clear sky and its myriad of bright, sparkling stars. Not something you could ever observe in the cities these days with their large scale pollution.

Around twenty-five yards or so along the alley from the rear of the Courtyard Bar, at one of its darkest parts, while she was still gazing up at the heavens he jumped out from one of the recesses in the wall behind her that led to some steps down to another of the alleys running into the centre of the village. His arm grabbed her around the neck from behind while his other hand, the right one, immediately thrust a gun fitted with a silencer against her right temple. He struggled to try to drag her back into the dark shadow of the recess. Even though she couldn't see his face she knew instantly that it would be the guy who sitting outside Pal's, the one who had been asking about an Irish woman earlier. Despite the dim shadow light she made out the black short sleeve of his polo shirt. She knew he was from MI6. He had to be.

As he attempted to drag her back into the recess, obviously intent on killing her, he stumbled slightly on the rough, worn ground of that part of the alley. That was her chance. She'd learned quite quickly from her two visits to the village that some of the paths could be treacherous, slippery, and shiny from the years of donkey hooves passing over them every day during the summer season. She had almost fallen foul of them in one place in the village during her previous visit in June. Now she was more than grateful for them, and the donkeys. This was one such path, or at least this part of it was, leading as it did from the donkey station in the Main Square up to the top of the village by the Atmosphere Bar and Lindos Reception. As she felt him partially lose his footing, and with as much strength as she could muster, she immediately pushed all her weight back onto him with a heavy thrust, while he attempted to steady himself and retain his arm-lock around her neck. The two of them fell backwards to the floor of the pitch black recess. As he fell he initially struggled to retain his grip around her neck, but as she fell on top of him she intentionally smashed the back of her head full into his face with as much force as she could summon up. The crack of his nose was audible, and he let out a voluble yell of, "Argh." Simultaneously, the back of his head hit the hard flagstone ground and a piece of loose broken stone which lay on it, causing trickles of blood to begin to flow from an open wound. The pain from the force of the crack on his nose from the back of her head, as well as the wound to the back of his head, caused him to release his arm-lock around her neck and to drop the gun to the ground out of his right hand. She quickly leapt up from her position on top of him on the ground and picked up the gun.

"You bitch, you fucking Irish bitch," he screamed at her while he writhed in agony on the ground clutching his face, now streaming with blood. His hands over his face muffled his scream somewhat. It was very unlikely that there would be anyone out in that part of the village at that time, but she was relieved that his scream of anger and agony was muffled and was not likely to be heard anyway.

She pointed the gun at him telling him quietly, but firmly, "Yes, I fucking am. A bitch, that's what those shits you work for trained me to be for twenty years. Bloody MI6, don't bother to deny it. I know your sort, can spot you a bloody mile away. I knew that as soon as I spotted you outside that bar earlier."

He now lay motionless on the ground. The full effect of her assault on him was beginning to kick-in and he was groggy from the blow to the back of his head, as well as the pain from his broken nose. Even if he had all his senses and could, he wasn't bothering to deny what she'd said, or even confirm it. She knew from her own training that he wouldn't. He would have been trained not to. Even though she needed to ask, she guessed he wouldn't answer her next question either.

"You here alone or are there more of you bastards here looking for me?"

She was right. He never answered. He just stared hazily up at her standing over him, his hands now covered in the blood from his nose, while that from the wound on the back of his head continued trickling down the back of his neck, soaking into the collar of his black polo shirt.

"I didn't think you'd tell me that. From working for those shits for years I knew you wouldn't. I guess you know that though. But I don't work for them anymore, so I don't have to pretend anymore. I decided I wanted my life back. In any case, in reality I never did actually bloody work for those sodding Brits with all their Secret Service games."

For some illogical reason he actually started to think that if she was telling him all that then she wasn't going to kill him. He was wrong.

"Get up, get up!" she told him forcibly. "Put your hands on top of your head," she added as he staggered to his feet to face her in the darkness while she remained pointing the gun at his face in her right hand. As he managed to stand up straight immediately in front of her she lifted her left hand, stared coldly straight into his eyes, and then, much to his surprise, stroked his right cheek tenderly. His eyes widened, completely uncertain and bewildered as to what was likely to happen next. As she finished stroking his cheek and continued to stare intensely into his fear riven eyes he started to ask, "What, what are you going to-"

He never got to finish. She allowed a broad smile of mischievous contentment to emerge across her lips, and then placed the index finger of her left hand on his lips in order to indicate he should stop speaking. Finally, she planted a tender kiss on his right cheek as she moved the gun to press on his left temple. He started to force a slight smile, anticipating relief that she wasn't actually going to kill him. No sooner had the smile started to spread across his lips though, and as her smile returned even broader, she brought her bare right knee up in a rapid action with great force into his balls. He groaned in pain and doubled over slightly. As he stumbled forward she followed up with a full bloodied kick to his groin area, landing her trainer covered foot with full force perfectly.

He let out another groan as she told him, "You're going to be my message to that 'old boys club' you work for. Don't bloody mess with me is what it'll tell them. Fuck off and leave me alone to get on with my life."

He was gasping for air having sunk to his knees and doubled over completely in front of her from the blows. His gasping for air and his groans of discomfort lasted only a second or so more, however, as she instantly reversed the gun in her right hand and smashed the handle of it into the rear of his skull with as much force as she could muster. She knew the precise fatal spot to aim for, close to the initial wound from his fall earlier when he cracked the back of his head on the flagstone and loose stone. Years of training by his 'old boys club' employers had taught her well.

He slumped further forward onto the ground in front of her with one final groan of pain and then lay there face down totally motionless. She quickly checked for any pulse and that he was dead. She knew instantly exactly what she was going to do next. The rough and shiny ground of the alleyway had not only provided her with the opportunity to escape his grasp, but now it was going to provide her with what she hoped would be believed as the cause of his death. She carefully lifted his body up from the ground, making sure none of the blood spread onto her clothes. Most of it had soaked into his polo shirt anyway. Then she manoeuvred it down the three small steps into the equally dark alleyway that led down into the centre of the village. She guessed it was one that wasn't used very often, by either locals or tourists. At the bottom of the steps she took his head and smashed it once more against the white wall shrouded in darkness and shadow. This time though it was the top of his forehead that split open, and as she allowed his body to fall to the floor at that spot she ensured that some of the blood from his forehead deposited itself on the wall above his body at head height. Her plan was that any possible police investigation would merely assume that he'd had too much to drink, lost his footing in the darkness and stumbled at the top of the steps, cracking the back of his head on the ground there, then tried to recover and get some help, but instead fell down the steps, cracking his nose and forehead against the wall. Through the window outside Pal's she'd noticed he was drinking what looked like at least three Gin and tonics or possibly Vodka and tonics. So, she knew he had alcohol in his system, and the police would no doubt discover that in any autopsy. Perhaps it wasn't going to be enough to suggest he was completely drunk, but it could, or should, be just enough to suggest that he lost his footing because he'd had a few drinks. In any case, she'd heard a few stories of tourists losing their footing in some places in the village because of the rough or shiny paths in the alleyways and suffering broken or sprained limbs, even during the day and not having had any alcohol. So, the scenario she had now contrived shouldn't be too hard for the local police to believe, accept, and come to that conclusion.

She still had to deal with the gun. She wiped the blood off as best she could with some tissues from a packet she always carried in her handbag. Now though, she had to dispose of the tissues, as well as having the question of what to actually do with the gun. She dismantled the silencer and carefully wrapped it and the gun in some more of her tissues, then placed them all in her handbag.

Finally, she checked the pockets of his chinos. There was nothing, except some Euros and a mobile, but no identification, not even any indication of where he was staying. Oddly there was no key of any sort or even a card from any nearby hotel or accommodation. She frowned, puzzled as to how that could be, but took the phone to check it later somewhere safe before disposing of it. It definitely wasn't an expensive one and from the look of it she guessed it was a 'burner' phone. She'd had plenty of them given to her when she worked for MI6; mobiles with prepaid minutes and definitely without any sort of mobile network supplier contract. She anticipated it would have very little information or contacts on it. Nevertheless, she hoped it might give some clue as to whether he was alone in Lindos or whether there were other MI6 operatives with him. It was turned off, obviously so there was no chance that it would make any sound while he was hiding in waiting to attack her. She knew better than to turn it on at this point in case there was any chance it could be tracked later by MI6, even if it was a 'burner' phone. She just placed it in her handbag, relieved that she'd actually chosen to use her reasonably sized one to go out with that night. She certainly wouldn't have been able to fit the gun, the silencer, the blood stained tissues and the phone into her other smaller handbag.

That thought made her realise that she was actually now surprisingly calm, remarkably so considering the turmoil and her actions of the last few minutes. Obviously some of the attributes and characteristics of her past life hadn't left her completely. She hadn't lost it. She still had all her old skills. Nevertheless, she took a deep breath to compose herself even more, at the same time realising that she needed to get away from there as quickly as possible before there was any possible chance that someone would actually be using that particular alleyway on their way to their apartment at the top of the village. Her first instinct was to head straight back to her own apartment, if nothing else in order to clean up the gun and stash it somewhere there before figuring out how and where to dispose of it. The sea was the obvious choice, but not now at that time tonight, although it would obviously have to be at night.

She checked her clothes and luckily found no traces of blood on them. She could feel, almost taste the smell in her nostrils though. It was a familiar one to her. It was the smell of death. She'd smelt it many times before. Others may not, but she could always smell it, on her, on her clothes, in her hair. It lingered. She searched for the small vial of perfume spray in her handbag, beneath the gun, the silencer, and the tissues. It wasn't a discernible odour to anyone else, the smell of death, but it was to her, probably merely in her mind. She squirted two short sprays of the perfume onto either side of her neck. It was just a reassurance really, a bizarre sort of comfort blanket.

Briefly she thought again of heading straight for her apartment. However, her past experience in these sorts of situations told her the best move now would be to be seen by a lot of people immediately; people who she would ensure certainly remembered her at this specific time should any possible police investigation develop. She would set about doing that, even though from the way she'd staged the scene of his death she was pretty certain the police would rule out any foul play fairly quickly, assume it was just a bad accident. Her past experience also told her that there was no way they would be able to pin down the exact time of death, only a broad period. Consequently, ensuring that she was seen by a number of people in a bar somewhere in the village soon would give her some sort of alibi, should she ever by any chance need one.

Where she was heading for when she was attacked, Arches club, would no doubt have people there who she could make sure remembered seeing her. But she decided that was not a good choice, for now at least. So she immediately ruled it out.

There was no way she wanted to be seen coming down from the top alley at this time by people going into the club or possibly even by club staff working at the entrance into the club's courtyard. That would place her much too close to the proximity of what she had just done.

Her brain was racing, figuring out what was her best next move. Instead of Arches, and the alley leading down to its entrance, she decided she would go back up to the top alley and walk further along there, once again fairly sure it was very unlikely that anyone would be coming along there at that time of night and see her. She would then go down the alley to the left after the one to Arches and into the Crazy Moon cocktail bar, which she was sure would still be open. She'd been there once before during her previous Lindos visit in June at around this time of night and there were some people still there having a late drink. Also she recalled that there was usually no one on the entrance there, which was also an archway into a courtyard from the alley. At that time of night she was sure that would still be the case. Consequently, as long as it was, there was no possibility that anyone would see which direction she came from, down from the top alley. So, that's what she did, after first checking closely once more that her clothes and the exposed parts of her body didn't have any signs whatsoever of any blood from the guy's wounds. There were none.

As she made her way through the stone archway of Crazy Moon, crossed the courtyard, and approached the inside bar a young blonde woman standing by the doorway, who she took to be a waitress, greeted her with, "Hi." Aileen responded with a, "Hi," of her own, followed by asking, "Is it too late for a drink, although I actually need to use your toilet first to be honest."

As far as Aileen could see as she stood at the doorway there were still eight people inside sat at the bar drinking, as well as the two couples she'd passed at the tables outside. So, the young woman, who was obviously English, told her, "No, it's fine, never too late in Lindos for a drink. What can I get you while you use the toilet?" She pointed and added, "It's over there in the corner of the courtyard."

Aileen told her, "A Gin and Tonic, please, with ice and lemon." She definitely needed another one now, and she'd already succeeded in making sure the young blonde woman would remember her by asking if it was too late to get a drink, as well as asking to use the toilet.

As soon as she got in the toilet she carefully firstly checked that there was no one else in there. After she'd made sure that was the case she quickly removed it from her handbag and washed the gun, removing any trace of any remaining bits of blood. She dried it with some toilet paper from the nearby cubicle. Then she flushed that and the tissues which she'd had the gun wrapped in down the toilet, along with the blood stained tissues she'd previously wiped it down with in the alley,. She placed the gun back in her handbag and re-zipped it. Finally, she looked in the mirror to check once again that there were no traces of blood on her clothes at all. Again, there wasn't.

As soon as she emerged from the toilet and went into the inside bar she set about quickly making sure that as many people as possible remembered her being in the bar at that specific time, just as she planned. Should the local police decide to investigate further rather than just accepting the guy's death was an accident and, by any chance she came under suspicion, she would have a good alibi. She was well aware that if they did do any sort of investigation at all that involved trying to find out who the guy was, and what his movements in Lindos were that night, then it was likely they would interview some of the staff and the owners in the bars. That meant those in Pal's Bar were certainly likely to remember him and the fact that he was asking about her, or at least, "an Irish woman." However, she felt that she was now totally in control of all eventualities, all circumstances, had covered all bases. She told herself that she obviously hadn't lost it, being completely cool and calm in tight and difficult situations under pressure.

So, she took a seat on one of the stools at the bar and as the blonde young woman delivered her drink she deliberately engaged her in conversation once again for any possible alibi, should she need one.

"Are you working here for the summer?"

"Well, yes and no really. I'm working here for the summer and every summer now, but I live here. My mother lives here, and my partner over there is a co-owner of the bar."

She pointed to a youngish Greek looking guy at the far end of the bar talking to a couple of customers.

Aileen took the opportunity to ensure that the young woman knew exactly who she was as she told her, "I'm Aileen by the way. Irish, as you can no doubt tell. Here for a couple of months, I think. At least I've rented an apartment here for that long anyway. I'm trying to trace some of my past family who were here. My mother worked here in the nineteen-seventies."

"That's sounds interesting. I'm Emily."

They chatted on and off for another thirty minutes while Aileen drank her Gin and Tonic. In between time, while Emily went off to serve some of the customers outside in the courtyard, she also made a point of introducing herself to a couple of middle-aged English women who were sat on the stools next to her at the bar. In turn, they introduced themselves as Gill and Anthea. She made sure she also engaged them in conversation. It was just standard stuff about Lindos and how many times they'd been mainly. They were regular visitors over many years apparently, often a couple of times each summer. They seemed to be enjoying their cocktails, and appeared to have had quite a few by that time of night.

By just after two-thirty she was satisfied that she'd done enough of making sure people remembered she'd been there at that time. Having finished her drink and paid she wished, "Goodnight," to Emily and the two women, then made her way back to her apartment.

As soon as she got back there she removed the gun and silencer out of her handbag and placed them underneath some of her underwear in the small chest of drawers. She would dispose of them in the sea off the rocks in St. Paul's Bay tomorrow evening, under the cover of darkness. Then she took the guy's phone and some Euros out of her bag, put them in the pocket of her shorts, and left her apartment. She headed to the entrance to the Arches Club in the centre of the village where the guy at the entrance to the club's courtyard greeted her with a smile and a, "Good evening."

She returned his smile, accompanied with a "Good evening," of her own.

"Can't stop, need the toilet urgently," she explained as she headed across the courtyard and into the women's toilet. As soon as she got into one the cubicle and locked the door she removed the phone from her pocket and turned it on to check the record of the guy's recent calls. As she expected it displayed that his last call was to an unidentified number. She adjusted the volume on the phone to its lowest point and then pressed 'Recall'. What appeared to be a well-educated voice answered, asking simply in a very low monotone bureaucratic manner, "Is there a problem?"

She hung up straightaway and immediately turned off the phone. She figured that even if MI6 were able to trace the phone's location by any chance - which she seriously doubted if it was a 'burner' phone - then from that very brief time she'd switched it on there was at least a chance that they might assume someone had merely stolen it from their agent, gone to Arches, and tried to use it. A tourist, perhaps, and even when MI6 did eventually discover that he was dead maybe they would simply assume that the phone had been taken from his dead body by some opportunist tourist passer-by.

She didn't recognise the voice that answered of course, but she was very familiar with the procedure and that monotone tone and phrase of response. It was definitely an agent's contact at MI6 – almost an MI6 'helpline' for agents in trouble, or at least facing what the Agency liked to refer to as, 'difficulties' or 'a 'problem'. She knew and recognised it because she had been familiarised with it herself when on missions, along with being issued a 'burner' phone. It was part of her training, and she'd even had recourse to use it a couple of times.

"Fuck, all this was supposed to have ended," she muttered quietly as she put the phone back in her pocket. She would dispose of it with the gun and the silencer, although separately. She flushed the toilet, just in case any woman was waiting outside to use it and had any doubt about what she'd been doing in there. Then she took another deep breath, uttered another quiet, "Fuck it," to herself, followed by, "A drink, I need another bloody drink." She opened the cubicle door to be confronted by a young English woman who had, indeed, been waiting. "About bloody time," she told Aileen as she brushed past and into the cubicle.

Aileen glared at her, but never bothered to respond. She'd had enough confrontation for one night. She walked quickly across the courtyard, waited for the outer sound lock door to be opened, and then headed inside for a final Gin and Tonic. As she made her way through the busy clubbing clientele towards the bar opposite the door she spotted the couple she been talking to in Pal's earlier, James and Katy. She went over to them to say hello, not least to add further to any alibi she may need later, and the guy insisted on buying her a drink. As she relaxed with them over the next hour - chatting, listening to the music and watching the clubbing dancers - she couldn't help thinking once again that at least there was one thing she was sure of from her evening's experiences. She definitely hadn't lost her nerve or her skills learned over the past twenty years.

The following afternoon she overheard what she took as verbal confirmation of that self-belief. She was relaxing on Pallas Beach after the stress of the night before. At the point of dozing off for a short nap after a swim she was disturbed and couldn't help but overhear a middle-aged English woman, and what she presumed was her husband, seated on nearby sunbeds speaking quite loudly to a similar English couple on the beds in front of them. She didn't hear the first part of the conversation, but what she did hear reassured her.

"They think he was drunk. That's what the woman serving in the supermarket told me this morning. It's slippery on the path up there and uneven, and there's not much light there at night apparently. That's what she said. She said she heard the police think he had too much to drink, fell down a few steps up there in the dark and hit his head on the stone path. She said one of the local women from the village, a cleaner in one of the bars apparently who lives in that part of the village towards the top, she found him early this morning on her way to work. She told the woman in the supermarket that there was a lot of blood on the path and on a wall. So, it sounds like he must have stumbled and then hit his head on there as well. Drunk and dazed, I guess. You have to be careful here with the paths, especially in the dark up there. There's not much lighting. Sad though, dying like that and on holiday."

Feeling reassured from overhearing that Aileen Regan drifted off into a warm and contented Lindos Pallas Beach slumber, although she knew there would be repercussions when MI6 back in London heard their operative had been killed. Her efforts at the scene of his death to make it look like an accident might fool the local Rhodes police, but she knew it wouldn't fool the Agency back in London. She knew how they operated from her nearly twenty years as an agent, infiltrating the Service for the IRA. They would most likely send another of their assets, an agent stationed somewhere nearby, to try again and finish the job. She may have been able to relax into a comfortable warm sleep on Pallas Beach at that time, but she knew she would have to leave Lindos, and Rhodes, quickly, soon, in the next day or so hopefully.

Actually though she didn't do that, not in the next day or so anyway. She had met an English guy in Lindos in June when she was on holiday there with Sandra Weston, and they had an affair, but subsequently she ended it and left him when they were back in England. She intended to leave Lindos on Tuesday 16th, although she hadn't finalised where to. On the Monday evening by chance she bumped into the same guy when she went into Jack Constantino's Courtyard Bar, He'd just returned to Lindos after a couple of weeks back in London, having spent most of the summer so far in Lindos. They ended up sleeping together that night and spent all day on Tuesday together at the Lindos Memories Hotel beach, where she persuaded Martin Cleverley to leave Lindos with her the next day, Wednesday 17th, for Crete.

Later, in the afternoon of that same day, the 17th, back at the River House in London the Mediterranean Section Head Director, Tom Fortescue, took a call that he really didn't want to get from a Supervisor in his Section.

"We lost him, sir, the operative, and lost her. He's been found dead in Lindos on Rhodes, and she's disappeared completely as far as we can see."

"How?" Fortescue asked curtly.

"We lost contact with him on Saturday night. The last contact was around three on Sunday morning from his 'burner' phone. But when our guy at the emergency contact desk at River House answered and asked if there was a problem, as per standard procedure, he, presuming it was our operative, just hung up. The report our people at the Embassy in Athens picked up from our Vice-Consulate on Rhodes was that an unknown individual, believed to be a tourist, was found dead in Lindos on Rhodes early on Sunday morning. Apparently local police enquiries in that village suggest he's a Brit. The Rhodes Vice-Consulate forwarded a photo of the deceased that they managed to get from them on the grounds that if he was a British person they may have been able to help with identification. One of our people in the Vice-Consulate sent it through to the Med Section, and it was passed to me in the belief it would be of interest to us, which, of course, it is, sir. It's not pretty, but it's definitely our man from Athens unfortunately."

"Any indication at all from our person in the Vice-Consulate that they have any idea what happened?" Fortescue asked.

"Not really, sir. He said that the local police seem to think it was an accident. After our Vice-Consulate contact confirmed to the Rhodes police after he got the photo that the victim was British they told him that the guy was pissed and first impressions at the scene were that he fell down on some rough steps and an uneven path in a dark part of the village cracking his head open and breaking his nose. The local Rhodes Police Inspector, Papadoulis, is apparently digging around, suggesting it may not have been an accident. He's not convinced it was our source at the Vice-Consulate is hearing from his Rhodes police contact. Obviously, the local police are not aware of all the facts and circumstances like we are, but it definitely sounds like the handiwork and m.o of our former Agent, our 'friend' Aileen Regan, sir. Too much of a coincidence I think, given that's who he was sent there to find and eliminate."

"Yes, seems pretty certain. Leave it with me. We need to clean up the mess quickly, which means stopping the local police and this Inspector Papadoulis digging around too much and trying to find who the victim, our guy, was and what he was doing there. I'll get on to the British Ambassador to the

Hellenic Republic, the British Ambassador to Greece, Peter Stanhope, Sir Peter Stanhope, to give him his full title. Used to work in this Section many years ago, know him well. Err ... erm ... anyway, I'll tell him we need to halt the police investigation and get the guy's body back to the U.K. straightaway. As the British Ambassador I'm sure he will be able to pull a few strings with the Hellenic Police Chief in Athens. I'll suggest Peter points out to him that it was obviously an accident and we don't want it getting back to the guy's family in the U.K. that he was so pissed; all too embarrassing and unnecessary in their hour of grief, etc. Not sure if he even has a family, but that should do it."

"Yes, sir," the Section Supervisor agreed.

Fortescue wasn't finished though.

"But what about bloody Regan? You said she's disappeared, gone from Lindos and Rhodes?"

"Yes, sir, unfortunately, gone without trace. We didn't have anyone else, any other operatives, on the ground on Rhodes. Even the dead guy came from Athens. She could still be in Greece, but we've no idea, so can't be sure."

"Bugger!" Fortescue exclaimed. "It'll be like trying to find a needle in a haystack now she's got wind we're looking for her. All we can do is put out a bulletin with a photo from our files and her description to all our operatives in and around the Med and as many places elsewhere we have any clue that she may have scuttled off to. I'm not hopeful though. She may have slipped away from us completely. But the Agency never stops looking, so maybe one day.

"Yes, sir, I'll get that bulletin sorted, and as you said, maybe one day we'll find her and get her."

One of the key things Aileen Regan knew and fully understood about MI6 was that they never stop looking. So, six years later they thought they had at last found her. Tom Fortescue was in his last year as Mediterranean Section Director before retirement. He could barely believe their luck when his P.A. informed him in mid-afternoon that the Section Supervisor wanted to see him urgently about Aileen Regan. They had been looking for her for six years, constantly hampered by cuts in their operational budgets year on year and ever decreasing limited resources. Fortescue told his P.A. to inform the Section Supervisor to come to his office straightaway. He had barely got through the door when Fortescue, standing in front of his large mahogany and dark green leather inlaid desk, asked, "What have you got?"

"Can I take a seat, sir?" the Supervisor asked.

"Yes, yes, of course," he replied and walked around to sit in his own large comfortable leather chair behind the desk before saying bluntly, "So?"

"Regan, sir, it's about Regan, although it seems she's using the name O'Mara these days, Kathleen O'Mara."

"And?"

"A source of ours on Rhodes reported to his contact in our Section that Aileen Regan had been spotted at Rhodes Airport Arrivals at noon today. The source checked with the taxi driver who he saw pick her and two other women up at the airport and the driver told him that he dropped them at a hotel just outside Lindos, the Lindos Memories. The source checked with someone he knows at the hotel and the three women checked in under the names Alison Lees, Suzanne Carmichael and Kathleen O'Mara. His hotel contact said O'Mara was the only Irish one, the other two are both English."

Fortescue got up from his chair and walked around to lean against the corner of his desk above the Supervisor in his chair as he asked with an element of circumspection in his voice, "Just how sure is this source that it's her? How reliable is he?"

"His contact in our Section said he's usually very reliable, sir, has given us plenty of good info."

"And that it's her? How sure is he of that?"

"The source said her hair is definitely different from the photo in the bulletin we sent out six years ago, short and blonde now, whereas it was long and dark back then, but he recognised her facially from the photo. According to what he told his Section contact the source couldn't be hundred per cent certain, but he said he's pretty certain it's her."

There was a distinctive trace of satisfaction in his voice as Fortescue replied.

"Let's hope he's right. I knew she'd surface eventually. We've been bloody looking for her for six years since she killed

Weston and then our agent looking for her in Lindos on Rhodes not long after. I was determined to find her, get her, before I retire, a perfect retirement present to myself."

He nodded slightly briefly as he instructed the Section Supervisor to, "Get one of our best assets from Athens to deal with it, deal with her, straightaway. And this time make sure they do it right and don't get killed by her in some sort of supposed bloody 'accident'."

"It was six years ago though, sir, so-"

He didn't allow the Section Supervisor to finish. Fortescue's pleasure over what he'd been told had quickly turned to an element of anger at his instruction being questioned.

"What's that got to do with it?" It's on my record here. It's a question of National Security. The Service will be a laughing stock if what she did six years ago, killing one of our former and then current operatives and getting away, ever by any chance gets out into the public domain. Not good for the Service at all, and not good for the government in terms of security. We will look stupid. Take her out now, immediately, before she disappears again. She probably thinks the trail has gone cold seeing as six years has passed, but the Service never forgets and never gives up."

He repeated his instruction. His firm voice made it sound even more like a clear order.

"Just get on and send one of our best operatives now and make sure they get the job done this time. Never forget, revenge is a dish best served cold."

15

The Bhoys (loyalty)

"Hi Kathleen, we wanted it to be a birthday surprise nearer the time, but Ali said I should check first that you can come before I go ahead and confirm it so-"

"Confirm what, Suzy?"

"I've got a deal for the three of us, you, me, and Ali, through one of my clients at the company. Five days, four nights in the sun at a Mitsis Hotel on Rhodes. It's one of the clients we do marketing for and they have some link with the Mitsis group. They got me a really good discount. Well, I suppose strictly speaking, darling, it's a discount for me and Ali because we decided we should pay for you to come. It'll be a birthday gift from both of us."

"Wow, yes, erm ... err ... wow! But I really can't let you two-"

"Yes, you can dear. We insist. It's the 2nd July to the 6th. So, we'll be there for your birthday on the third. I couldn't really get to choose the hotel, just took what the client said he could get a good discount on for us. Looks good though, beautiful setting, nice beach, two pools, officially it's classed as what the Greek say is a four-and-a-half star, and at that time of year the weather will be nice and hot."

"Well, yes, sounds great Suzy, but it's only a month away, just less, and what about work; the three of us being away at the same time?"

"All sorted, darling. Spoke to Tony Evans and he's fine with it as it's only five days, and two of those are the weekend. He may be our boss, but you know he has a soft spot for me, and that means I can twist him around my little finger. I think he actually has a thing for you too, so when I told him it was for your birthday he wasn't going to say no was he?"

"Where is it though, Suzy? Where on Rhodes?"

"Lindos, Lindos Memories Hotel. Check out the hotel website, looks great. I checked out the flights too, and no problem getting on B.A. to Rhodes from Heathrow. So, come on Kathleen, it's not every day your forty-four, just say yes and I'll get on to my clients and get them to book it for us so we can get the discount. We can celebrate your birthday in style there in the sun, and with a few nice cocktails."

"Err ... yes ... I suppose that would be nice but ... erm, won't it be a bit hot at that time of year there?"

"Hope so, that's what we're going for isn't it? Get away from all this bloody rain here."

"Yes, I suppose so."

Suzanne Carmichael was picking up that Kathleen's voice wasn't exactly exuding unbridled enthusiasm.

"Ali and me thought you'd be pleased, a nice surprise birthday present for you, maybe even a little excited? You don't sound very ... you been there before? Is it not very good, not very nice, Lindos?"

"No, no, I haven't, why would you think that? I'm sure it's very nice."

"Just you going on about the heat that's all."

"Everyone knows Greece is bloody hot in July and August, that's all."

She took a deep breath, then trying to sound more positive added, "But I'm sure it'll be fine. Thank you both so much. I'll look forward to it. It'll be great; sun and cocktails with two good friends. I'm sure the three of us will talk about it lots in work and over a few drinks before we go. So, yes, thank you."

"I'll get on to my clients and sort it then, and the three of us can go and see Tony together in work, use our charm, just in case he changes his mind."

Kathleen let out a slight laugh before Suzanne said, "Bye, see you in work tomorrow. We can go for lunch with Ali and start planning four nights of partying and sun."

She may have let out a small laugh as the call ended, but inside she wasn't anywhere near so relaxed about her surprise birthday present from her two friends. It certainly wasn't the July Rhodes heat she was worried about. She had another, much darker, reason not to go back to Lindos. Her initial reaction was worry, worry that someone there might recognise her.

As she poured herself a glass of white wine she tried to rationalise and control her fears. It had been six years. She didn't look the same. She'd made some changes to her appearance, her hair colour, style and length. It was short and blonde now, not dark and long as it was back then. And she was six years older, so .... maybe she was simply worrying unduly. And anyway, what if someone did recognised her? What would that mean? So, there was a death there six years ago. So what? Everyone said it was an accident didn't they, even the Greek police eventually came to that conclusion, that verdict. She knew that. So, why would anyone in Lindos connect her with an accidental death there six years ago, even if they did recognise her?

She sat back on her comfortable sofa, lifted both her legs up on to it, drank her wine, poured another large glass, and had convinced herself she was worrying unduly. Suzanne Carmichael and Alison Lees were relatively new friends of hers; friends through work over the past two years. Their friendships developed over a number of long after work drink evenings, as well as theatre and cinema visits, and weekend visits to a few spas. After all, it was very generous of them to buy her such a lovely birthday present. She should just go, would just go to Lindos, and enjoy herself and her birthday with her two friends in the village and in the comfort of the Lindos Memories Hotel. No one there could possibly connect her with the MI6 guy's accidental death. They hadn't then, so why would they now, six years later? She hadn't even told Martin Cleverley the full truth about her background, and certainly nothing about her killing the MI6 agent – his 'accidental' death - sent to Lindos to find her in August 2016.

When Aileen Regan told Martin Cleverley in Lindos in August 2016 about her background as an MI6 agent for the past twenty years - something he subsequently relayed to Inspector Yiannis Papadoulis on Crete six years later - she was being economical with the truth. She deliberately never told him the full story. She omitted one crucial fact.

It was true that she had operated as an MI6 agent, ostensibly at least. She'd been recruited to MI6 near the end of the first year of her media studies degree in 1997 at Bristol University by a student on the same course, Sandra Weston. Sandra had deliberately developed what she thought was a deep student friendship with her throughout that first year. She'd been recruited herself into the British Secret Service a year before, having been identified by them while still in her private school sixth form as having the right attitudes and political beliefs for possible recruitment and training as an MI6 operative. In fact, it was one of the teachers at her school – a Secret Service contact and associate – who identified her and recommended her. She was already very active and prominent in the Young Conservatives group in the school, and the Conservative Association locally. She was very vocal in both those arenas in her support for Britain and British, particularly English, nationalism. She hated the Irish with venom that was unusual in a seventeen year old. That had its origins in her family British military background. At that time, in the mid-nineties, MI6 was developing a programme of identification and recruitment of exceptional young people with what Sandra's teacher described as, "the right sense of patriotism". Apparently she was one of those young people. Their role and purpose was to infiltrate the student movement at various key universities, identify like-minded sympathetic students, and change the political climate and agenda within the student body.

Despite her southern Irish origins and distinct accent Aileen Regan quickly became Sandra's prime target and she keenly cultivated their friendship during that first year. They became inseparable. Sandra pursued her aim carefully and slowly, just as she had been coached and advised to do by what was by then her MI6 handler. She occasionally made a few carefully placed right-wing politically loaded remarks throughout that first year, just to test the water. Aileen always appeared receptive and in agreement, even when Sandra was deliberately scathing about Irish nationalism. She was from Bantry Bay in West Cork, often referred to as 'bandit country', but Aileen never betrayed any indication to Sandra that she disagreed with anything derogatory that Sandra said on the subject of Irish nationalism.

So, by late March 1997, after various consultations with her handler and numerous MI6 investigations and background checks on Aileen, Sandra was given the official go-ahead by her handler to put the suggestion of MI6 recruitment to Aileen. It turned out to be not at all difficult or awkward. She was very receptive, even though she feigned some surprise initially and then a little apprehension.

What Sandra didn't have a clue about at the time was precisely the same thing that Aileen omitted telling Martin Cleverley on that night in Lindos in August 2016; that all along it was the aim of Kathleen O'Mara, in the guise of Aileen Regan, to allow, and even provoke Sandra to recruit her for MI6. Kathleen's true allegiances certainly never resided with the British State, let alone MI6. They lay elsewhere. In fact, her purpose and mission was to infiltrate that organisation as a 'sleeper' for her Irish nationalist heritage and the IRA, of which she had been a secret member since she was sixteen. In that aim she was successful, thanks to Sandra Weston. Aileen maintained that deceit for almost twenty years, including within her continuing supposed friendship with Sandra.

Her fierce support for the Irish Nationalist cause, and hatred of the British Security Services, particularly Sandra Weston, increased even more so when it was revealed to her by the bhoys in 2004 that they had a good source confirming that the assassination by MI6 in 2002 of the Irish man she knew as her father was coordinated in MI6 by Sandra Weston. At that time she knew him as her father simply because he was married to her mother, although it stated on her birth certificate, 'Father unknown'. She had asked her mother about that a number of times before she died, but got no explanation. Later, after his and her mother's death, she discovered he was, in fact, her step-father. That didn't make his assassination any less painful. Kathleen was always both of them's daughter, not just her mother's. It was that way in the Ireland of that time.

Kathleen was told by the bhoys that their informant told them that it was definitely Sandra who had set up the killing of her step-father. Because of Kathleen's false identity and name as Aileen Regan, Sandra had no idea that it was her step-father. There had been a bombing in a part of Belfast. Kathleen was convinced that although they had no clues or evidence as to who was responsible the British Security Service was determined to have a sacrificial lamb, even though there was clear evidence her step-father was nowhere near the bombing. The evidence, and his alibi, was there plainly for them to see, but they hid it. Then Sandra Weston let loose one of their death squads on him, even though it was five years after the Good Friday Peace Agreement. Because of that it was all kept quiet under the Official Secrets Act. Even though Kathleen, as Aileen, was working for MI6 at the time, or at least they thought she was, it was all kept so tight security-wise that she never even got a sniff of it, and nor did many people at all, except for Sandra and those close to her in her team, her Section. She was right at the heart of it, coordinated it all, according to the bhoys. Because of the sensitivity of it being well after the peace agreement Sandra kept it all to herself and her tight, small MI6 team, which Aileen wasn't part of at that time. All she understood at the time was that the man she knew as her father had committed suicide. Such was her undercover identity that she could not even attend his funeral, for fear of that being discovered by MI6. The Bhoys made sure she kept away, as she was ordered to do.

Just before Christmas 2015 Kathleen, as Aileen, finally embarked on a mission she was given by the bhoys to secure the ultimate complete revenge for herself, as well as for the bhoys, on Sandra and MI6. It was an act of personal revenge for her that she'd worked towards as an IRA infiltrator. The vehicle initially for that was her affair with Sandra's arrogant womaniser husband, Richard Weston. The overall aim was to destabilise Sandra psychologically by destroying her already fragile marriage, and then discredit her professional reputation with MI6. It was revenge for the bhoys after all the problems and troubles Sandra had unleashed on them as an agent in the 'Irish Section' of MI6 over the years. That revenge was twenty years in the making, beginning with Kathleen befriending Sandra at university as Aileen, and eventually allowing her to recruit her to MI6. Finally, the plan required Aileen being eventually revealed as an IRA infiltrator after she had disappeared, one recruited by Sandra, which would ultimately in turn discredit Sandra professionally within MI6, and ruin her professional life as well as her personal one.

Aileen decided all of that, her IRA infiltration of MI6, was best kept to herself. Consequently, she only told Martin Cleverley part of the truth that night in Lindos in August 2016; the part about her being a former MI6 agent, as well as that it was her final mission for them to embark on an affair with Richard Weston. She dressed the affair up as part of an MI6 operation to discover if he was a Russian agent. There was no such operation, not an official MI6 one anyway. It was her personal mission of revenge on Sandra. Aileen never told Martin that either, as well as nothing at all about being an IRA infiltrator of MI6. She never even hinted at it. Not least because she never wanted to get Martin dragged into any of that stuff in her background, and most of all because she always remembered what her IRA handler, Michael – she never knew nor wanted to know his surname, and was certain that Michael wasn't even his real first name – she always remembered what Michael told her when she told him killing Sandra would be her last job for the bhoys. She was quitting.

"It's about loyalty for the bhoys, Kathleen you know that. So, you know you can never leave, don't you? It might be many years that have gone by, but if they need you they will pull you back in, at anytime, anywhere. You know too much about the organisation. Don't forget that, and don't, whatever you do, do anything stupid, even accidentally or inadvertently, that might threaten the organisation and the people still operating in it. For your own safety."

Almost six years later, in the third week of June 2022, Michael's words, "if they need you they will pull you back in," came back to haunt her.

"Kathleen, it's Michael."

"Yes, I saw, your name came up on my phone screen, Michael."

"Still got my number in there then, in your phone. Wasn't sure your number would be the same after six years. Thought you would maybe have changed it."

"Yes, Michael, yours is still in my phone contacts, and no, I haven't changed this number. Why would I? Back then six years ago only you as my handler and a couple of the other bhoys contacts were the only people who had this number. So, there was no danger of anyone contacting me who I didn't want to. This phone and number was only for work for the bhoys. Missions or operations, wasn't that what you used to call them? Got quite a few more numbers in it now though, Michael. Got quite a few more friends in the real world."

He ignored all that and simply asked with a certain lilting charm in his voice, "So, how you been keeping, Kathleen. How's you?"

His broad West Cork Irish accent instantly made his question sound insincere. That was hardly the effect he was aiming for.

"Cut the blarney, Michael. What do you want? It's been six years and now suddenly you call me out of the blue. I'm not stupid. There must be something you and the bhoys want."

He chuckled slightly down the line.

"Jesus, Kathleen, you've not changed. Still as blunt as ever, and at the same time as sharp as a kitchen knife in O'Connors in Bantry."

"Stop with the West Cork charm. You know it doesn't work on me, never has, never will. Look, Michael, get to the point, what do you want, or really I'm thinking what is it the bhoys want of me, from me, after all this time?"

He let out another slight chuckle down the line.

"Well do you remember what I told you when you quit? That for the bhoys it's all about loyalty. So, you can never leave. I told you that it might be many years that go by, but if they need you they will pull you back in, at anytime, anywhere."

She stayed silent. She knew for certain what was coming, what he was going to say next. She'd actually been expecting it all the time, at any time over the past six years. Eventually, after a ten second or so pause he broke the silence with the words she hoped she'd never hear.

"Kathleen? You still there?"

"Yes," was all she replied, and waited.

He tried to use his charm again, or what he thought was his charm.

"It's Hotel California time for you, Kathleen. You know what that means don't you?"

"What, Michael? What are you on about?"

"You know, Kathleen, surely you do, know the song, or the line in it anyway. You can check out any time you like but you can never leave. That 'anytime, anywhere' that I told you about six years ago is now."

"Yes, very interesting, Michael, thanks for the culture and popular music lesson. I see. Time for what? What do they want me to do?"

"I knew you'd see sense. I told the bhoys you would. You ruffled a few feathers you know, upset a few of the bhoys, with the actions of your rogue private vendetta against the Weston woman, and then when you took out that MI6 agent on Rhodes who came looking for you, Lindos wasn't it?"

She never answered, said nothing.

"Don't get me, or the bhoys wrong, Kathleen, the Weston woman had it coming. We all agreed on that. That's why she was on the hit list, and you wanted it remember, wanted to be the one to do it. When I told you it was all set up and ready to go, you asked me to ask the Bhoys to let you be the one to do it. But an affair with her fucking husband, that was another thing altogether. That wasn't authorised by the bhoys was it? That was part of your personal vendetta against her. And then especially what you did to that MI6 guy on Rhodes. That was unauthorised too wasn't it, and after you'd quit from us."

This time she did say something.

"That was self-preservation, Michael. What was I supposed to do? He was going to kill me. That's what he was sent there for. Unauthorised? You said yourself I'd quit. I wasn't even an operative, an agent for the bhoys any more at the time. Was I supposed to ask the MI6 goon to hang on while I got a chitty from the bhoys, who I didn't work for any fucking more, before I killed him. He had a bloody gun to my temple. I got lucky. He fell backwards on a loose part of the path, and I did what I had to do to survive. That's what I was trained to do for twenty bloody years remember, trained by the bhoys to do and sodding MI6; trained in self-preservation, and I survived."

"Ok, Kathleen calm down. I'm just telling you that what you did on your own imitative with the affair with Weston's husband which wasn't in the mission at all, and then killing the MI6 agent in Lindos, ok having to kill him to survive, ruffled a few feathers and upset some of the bhoys. There were repercussions Kathleen, particularly from the Rhodes incident. We didn't have many people on Rhodes at the time, just three 'sleeper' agents living there for a while, taking a bit of a break. Good people. And after what happened to the guy MI6 sent looking for you MI6 sent a couple more. You'd gone before they got there, but we lost one of our 'sleepers' when they took their anger and revenge out on him."

"Oh, I didn't-" she started to say with a lot more contrition in her voice.

He, and the bhoys, wanted her to do something for them so his tone changed to a more conciliatory one at that time as he interrupted her. He'd made his, and the bhoys', point. Given her something to owe them for, to be in debt to them for.

"Ok, you didn't know? Why would you, Kathleen? How could you? You'd quit by then, as you said, and it was about self-preservation with the MI6 guy. I told the bhoys it would be something like that; him trying to kill you and self-preservation on your part. You wouldn't even have known at the time that we had three 'sleepers' living on Rhodes. You know that's how we operate, on a need to know basis, particularly where our other agents are concerned. And you only went there searching some of your family history anyway, didn't you."

"Yes, that's true, Michael. I didn't, I didn't know about any agents on Rhodes, any 'sleepers'. But how do you know that's why I went to Rhodes and Lindos. I just told you I was quitting. I didn't say I was going to trace my family history and go to Rhodes?"

He practically ignored her question. Only gave her a half answer at best, and then changed the focus of her thought process. It was what he'd been well trained to do.

"We have our ways of knowing these things, Kathleen, our sources. We had three 'sleepers' there remember, and you were spotted, one of our people picked up why you were there. Anyway, yes the bhoys weren't over happy with you back then six years ago when you quit and that incident in Lindos occurred, but it was partly because they don't like to let the good ones go easily, and I told them, Kathleen, told them you're one of the best."

"Thanks, Michael."

That was when he got to the heart of what his call was really about. He'd softened her up a little with all that previous talk. Now he'd get to the point.

"Yes, I told them then that you were one of the best, right up there when it came to completing missions, following orders, eliminating people for the cause, supporting the struggle. And I told them recently that I knew you would still be now, one of the best, right up there. You don't lose those sorts of talents, Kathleen. You were a good learner and you continued to hone your skills on what you did."

She waited, let him talk. She knew this was just him softening her up, flannelling her even, to get her to agree to whatever they wanted her to do.

"That's why I told them you'd do this for us, Kathleen. It's simple, straightforward, no killing involved. I'm sure you could do it with your eyes closed. I told the bhoys that when I suggested you."

She was stifling a slight laugh. In reality she knew a lot of that was bullshit, but his West Cork charm and flannel had calmed her down and got her mood to precisely where he wanted it.

"So, come on then, Michael, you've done the prelim stuff, suggested me for what? What do they want me to do that is so simple and straightforward? And no killing you said?"

He still didn't answer her question directly

"A little bird told me you're taking a trip soon. Going back to Rhodes and Lindos they said."

Although she began to feel a little uneasy again that he knew that, and was wondering who from, she tried to make a joke of it, playing him at his own game, trying to loosen him up and perhaps give away something that would be a clue for her to figure out who it was that he found about her trip from.

"You sure it was a little bird, Michael, and not a leprechaun?"

"Could have been, Kathleen, could well have been. There's a lot of them about these days, leprechauns."

He wasn't giving anything away at all so she just told him, "Yes, the little bird or the leprechaun, or whoever, told you, was right."

He surprised her even more by adding, "For five nights isn't it, with two friends from work for five nights?"

It wasn't really a question. He knew that was the case. She didn't want to give away her bewilderment over how he knew so much about it so she didn't respond.

"Beginning of July, the second, should be nice, Kathleen, nice and hot, and who knows maybe you'll see some old friends there and catch up with them."

Now she was really worried. What exactly did he mean by, "old friends". Perhaps agreeing to the trip wasn't such a good idea after all. She still decided to play it cool, or at least try to.

"Perhaps, Michael, yes, perhaps I will."

"That'll be nice, Kathleen, after six long years."

There was clear sarcastic edge in his voice. She'd had enough of his game playing.

"Look, Michael, yes I'm going to Lindos, yes going back for five nights from the second of July with two friends from work. It's a birthday present from them. Now just bloody tell me what you and the bhoys want from me now and stop playing your games. Is all this about me going back to Lindos really just your West Cork bandit country idea of small talk or is there some point to it? Because if it is what you think of as small talk in that part of the old country we both come from I can tell you it's bloody crap. Was crap when I grew up there and heard similar shit from plenty of pissed 'Mick bayturs' in the pubs and bars on Friday and Saturday nights thinking they could tell me a few pleasantries and that would get them into my knickers. And it's even more crap now I'm older and wiser. So, what the bloody hell do you want? I know you've not suddenly called me after six years to talk to be about my birthday break. Credit me with some intelligence, Michael. I was in and around the organisation for twenty years feeding the bhoys stuff from MI6. I'm not fucking stupid. I know how this works. So just tell me, and no killing. I'm not doing that any bloody more. I've had enough of it, even for the bhoys."

Now she was very angry and she was letting it show. He'd rattled her and he knew it. He tried to add one more attempted light hearted comment, just to keep her off balance.

"Why do you think this about me wanting to get in your knickers, Kathleen? We know you've let a few in the past, like that Cleverley guy, and of course, Richard Weston, but-"

He'd tipped her over the edge. He'd been her IRA handler for the bhoys for over ten years before she quit, so he knew exactly how to 'push her buttons', what got her mad and destabilised. He'd certainly done that.

"Fuck you, Michael! Tell me right now what you and the bhoys want me to do or I'm hanging up right now."

"Ok, ok, just calm down, Kathleen. It's very simple. You're going to Rhodes, to Lindos on holiday soon, in around a month, and when we found out that we thought it was just a perfect opportunity for you to do something for us that we need doing."

"Michael!"

"Yes, yes, ok Kathleen. As I said it's not killing. There's no killing involved. Look, we've still got two 'sleeper' operatives there 'resting', in a small place called Lardos, near to Lindos, not that far from the hotel you'll be in. So, it's just a courier job, Kathleen. The bhoys want you to a take a package to Rhodes for the one of the operatives when you go on your holiday."

There was a short silence. She was obviously thinking over what she'd been asked, probably told, to do. In reality, she knew she didn't have a choice, but she wanted to know more.

"Kathleen?"

"Yes, Michael, I'm still here."

"It's just a small package Kathleen, quite small. All you've got to do is take it to Lindos with you and you'll be contacted the first night you arrive for someone to pick it up. That's all. It's simple enough. You don't need to know anything more, honestly you don't."

"What's in it, Michael? Not anything that's going to get me stopped and searched at security at Heathrow or at Rhodes airport is it? Am I being set up here? Something you're not telling me?"

"No, you're not being set up at all. It's quite small. Put it in your case for the hold of the plane. It won't be flagged up as a security risk when it goes through the scanner for that, because it isn't. I presume you'll be taking a bag or a case to check-in?"

"I wasn't intending to. It's only five nights, four days, but it appears I am now going to have to. Might make the other girls raise their eyebrows, but ..."

"Ok, do that then, Kathleen. It'll fit in your case easily, won't take up any room at all."

"So, come on, Michael, what's in this package that me and B.A. are going to be transporting?"

"Better you don't know. As I said it's only small. One of our people will drop it off to your place the day before you go. Thanks, Kathleen. The bhoys will appreciate it. It'll earn you some 'brownie points' back with them, help them forget and forgive what you did back in 2016 off radar and all the repercussions from that."

She wasn't happy that, from what he said about someone dropping the package off to her place, he obviously knew where she lived. But he'd diverted her from any concern about that again back onto the issue of what happened back in 2016. She took the bait.

"Look, Michael, I told you, that was-"

She was determined not to leave the 2016 stuff the way the bhoys, and obviously Michael, really saw it. But, having used that to successfully divert her away from any concern she may have had over him knowing where she lived he wasn't really going to let her go on any more about 2016 and what happened. His voice got softer and his Irish brogue was prominent once again as, typically for him, he told her a piece of information that appeared at first to be completely unrelated to what they'd been talking about, completely off the subject. She'd heard him do exactly the same thing quite a few times in the past as her handler. There was always eventually a relevant point to it. This time was no exception.

"Do you know anything about bridges, Kathleen? About building bridges?"

"What? No, of course not. What's that got to do with anything, Michael, to do with me and the bhoys?"

"Bridges exist, remain standing, through a never ending struggle between tension and compression, with the two sides constantly pulling away from each other. So, someone, the overall designer, has to manage the demands of those two opposing forces, two opposing sides, or the bridge would buckle or collapse completely."

"All very interesting, Michael, is that your hobby?"

Now it was her turn to be sarcastic. He was serious though, deadly serious and trying to make a serious point to her.

"Had no idea you were an engineer. Thanks for the insight."

She continued to sarcastically dismiss what he presumably was trying to get at, warn her about.

He totally ignored her sarcasm and just continued.

"So, some tension is clearly important in keeping a stable structure together, but just not too much, Kathleen."

Then he got to his point and his voice got much, much firmer.

"And that's life in our organisation. Tension has to be balanced between sides, between operatives, between us handlers and operatives, our agents, for the good of the cause. Consequently, some tension is good in order to maintain the structure and the aims of the organisation, the cause, the struggle, so long as it's balanced."

There was an edge to his voice, louder and clear menace, as he added, "That's what people like me do, Kathleen. What people like me in the organisation are here for. To manage the tension and keep the structure of the organisation stable for the bhoys. We don't like unscheduled, unauthorised, off radar rogue actions by operatives. That leads to chaos and mayhem, and always unpleasant and unfortunate repercussions which usually cost people their lives, some of our operatives, good people, good assets for the cause. You know what I mean don't you, Kathleen? What you did back in 2016."

She remained silent. She knew from his tone of voice, and her past experience of him being her handler for a long time, that now was not the time to say anything. That would not be wise at all.

After a few seconds he added, "So, be careful, Kathleen. You only get one chance in the organisation. We all do, including me. You had yours back then in 2016 when you made those veiled threats to me when you told me you wanted to quit or else. That was what you said remember. Then went and did what you did off-script.."

All she could say in a serious and solemn voice was, "Ok, Michael. I hear what you're saying. Thanks."

"Good, just don't forget it, Kathleen. Be aware of all those around you in Lindos, and trust no one. I'll keep my ear to the ground, keep in contact with one of our 'sleepers' in Lardos beforehand and while you're there in Lindos, just in case they get any sniff that someone has recognised you or there's anything they pick up about you and the death of the MI6 guy six years ago."

With that the line went dead.

She immediately guessed that the package she had to deliver must contain drugs or cash, but if it was so small it wouldn't take up much space at all in her suitcase why was it so important? It couldn't be a very large amount of either.

The afternoon before she was leaving for Rhodes and Lindos the package was delivered by a motorcyclist at her door. They deliberately never removed their helmet or lifted up the visor, nor even spoke. So, there was no chance of her identifying him or her, It was, indeed, not very large at all, less than six inches by six inches and around two inches deep. As she was only going to be there for four days and five nights she wasn't intending to take a lot of clothes anyway, especially given that it would be hot during the day and still warm at night. So, the package was easy to fit in her case.

Suzanne Carmichael and Alison Lees did raise their eyebrows in surprise when she turned up at Heathrow and needed to check her case in. Alison actually said, "If I'd had known you booked a case to check in I would have brought a few more things and could have put them in your case. Luckily she didn't know that, and Kathleen made some excuse about that being the smallest case she had. It wasn't exactly large, and it was by no means full, but it was too large for a 'carry on' bag. There was no problem with the checked in case at Heathrow or at Rhodes airport though. So, presuming it had gone through a scanner at either or both of those, she assumed the package wasn't drugs. Money maybe, but not a large amount obviously, and there was no way she even thought for one moment about opening it to find out when she got into her room later at the Memories Hotel. She just put it straight into the safe in the room, along with her passport, bank and credit cards, and some cash.

Despite his threat and warning on his call to her just under a month or so before that she would only get one chance, as her handler Michael kept his word about 'watching her back' by letting her know if he heard anything about anyone recognising her while she was in Lindos. At least he thought he was 'watching her back' when he tried to call her twice early on Saturday morning, at six-fifteen and six-thirty five on the 3rd of July, by which time she was already dead. He wanted to warn her that he'd been informed by the bhoys 'sleeper' operative in Lardos that she'd been spotted and recognised when she arrived at Rhodes Airport with Alison Lees and Suzanne Carmichael the previous afternoon. When he couldn't get any answer for his six-fifteen call, on the one he made at six-thirty-five he decided to leave a short voicemail message, simply saying, "Be careful Kathleen. Is it done?" He decided it wasn't wise to leave any more detail on her phone about how she'd been recognised as he knew it wasn't a 'burner phone' and so wasn't entirely sure how secure it was. He'd try her later instead. By that time it was too late.

PART THREE

THE MURDER

16

Ημέρα τέταρτη (Day 4)

Tuesday July 5th 2022

The gloomy blackness of the nearer he got to Lardos on his Monday night drive, as well as the looming darkness of his affair with Sally Hardcastle, was replaced by bright July early sunlight and clear blue sky as he drove to Lindos on that Tuesday morning. When Papadoulis arrived in the small office at Lindos Police Station at just after eight-thirty Georgiou was already there making some coffee. He had a surprising and unexpected question as he handed one to the Inspector.

"Were you interviewing someone in Lardos about the case last night, sir? Someone from something you picked from Cleverley on Crete?"

Papadoulis was caught a little off-guard and hesitated slightly while he took a sip of his coffee.

"Err … no Sergeant, what makes you think that?"

"An officer here in the Lindos station said he thought he saw your car parked in Lardos last night."

"No, no, he must have been mistaken," the Inspector told him firmly and then quickly changed the subject.

"Here are the notes the Crete officer who sat in with me took while I talked to Cleverley yesterday. Have a look through them. See if anything jumps out at you. Quite revealing, but nothing there really points to Cleverley as our killer now his alibi checks out. Anything from Kyriakopoulis on Richard Weston?"

"Yes, he's in Moscow, sir."

"Really?" Papadoulis raised his eyebrows.

"Yes, Kyriakopoulis said the British police came straight back first thing this morning, quite a high up officer apparently, said he defected in 2017. The only other thing Kyriakopoulis could get out of them was that he'd been on the radar of the British Security Services for some time, but the British police officer said it was all classified. Kyriakopoulis said he even joked that we might be able to get access to it all, or at least some of it, in twenty-five years."

"That's interesting. Cleverley told me that Regan told him just before they left Lindos in 2016 that she worked for MI6 for twenty years and her last mission, assignment, was about Richard Weston. It's all in the Crete officer's notes. It was just before her and Sandra Weston came on holiday to Lindos in June that year. MI6 thought that Richard Weston might be getting stuff, information, through his wife, Sandra, with or without her knowledge. Part of Regan's mission was to have an affair with him, because MI6 had a tip-off that he was passing information to the Russians and-"

Georgiou interrupted, "So, they were right. Did Regan expose him then? That would be a motive for him to kill her wouldn't it?"

"No, Sergeant, they weren't right, or at least their tip-off wasn't right, at least it wasn't at that time obviously. Regan told Cleverley that she couldn't find anything suggesting Richard Weston was passing stuff to the Russians. So, the mission was stopped."

The Inspector let out a long sigh before he continued.

"So, Richard Weston isn't our killer either then, couldn't be because he's in Moscow, and I can't see him popping over from there to here to kill Regan after all this time. I was really beginning to think there was a strong possibility he could be."

Papadoulis had successfully diverted the conversation away from Georgiou's question about the Inspector's car being seen in Lardos. It hadn't though diverted, or removed, a thought about Sally Hardcastle that had been nagging away in his brain on his drive from Lardos to Lindos that morning. It was proving a dilemma for him. Why really did she ask him so many questions about the case each time they met? It could, of course, simply be that she was curious about it. However, there was something in some of her questions that started the suspicious detective part of his brain ticking over. Then there was the fact that she seemed to already know quite a few things about it, things that he hadn't told her, like the victim was an Irish woman, like he'd gone to Crete to see Martin Cleverley. No matter how much he told himself that it was all about Lindos and Lardos being small places full of rumour and gossip, and that she worked in a café in Lindos which no doubt would be a hot bed of those sort of things, he couldn't shake the smallest element of suspicion out of his mind.

Ultimately that was what was raising a dilemma for him on his drive to Lindos that bright sunny morning. He wanted to raise it with the two Sergeants, and even get Kyriakopoulis to do some background checks on her. Maybe it was nothing but her curiosity after all, but somewhere deep in the back of his brain he knew he should. His dilemma, his problem, his difficulty, was that he knew one of the two Sergeants, Georgiou certainly, and maybe even both, would ask why her; why background checks on a Sally Hardcastle? What had she got to do with the case? What was her involvement? And if they discovered, maybe in the background check itself, or through other sources, that she was living in Lardos, one of them was bound to put two and two together and connect it to his car having been seen by a Lindos officer in Lardos on Monday night. That might open up a whole 'Pandora's box' of difficult questions and issues for him. That was even worse after he got to Lindos station and lied to Georgiou in denying his car was in Lardos the night before. He also knew that police officers were notorious gossips and both the Sergeants lived in Rhodes Town. He couldn't take even the slightest risk of any talk of him being in Lardos on Monday night getting back to his wife Dimitra when he'd told her he had to stay over on Crete. That wouldn't help his current marriage difficulties at all. But then, nor would him cheating on her. So, the dilemma he couldn't remove from his brain came down to the contradiction that he knew professionally he should probably get Kyriakopoulis to do some background checks on Sally Hardcastle, but personally that might not help his marriage situation, damage his marriage even further, were any gossip about him being in Lardos on Monday night and about Sally Hardcastle to get back to Dimitra. What's more it was all beginning to weigh heavily on his conscience; the dilemma, plus at the bottom of it, what he'd been up to with Sally again.

That didn't exactly get any easier when Dimitra called him at lunchtime and asked him, almost quizzed him he thought afterwards, about Crete, particularly where did he stay on Monday night on Crete. He was deliberately evasive, telling her the local police fixed him up with a hotel in Heraklion without giving her a name of one, not least because it wasn't true of course, but also because he didn't actually know the name of one there. He never gave her the chance to ask the name, even if she intended to. Instead he just carried on speaking, explaining that he stayed over because he wanted to check out a few things on Crete which the guy he went to interview told him that were relevant to the case. She seemed convinced and told him she looked forward to seeing him later and hoped he wouldn't be too late at work.

As it turned out he soon knew he probably wouldn't be very late because of any further work on the case. His day didn't get any better at all when he got another call in the middle of that afternoon. Initially it was a female voice he heard when he took the call in the Lindos Police Station office. It really was a case of déjà vu from six years previously.

"I have Police Lieutenant General Kouris, Chief of the Hellenic Police, calling from Athens for Detective Inspector Papadoulis."

He thought it was almost word for word the opening comment of a call he took back in August 2016. Could even have been the same female voice of the same woman. It certainly was the same Chief of the Hellenic Police she was about to put him through to after he replied, "Yes, Inspector Papadoulis speaking."

"Hello Inspector Papadoulis," after short silence a very important sounding, and very formal, male voice came down the line.

"Good afternoon, sir." Now Papadoulis was wondering what exactly this call would bring. He didn't have to wait long.

"I recall we spoke about six years ago, Inspector, about the case of a death in Lindos you were investigating."

"That's right, we did, sir. I remember that well."

He did, very well in fact. Papadoulis was being polite to his superior. It wasn't what he was thinking at all.

"Now you're in charge of the investigation into the dead body of a tourist found in Gennadi on Saturday morning, I understand? An Irish woman, name of Aileen Regan I believe?"

"Yes, sir, that's correct, I am, and yes, we've ascertained that the woman was Irish, Aileen Regan, but also-"

The Inspector was about to explain about her also being known as Kathleen O'Mara, but never got the chance. It didn't appear that the Police Chief was interested at all in hearing that as he interrupted in a much firmer and even more authoritative voice.

"I understand one of your officers made some background enquiries about the victim to the British police in London in your investigation, as well as about a British married couple Richard and Sandra Weston."

"That's right, sir."

He wasn't completely certain, but based on what happened in August 2016 Papadoulis feared what he was about to be told to do, what was coming. He was right to.

"I got calls about it, your enquiries to the British Police, from the British Security Services asking why your officer was making enquiries about those people, and then from one of our government Security Ministers telling me to do whatever the British Security Services required, particularly in respect of providing them with any information we, you, had about Regan and any people she had connections with on Rhodes or in Greece generally."

"I see, sir, well, we discovered that-

Once again Papadoulis tried to explain that they'd discovered Aileen Regan was also going under the name of Kathleen O'Mara, but he was cut short once more."

"You've stirred up a real bloody hornet's nest with those background enquiries about that woman Regan, Inspector, as well as about Sandra and Richard Weston. It not only involves the British Security Services, MI6, but also the IRA."

The Inspector knew about MI6 involvement in Aileen Regan's background from what Martin Cleverley told him, but the IRA involvement was new to him. He thought it best to stay silent though and not interrupt his superior officer at that point.

"The British Security Services told me they've been looking for Regan for six years."

That was something Papadoulis surmised from what Cleverley told him, but he didn't think or know from that MI6 were looking for her for the reason the Police Chief was about to inform him of.

"That guy who died in the supposed accident in Lindos in 2016 which you were in charge of investigating was one of their operatives, an MI6 agent. They knew she was on Rhodes in 2016 and as one of the British Security Services chiefs who called me put it, 'They were anxious to interview her back then'. He didn't say why, and I didn't ask. No doubt he wouldn't have told me anyway. Their operative, the guy who died, was sent to find her. They are convinced Regan killed him and it wasn't an accident. So-"

Papadoulis decided to chance his arm and speak out. He'd not had a great day so far, what with his dilemma over Sally Hardcastle and the case, as well as his situation with his wife. What had he got to lose? He couldn't hold his tongue any longer. The long-time straight up and down, 'play it by the book' Inspector Yiannis Papadoulis was disintegrating fast.

"Well some of us did think that at the time, sir, remember, that it wasn't an accident. But interestingly at their request, the British Security Services, you shut down the investigation."

The Police Chief wasn't happy at all with that somewhat unsubtle outburst. It was fully reflected in his raised voice and strong blunt response.

"Yes, Inspector, well she's dead now so your investigation stops right now. That's an order. And send all you have on Regan to me straightaway so I can forward it to the British Security Services and brief our Security Minister. This stops now, Inspector, not least because the last thing we want in our present economic situation is any public fall out from this, her murder, damaging the tourist industry on Rhodes for the rest of the summer."

"But this is the second time I've been ordered to close a case without conclusion that involves this dead woman, sir. We've managed to discover that the victim was also known as Kathleen O'Mara, and we now know, have discovered from a reliable witness, that she at one point as Aileen Regan worked for the British Security Services for many years."

"Yes, Inspector, and that's precisely why we have to shut down the case, because she worked for them. We will never find the killer, never be allowed to find the killer and get to the bottom of it. The British Security Services have been looking for her for the past six years in connection with at least two murders, one of their agents and a former agent, possibly a lot more they told me. Yes, of course, they may have finally succeeded and found her. It may well have been them, one of their agents, who eliminated her, killed her. But we will never know, never get to the bottom of all that. Shut the case down now, Papadoulis. That's an order. If you value your career that's exactly what you'll do right now, this afternoon."

He knew he had no choice but to do as the Police Chief ordered. He had plenty of other things on his mind to struggle with, particularly his marriage, without going against the order of the highest police officer in the country and putting his career in jeopardy. And in an ironic way the Police Chief's order removed his dilemma. Carrying it out and shutting down the case meant there was no need to even consider getting Georgiou or Kyriakopoulis to do background checks on Sally Hardcastle for the case. However, he was still curious about one thing and he couldn't resist asking the Police Chief it.

"Just one question if I may, sir," he asked tentatively, trying not to anger the Chief any further. "Did they seem surprised, sir? That she was dead, I mean, the British Security Services?"

"No, actually now I come to think of it, no they didn't really, Inspector. That's a good question, but just another we are not going to find the answer to I'm afraid. But then it's not easy to gauge the reactions of the British Security Services. 'Stiff upper lip' is what they call it, I think. Keep things close to their chest the top people in that organisation, give as little as possible away, and not just in terms of information, but also in terms of their reactions. Usually all the same, their reactions, to good and bad things."

He hesitated for a second or to having said more than he should or had intended.

"Hmm … yes, that about really describes them, but now I'll let you wrap this up, the case, as I ordered. Goodbye Inspector."

As soon as he finished the call Papadoulis told Georgiou "We've been ordered to shut the case down by the Hellenic Chief of Police in Athens, as you probably gathered from that conversation. So, we have no choice. We will have to, but one thing's interesting. When I asked he said the British Security Services weren't surprised that Aileen Regan is dead. Very interesting that, Sergeant, don't you think?"

Georgiou simply raised his eyebrows slightly then asked, "Do you think they could have killed her then, sir?"

"Maybe, Sergeant, maybe. It's definitely a possibility don't you think after what Cleverley told me she'd told him about working for MI6."

17

The night of Friday July 1st 2022

Kathleen O'Mara was in Pal's Bar in Lindos with Alison Lees and Suzanne Carmichael quite late on the Friday night, the day they arrived. It was around midnight when they came into the bar and got some drinks. It was only a small bar and very busy. One of the barmen, Stelios, engaged Alison in conversation while he made their drinks, as he always did with customers old and new. When he handed her their drinks, three cocktails, he added three free shots for them. While they talked Suzanne asked her to ask him where the toilet was. He pointed to the far corner of the bar and a winding iron spiral staircase, telling her over the loud music, "Up there." Suzanne went off to tackle the narrow staircase, while a guy behind Kathleen motioned with one of his hands requesting her to move back from the bar so he could also get served. So she did straightaway. As she did a slim woman in a baseball cap, a tight dark t-shirt, black jeans and trainers, making her way from the direction of the toilet through the crowd of customers, placed her hand gently on Kathleen's back to move her aside slightly in order to get past. Kathleen never turned around initially. She didn't need to do so to allow the woman to pass her. She just moved forward slightly back towards the bar so the woman could pass behind her. She thought the woman was leaning towards her from behind as she passed to simply thank her for moving. She wasn't. Even though the music was loud Kathleen still heard the woman rapidly say quietly in her ear, "Don't turn around. Later at your hotel for the package. Don't get pissed or go to bed as soon as you get back there." With that the woman barely paused and quickly manoeuvred her way through the rest of the customers in the bar and out of one of the doors into the alley.

As she was told to do Kathleen didn't turn around at all. She knew what it meant, what it was about.

Just over four hours later the same woman, dressed in the same clothes, but now with the baseball cap pulled right down to just above her eyes, knocked softly once on the door to Kathleen's hotel room just a few minutes after she'd said goodnight to Alison and Suzanne as they made their way to their adjacent rooms.

Before Kathleen could say anything as she opened the door the woman asked somewhat sarcastically, "Kathleen, or should I call you Aileen or maybe even Sheila?"

Kathleen ignored the question initially, instead telling her, "You didn't wait very long.," and then added, "Kathleen will be fine. Didn't expect a woman. You are?"

"You don't need to know. I was waiting and saw you arrive. Was hoping you might be back a bit earlier with those friends of yours so I wouldn't have to wait so long sat in the bloody car park."

She didn't sound pleased at all as she added an abrupt, "You got it?"

"Yes, come in," Kathleen told her, aiming to hopefully relax the obvious atmosphere between them somewhat. It didn't work.

"Just get it and come with me," the woman told her just as bluntly remaining at the door.

While the woman waited Kathleen went to get the package from the room safe. She didn't know what she meant by, "Come with me." Where? That wasn't what Michael told her was part of the job. When she came back with it Kathleen told her as she tried to hand it to her, "Here, you just take it."

She wasn't expecting the woman to tell her, "No, I'm not touching it. You have to deliver it. That was the deal. That's what I was told, my orders. You have to deliver it in person. Those were my instructions, and I always do as I'm told, what I'm instructed and ordered to do by the bhoys,." She added a very firm, "unlike you."

There was a threatening edge to her voice as she said that last part, and then said, "I'll take you. Get what you need and come with me."

"Where?"

"What? Just get what you need, your room key and whatever."

"Where, where are we going?"

"To the bloody car in the car park, and then to deliver the package you were asked to, told to deliver."

The woman was getting angry.

"Who to?"

"What?"

"Who to? Who are we delivering the package to and where?"

"What? I was told that you used to be one of our operatives. So you really expect me to tell you that, who it is you're going to deliver the package to? Are you bloody stupid? Do you think I'm bloody stupid? You know I can't tell you that, even if I knew their name, which I don't. You should know better than to ask. You don't need to know, and nor do I. And in case you're wondering, no I don't know what's in it, and I'm guessing nor do you, and I don't want to know that either and nor should you. Now let's bloody go, before it gets too light."

Kathleen decided it was best to do what the woman told her, rather than making her even more agitated and angry by asking any more questions. That was pointless anyway as she was clearly determined not to answer any. It was turning out to already involve a lot more than what Michael had told her the job would be though, "just a courier job". Not as simple and straightforward as he made it sound.

When they reached a black Mercedes SUV in the hotel car park and Kathleen got in the front alongside the woman she immediately realised there was another person in the back seat – a large man wearing a baseball cap also pulled right down over his eyes. When the woman started the car the instant air-conditioning was a relief from the stifling warm sticky summer heat of the Rhodes night, but not completely for Kathleen. She was feeling decidedly warm and uncomfortable, apprehensive to a degree, and not just from the Rhodes night heat.

She decided the best thing to do was to try and engage the woman in conversation, even some small talk, which might possibly at least take the edge off the clearly menacing atmosphere.

"I expected you'd be Irish, but you're English," she told the woman.

Perhaps Kathleen was right about the small talk as the woman let out a slight laugh before replying, "Part Irish, I suppose. It's in my blood. My parents were from Kilkenny, but moved to Manchester before I was born."

Kathleen couldn't actually come up with any more small talk ideas so they sat in silence as the car headed through the darkness on the road towards the south of the island. It was the woman who broke the silence after ten minutes. Her voice seemed more pleasant, as though her impatience and anger had subsided.

"You were here in 2016 weren't you? When that guy had the accident in the back alley in Lindos, the British Security Services guy?"

"How do you know that?"

"We have our sources. It's a village, Lindos. You can find out anything if you really want to you know."

"Really?"

The woman very briefly glanced sideways into her face. She was toying with her, playing a game, enjoying being in control, and could sense Kathleen's uneasiness over the situation in which she now found herself. As she turned her head back to look at the road ahead she replied, "Oh yes, really, even the police here leak like sieves"

Kathleen just shrugged her shoulders slightly, still wondering where they were headed, but realising there was no point in asking again. At least from her last couple of comments the woman seemed more relaxed and asking again where they were headed might only break that mood. Anyway Kathleen fully realised by now she wasn't going to get an answer.

The darkness shrouding the road ahead was just beginning to be very lightly threatened by the barest hint of the eventually rising sun and dawn breaking, bringing with it another scorching hot Rhodes summer July day. The guy in the back seat said nothing and the three of them sat in silence for another ten minutes.

Eventually the woman decided to embark on her little game once more.

"You came across a Rhodes Inspector back then in 2016 didn't you, Papadoulis? Yiannis, nice guy for a copper. That's when I first met him, back in 2016 when he was investigating the accident, the British Security Services guy's accident. Yiannis used to come into the place I was working at in Lindos then while he was on the investigation. It got quite regular, his visits, if you know what I mean."

She glanced over again briefly at Kathleen and raised her eyebrows slightly in a knowing sort of way.

No, Kathleen didn't know what she meant for certain at all, but she wasn't going to ask. Clearly it was something the woman was hinting at quite heavily regarding the Inspector, something she wanted to get over to Kathleen; that she knew a lot more than her about the 2016 investigation into the so-called accident, and had her source close to the investigation.

Kathleen simply remained silent, wondering quite where this conversation was going, what was the point of it? The woman was determined to pursue it, however, and make Kathleen aware she knew a lot more about her and what happened in 2016.

"We heard he interviewed you about the accident, but then the investigation was pulled. All too embarrassing for MI6 apparently. One of their agents getting bumped off like that so easily, definitely all a bit embarrassing don't you think? Especially as we know you were actually here. Doing your own little private investigation of your family history wasn't it? Not actually working for anyone at the time I mean, not working for any organisation at all?"

Now Kathleen knew precisely what the woman's comments were really about; where she was going with them. It was exactly what Michael had warned her about. Now she was even more apprehensive about the situation in which she found herself. She decided the best thing was to continue to stay silent and not even attempt to answer, or comment on, the questions which the woman obviously already knew the answers to.

"So, someone spotted you in Lindos back then in August 2016, tipped off the British Security Services, who were desperately looking for you, and the MI6 guy was sent from Athens to deal with you. Consequently, you did what you thought you had to do, arrange, is that the right word, arrange the accident. But then you disappeared with that writer guy lover of yours. To Crete wasn't it? One of the bhoys came across a very interesting little novel he wrote. Very interesting story it was, included a woman as one of the main characters who was living on Crete. An Irish woman wouldn't you know."

She glanced sideways at Kathleen briefly once more before continuing.

"But then, of course, you guessed that didn't you, that one of our people might eventually pick up the woman was based on you? That's why you left him, left Crete. Bit of a stupid thing for him to do really, putting that Irish woman character in his novel. These things have consequences, Kathleen. You should know that. You've had to face them all the time over the years you worked for the bhoys. What you did in Lindos in that summer of 2016 on your own private little trip was on your own private little initiative after you'd left the organisation, just as you wanted to. Of course, as you know, no one actually really ever leaves the bhoys, is allowed to leave completely. The MI6 operative you killed that August was only in Lindos looking for you because of what you did for your own personal vendetta. That was an act of vengeance a few weeks earlier in London, killing the bitch Sandra Weston. She wasn't even working for the Security Services by then though. Her personal life, as well as her professional life in MI6, had already been ruined earlier that year through what you did with her husband; your affair with him that you made sure she found out about on your holiday with her in June in Lindos. By accident wasn't it? You made bloody sure she found out, but made it look like it was an accident that she did."

She glanced across at Kathleen again as she added spitefully, "You're good at arranging that things happen by accident aren't you."

She looked back at the road as she went on.

"That wasn't actually in the assignment though for the bhoys was it, you having an affair with Weston's prat of a husband? That was all your idea, all part of your vendetta against the bitch Weston, wasn't it? That wasn't enough for you though was it? You wanted more, wanted her dead, despite what that might stir up, despite any consequences for anyone else in the organisation. Those sort of things weren't supposed to happen after ninety-eight though, and the ceasefire and the peace agreement. Consequently, MI6 weren't going to let the bhoys, and someone they thought was still one of the bhoys' operatives, you, get away with that, bumping off one of their agents even after they'd left the service, especially when they realised you'd been infiltrating the British Security Services, MI6, for twenty years as an agent for the bhoys. And the consequence of that led to you killing another one of their agents in Lindos that August."

She hesitated for a few seconds and then said in a firm voice, "Consequences, Kathleen, there's always-"

Kathleen didn't let her finish.

"That was an official operation from the bhoys, killing Weston. Yeah I volunteered for it, of course I did. Of course I would when I'd been told by the bhoys that Weston led the team that assassinated my stepfather back in 2002, despite him having a solid alibi. Weston and MI6 knew that. There was solid evidence that he was nowhere near the bombing they fitted him up for. So, he bhoys sanctioned killing Weston."

The woman glanced over again. Now anger was clearly growing on her face.

"You wanted it though, and they never sanctioned the affair did they? That was all your idea wasn't it? Your initiative for your own personal interests. You were desperate to do the killing though, wasn't you. And that had consequences, consequences for all of us here eventually. Because after you killed Weston you came here in August 2016 thinking all would be forgiven and forgotten by MI6 while you went tracing your family history here. You thought you could just walk away, just decide that was it for you with the bhoys and MI6 after you killed Weston and got your own little family vengeance. You decided you'd go on your own little family history investigation on Rhodes, in Lindos, but that resulted in you killing that MI6 agent there that night."

The woman stopped talking for a moment, waiting to see if Kathleen would react further. She didn't. She just sat staring ahead out of the windscreen at the slowly emerging light of the new day while clutching the package in her lap.

So, the woman asked, "You know what MI6 call their agents, Kathleen, don't you? Of course you do, you were one for twenty years weren't you."

This time Kathleen responded, but not to the woman's question.

"Look, much as I'm sure you believe this is an interesting conversation … erm … what did you say your name was?"

"I didn't," was the woman's abrupt reply. She wasn't going to be caught out like that.

For twenty years Kathleen's greatest weapon in her professional life, her strength, was her silence. Listening, observing, being aware of all those around her, and everything around her, mostly while operating undercover. She'd allied that successfully to her cold, ruthless, dispassionate, minutely planned and detailed methods. But now, six years on, a lot of that, that vigilance and awareness, had drifted away and she was getting increasingly anxious over the unpredictable situation she found herself in, had let herself be in. She didn't know the island at all, let alone the further south they appeared to be heading. She had no idea where they were, or indeed where they were headed.

She tried another approach.

"Ok, look where are we going exactly, and who am I meeting to deliver the package if it's not one of you two?"

The woman ignored her questions once again, instead continuing with what she had been saying.

"Assets, agents are assets aren't they Kathleen. That's what the high-ups at MI6 like to call them, one of those obscure meaningless, impersonal words, so they can easily think of them, the agents, people, as disposable objects, disposable assets. Some of the bhoys like to use that word too unfortunately, asset."

She briefly looked over at Kathleen yet again, who remained silently staring straight ahead and clutching the package. Through the barely half-light Kathleen thought she made out a sign saying Gennadi. She had no idea where that was on the island. She presumed in the south. Then the woman suddenly rapidly swung the car off the main road and on to a narrow road to the left that had a sign saying 'Beach'.

The woman continued, her voice becoming increasingly agitated again.

"The problem with that Kathleen is that an asset is not that, an asset, when it becomes a liability is it? Don't you think? And you became that, no longer an asset but instead a liability when you went pursuing your own little personal vendetta and then wanted to quit. What you did back then in 2016 in London, having an affair with her husband, killing Weston, and then that MI6 guy in Lindos, without an iota of thought about the consequences for the organisation, stirred up a real load of shit for us, the three of us taking time out here on Rhodes as 'sleepers' for the bhoys at the time. MI6 came here looking after that, for you mainly of course, but you'd gone hadn't you, pissed off to Crete with your writer lover. Didn't stop those bastards from MI6 getting retribution though, taking their revenge, Kathleen. We lost two good operatives, thanks to you."

She paused for a couple of seconds before looking across at Kathleen and adding with venom, "One was my brother by the way. Small world isn't it."

She shook her head once and added in a venomous tone, "Well, now this is my own little piece of family history vengeance, Kathleen."

As she finished she nodded slightly, and with that the silent guy in the back seat produced a hand gun and landed a very firm crushing blow to the back of Kathleen's head with the pistol's handle.

18

Why Gennadi?

The case was officially closed, shut down, as Papadoulis had been ordered to do. But it wasn't closed in his head. He couldn't let it drop, or at least not certain unexplained elements of it. It was shut down as the Chief of Police had ordered, but there were things on the case nagging away at him which Papadoulis couldn't get out of his head, couldn't stop thinking about. They didn't even appear to be very important things in the investigation. One of those, something in particular, was still bugging him; why was Aileen Regan's body dumped in Gennadi? Why there? Was there any significance in respect of who was the killer?

A week after he was ordered to close the case the Inspector came out of his office in the Rhodes Town Police Station and walked over to Georgiou's desk. To the Sergeant's surprise he suddenly said to him, "Why Gennadi?"

Georgiou looked up bemused.

"Why Gennadi what, sir?"

"Look I realise the case is closed, Sergeant, but why Gennadi? Why did the killer choose to dump the body there?"

Georgiou shook his head once and grimaced a little. Why was the Inspector still dwelling on aspects of the case when he'd been ordered to close it?

"Err ... perhaps the killer just thought it was a remote spot? Certainly more remote than some of the places around Lindos, sir. Just wanted to find a remote spot of rough ground with some tree cover to dump it? But as you said, the case is closed. That's what we were ordered to do."

"Yes, yes, I'm well aware of that, and it is, closed. It's just that business about where the body was dumped has been nagging aware at me for a few days now, I can't seem to drop it or ignore it."

"I see, sir, but do you think it's wise to be even discussing the case now, and here in the office? You, we, could be in a lot of hot water if it got back to our superior officers that we were when you were told by the highest one to shut it down?"

Papadoulis nodded. "Yes, you're right, Sergeant. Let's go into my office." He added in a much quieter voice, "There's no danger we'll be over heard there."

That wasn't exactly the response Georgiou wanted to hear. Nevertheless he got up from his desk and followed the Inspector into his office.

As he closed the office door the Sergeant thought he would try once more.

"Sir, I don't think-"

However, Papadoulis was insistent as he interrupted with, "Just sit down and hear me out."

Georgiou did as the Inspector insisted as he sat down at his desk.

"Look, Sergeant, everything we learned about the case pointed to the killer being meticulous, everything they did being organised, timed, planned. We came to that conclusion early in our investigation. They knew where the victim was staying, which hotel, probably even which room. They knew what time she got back there in the early hours of Saturday morning, knew enough to wait for her and then leave with her a few minutes later, around twenty-past four. They must have known she was going to be staying at the Lindos Memories hotel on a holiday break on that particularly date. We know from the CCTV images from the car park that when she left the hotel with the person we presume was her killer it certainly didn't appear that she was being forced to do so. There was no sign of the person with her having or holding a gun to force her to leave with them. So-"

"Well, the CCTV wasn't really that clear on that, sir. They could have had a gun in there trousers pocket perhaps or hidden somewhere on them?" Georgiou interrupted.

"Ok, Sergeant, yes, maybe, but my point is that her killer, presuming the person she left the hotel with was her killer, had all that information about where she was staying, which hotel, which room, and when, the date she was arriving. How did they get that and-"

The Sergeant interrupted once again.

"Perhaps from her, Aileen Regan herself, sir?"

"Precisely, Sergeant, from Regan herself, which means she must have known her killer and expected them to make contact with her soon after she arrived, even that night or as late as the early hours of Saturday morning."

"So, that could even be someone working for the British Security Services, sir, given what Cleverley told you Regan told him."

"Yes, Sergeant, or even-"

"Even what, sir?"

"Something the Hellenic Police Chief said in his call to me which I never really picked up at the time, or thought might be important, particularly when he ordered me to shut down the case. Can't remember it word for word, but he said something like our enquires to the British Police about Regan, Sandra and Richard Weston had stirred up a lot of problems, a difficult situation, a bloody hornet's nest, yes that was exactly what he said. He said that not only involved the British Security Services and MI6 ..."

He hesitated for a few seconds for emphasis before adding, "But also the IRA. He meant the Irish Nationalist Republicans, although he didn't actually say those words I'm sure.. This difficult situation he was on about also involved the IRA. But we never came across any mention of them, any involvement of that organisation, or even a hint of their involvement in Regan's murder in any of our enquiries. Cleverley never mentioned them, never told me that Regan told him she'd been involved with them at all. There was no mention of them, or connection to them, that came up in our 2016 case investigation into the guy's death in Lindos either. The only thing that could even remotely linked Regan with them was the small tattoo of the Irish flag on the victim's inner thigh."

"That's a bit of a stretch though, sir, just because she had a small tattoo of the Irish flag."

Yes, I agree, but if we think about what the Hellenic Police Chief said about the difficult situation our enquiries to the

British Police stirred up, involving MI6 and the IRA, then it could have been that the person who knew all that information about where Regan, in the name of Kathleen O'Mara at the time remember, was staying, as well as her movements earlier that night, her killer, was, as you said, someone working for the British Security Services or even the IRA?"

"But as you said, sir, we came across nothing in respect of Regan and the IRA; nothing that led us in that direction in our enquiries."

"That's right, Sergeant, we didn't, because it appears even Cleverley knew nothing about Regan's past, or even present involvement with them. Or at least if he did, and Regan told him, he never told me."

"What about the voicemail message on her phone though, sir? The one from the elusive Michael at six-thirty-five that Saturday morning. He definitely had an Irish accent when he left that message of 'Be careful, Kathleen. Is it done?" We never found him, and never figured out what was meant by his message, although 'Be careful' could have been some sort of warning to her that someone was looking for her to kill her couldn't it? Perhaps, he meant someone from MI6 though, which just leads us back to them doesn't it?"

Papadoulis took a deep breath and then agreed, "Yes, I suppose it does. Not the IRA then, but MI6 were her likely killers."

Georgiou scratched his head and went to get up as he said, "That's all very interesting, sir, but you started out asking 'Why Gennadi', why was her body dumped in Gennadi, remember?"

"Sit down, Sergeant, and bear with me for a moment more," Papadoulis told him.

He did.

"That's the point of all this. As I said before her killer, whether they were from the British Security Services or the IRA knew all those things about when she would arrive, what date, where she was staying, even when she got back to the hotel. Perhaps, as we suspect, she told them, because she knew her killer. But, Sergeant, her killer had it all planned out, even down to how long to wait after she got back to her room that night and that they knew she would go with them, without any force being required it appeared. And, let's not forget the KCN cyanide tablet that the killer used. Not something you just happen to carry around on the off chance is it, Sergeant? The planning and timings were meticulous."

Georgiou scratched the back of his head once more

"Yes, sir, you said all that before, and it doesn't really tell us if it was an MI6 person who killed her or someone from the IRA does it, or even someone from neither of those?"

Papadoulis got up and walked around his desk to perch on the corner of it.

"No, it doesn't, Sergeant," he began firmly, "but if all that was meticulously planned it doesn't suggest does it that the dumping of her body on that rough ground under the trees in Gennadi was just a random choice by the killer either."

"Well, maybe they-"

Papadoulis interrupted. He wasn't about to let the Sergeant pour cold water on his theory.

"The body was dumped there, in Gennadi, for a reason, Sergeant. Yes, the killer almost certainly knew the area, but I think this meticulously planning killer was trying to make a point, trying to tell us something, some sort of clue, not who the killer actually was, but playing a little game with us as to why they chose Gennadi as the place to dump Regan's body. There has to be some sort of connection between Regan, or O'Mara as she was known when she was killed, and Gennadi."

As he finished he walked back around his desk to sit in front of his computer and turn it on while Georgiou told him, "But, sir, we found no connection between O'Mara and Gennadi. As far as we know she'd never even been there, not even on each of the times she was previously on Rhodes and in Lindos in June and August 2016 using the name Aileen Regan."

Papadoulis sat back from his computer in silence for a long ten seconds stroking his chin with his right hand. Then suddenly he leaned forward again to tap something on the keyboard, muttering, "Yes, I wonder, maybe, I wonder."

He pulled up a search engine on the computer screen, then stopped peering at the screen before he could type in the name of what he was looking for when the Sergeant said, "Sir, sir, wonder what?"

Papadoulis sat back in his chair once more, away from the computer screen and started to tell Georgiou, "When I was Inspector Karagoulis' Sergeant after he was transferred here from Athens I soon came to accept some of his more unusual investigative ways and comments. I was a relatively young, keen police officer then, born and raised in Rhodes Town, and much more used to doing things by the book."

Georgiou looked bemused, completely unsure where his Inspector was going with what he was telling him, and how it was relevant in any way to what they'd just been discussing.

Papadoulis continued. He knew exactly what he was trying to say; the point he was about to make.

"Even so, I quite soon adapted to some of the more alternative approaches and quirky comments of Karagoulis. In fact, I soon grew to like and enjoy them. I not only respected him as my superior officer, but actually liked him and admired some of his ways. The Inspector was always searching for an alternative explanation to the one that appeared most obvious for solving the crime he was investigating. Sometimes that did put him at odds with me and my more regular ways of investigating, but I got used to it, learned to live with it. That particularly included his flamboyancy when it stretched to his fondness for referring to, and quoting from, Greek mythology and Greek philosophers at every opportunity. I quickly adapted to it and grew to accept it, or maybe I soon eventually did, is a better way of putting it, even though it still brought a smile to my lips every time the Inspector did it. Even all these years after Karagoulis' death on a case we were on together in 2010 I've never forgotten my former boss and his quirky leanings towards Greek Mythology in solving cases."

"Of course not, sir, of course you wouldn't forget him, none of us has."

Georgiou was still wondering quite what all this reminiscing had to do with what they'd just been discussing.

Papadoulis leaned forward again to type something into the search engine as he said, "So, what would Karagoulis say about it, Sergeant? That's what I'm thinking. What would he say about why Gennadi, and why the body was dumped there? What would he say Gennadi has to do with Aileen Regan or

Kathleen O'Mara? In his own quirky way I'm sure he'd be employing his Greek Mythology obsession to answer those questions."

The Sergeant was frowning heavily as he replied, "I've really no idea, sir, what would he say?"

But Papadoulis wasn't really listening. He was busily scrolling down a page in the search engine. Georgiou sat in silence, unsure of whether to say or ask anything more, or simply get up and leave the office.

He was about to ask if he could go back to his desk when Papadoulis exclaimed loudly while pointing to the computer screen, "There, there, there it is. I knew it."

"Sir?" Georgiou asked.

"Here, here, look at this, Sergeant," the Inspector told him pointing to the screen again. "We've been looking at the wrong thing, whether or not Regan, even as O'Mara, had ever been to Gennadi. But it's in the bloody name, Gennadi. The link's in the name of the place, Gennadi. That's what the killer was indicating when they chose to dump O'Mara's body there, thinking they were being clever, playing a game with us."

Georgiou got up out of his chair, walked quickly around the desk, and then leaned down to peer at the screen as Papadoulis read out, "One origin of the name Gennadi is that it is said to be derived from the name of the Ancient Roman Sun God, Janus, the guardian of beginnings and endings, and as such is a variant of the Latin, Janus. Janus is usually depicted as having two faces."

The Inspector slumped back in his chair and puffed out his cheeks.

"The cheeky bastard. The killer was playing games with us; Gennadi, Janus, two faces, two personalities, two for the same person, Sergeant. That's what our killer was telling us in choosing Gennadi to dump the body. They couldn't resist having their little riddle, trying to show how clever they were. Dumping the body at Gennadi, so far from Lindos that night, wasn't a coincidence. It wasn't just some piece of deserted rough ground they'd checked out before. It was a little game to play on us, demonstrating something they knew but thought we didn't. Whoever the killer was, and from whichever organisation or none, they definitely knew she had two identities; two faces of the same person, Aileen Regan and Kathleen O'Mara. That was what they were saying in choosing Gennadi."

Papadoulis shook his head slightly and allowed a small smile to cross his lips as he added, "He would have liked that, that little riddle, that little puzzle, the Inspector. The ways of Inspector Dimitris Karagoulis, and what he taught me, have never let me down, even if it took me a while to realise it in this case."

Printed by BoD™in Norderstedt, Germany